Praise for *Alphabe*

"Page throws hope into a mixed-up world where only fantasies and delusions dare to grow." — *Globe and Mail*

"A complex book, and splendidly written, *Alphabet* is an intensely compelling reading experience that speaks to the power of words and the significance of language in all its dangerous subtleties." — *The Edmonton Journal*

"One of the most complex characters I've ever met in a novel. His attempt to win redemption is totally engrossing."
— *Victoria Times Colonist*

"It is a bracing study, emotionally nimble and intelligent, and forms a very fine novel." — *Daily Telegraph*

"It is a wonderful book, peculiar, intense, revealing, challenging and above all riveting…I kept saying to myself, how could she know this?" — Erwin James,
Guardian columnist and author of *A Life Inside*

"Sometimes novelists go too far — and sometimes they manage to demonstrate that too far is the place they needed to go."
— *Time Out*

"Simon is real. Simon gets under your skin. You'll keep reading *Alphabet* because you'll want to understand how Simon got to Z from A."
— *Times Colonist*

Praise for *The Story of My Face*

"An elegantly compelling story of how a young girl's obsession forever changes the lives of those around her...a disciplined exploration of the complexity of human motivation and our need for redemption." — *Vancouver Sun*

"A compelling and unpredictable journey...beautifully written, rolls on at a rapid pace and delivers a satisfying punch at the end." — *Globe and Mail*

"Skillfully written and a most impressive achievement."
— *Sunday Telegraph*

"One of the most compelling, unsettling novels I've read in ages, which should appeal to fans of classy thrillers and literary fiction alike." — Sarah Waters

"A moving, absorbing story...Kathy Page writes beautifully."
— Helen Dunmore, (author of *A Spell of Winter*)

"Natalie's character is a triumph . . . It's rare to find a book that can not only move and thrill but also asks fundamental questions about religious belief and the nature of virtue and sin."
— *Good Books Guide*

"[Page's] writing, mostly in the present tense, is lit with an immediate sense of period, summoning images which are by turns softly painterly, sharply filmic or as murky as those first television images of the moon landing."
— *Times Literary Supplement*

THE FIND

ALSO BY KATHY PAGE

The Story of My Face
Alphabet

THE FIND
KATHY PAGE

McArthur & Company
Toronto

First published in Canada in 2010 by
McArthur & Company
322 King Street West, Suite 402
Toronto, Ontario
M5V 1J2
www.mcarthur-co.com

Library and Archives Canada Cataloguing in Publication

Page, Kathy, 1958–
The find / Kathy Page.

ISBN 978-1-55278-837-0

I. Title.

PR6066.A325F46 2010   823'.914   C2010-900584-8

The publisher would like to acknowledge the financial support of
the Government of Canada through the Canada Book Fund and the
Canada Council for our publishing activities. The publisher further wishes
to acknowledge the financial support of the Ontario Arts Council
and the OMDC for our publishing program.

Cover and text design by Tania Craan
Typesetting by Mary Bowness
Printed and bound in Canada by Webcom

10 9 8 7 6 5 4 3 2 1

Mixed Sources
Product group from well-managed
forests, controlled sources and
recycled wood or fiber
www.fsc.org Cert no. SW-COC-002358
© 1996 Forest Stewardship Council
FSC

99%

ANCIENT FOREST ™
FRIENDLY

For Richard

1

──────◆──────

SCOTT WOKE JUST AFTER FOUR. Rain lashed at the house. Rivers ran down windows; the blackness outside had a fierce, violet tinge. There was a steady drip, drip, that could only be from somewhere inside. In the bathroom, the floor was awash. Brownish drops oozed steadily from a bulge in the ceiling, just below the skylight. He climbed on the edge of the bath to pierce it with a skewer — realised as it collapsed, drenching him in a gritty gush, that they'd better get a tarp on the roof. They? Dream on. He pulled on jeans, sweater, waterproofs, threw open the door.

Outside: a wall of water, the deafening roar of a million tiny parts. The rain sang and drummed, raced downwards, pooled, spurted from guttering, burst in gurgling torrents from downspouts, bubbled from blocked drains.

He struggled from the workshop with the ladders, hammer, nails and tarp; water coursed down his neck and up his arms as he hooked the roof ladder on and climbed up, pulling the tarp behind him on a rope. He heaved it over the skylight and the ridge, battened it down, had to keep shifting the ladders. It took almost an hour to get it done. The darkness was just beginning to break up when, on the way down, he reached out his foot and the ladder, which was propped against the gutter, slipped away: he was stuck on the roof, held only by his hammer, face pressed into the decaying asphalt tile, with the rain beating on his back and his hands going numb.

He leaned south and gripped the guttering, which gave way and slapped him across the head as he fell. His right foot hit the capsized ladder; he landed on his left side, jarred his hip and crushed his arm. For a few moments, nothing hurt, and there was just the sound of the rain. Then came the beginnings of pain. He crawled back to the porch, and once inside fumbled, blue-fingered, on the shelf for Advil. All gone. Half-dry, shivering, he struggled into new clothes and in the kitchen watched TV images of meltwater and rain in a foaming brown torrent, full of rocks and grit.

In the lower valley, towards the old port, water rippled across the surrounding fields. Homes were waist-high in water. The bridge was gone. Residents, the announcer said, had been told to dress warmly, go to the community centre taking with them nothing more than a day pack and a sleeping bag.

The smell in his father's room, animal and chemical combined, hit the back of Scott's throat. The pain made him sick too.

He clicked on the light: saw grey stubble, the burst-looking nose, the eyes clenched shut. Mac rubbed his face, turned away. Scott shook, then slapped.

'Wake up, Mac! I'm hurt. You might have to drive.'

'Drive?'

Back in his room, Scott packed his computer into the original boxes. It was a new system, bought on sale not long ago. Half-price but still three thousand dollars that he would be paying off forever at eighteen percent, so, he thought, the Door to the Universe had better be okay. He heaved the chest of drawers on top of the desk and put the boxes on top of them both. He took his tin out of the desk drawer, sat with his leg on the bed and rolled four joints to take with him. His ankle was enormous, twice the size of the other one.

He staggered outside, back into the rain. Mac sat in the Ford with the engine on, frowned at the wheel.

'Scotty,' he said. 'I think I might have forgotten something.' They both knew what he meant: there was no drink in the house for him to bring, could they somehow get some, or what the hell would he do?

'Just go, Dad—' Scott told him and the car jerked forwards. He felt as if someone was sawing off his foot. At the dip by the first junction, the pooled water, pocked with constantly falling drops, covered twenty or thirty metres of road. A great wake spread after each vehicle that crossed.

When they reached the community centre, Mary Divers strapped up his ankle and handed over four Tylenol 4 to last all day, along with her umbrella to use as a walking stick. The ankle could be broken, she said; keep it up and rested for now.

In the main hall, families marked out territory with chairs, unrolled sleeping bags and piled up their sweaters and coats. The heat was full on, the windows flung wide to combat the damp rising from clothes and hair, the water people breathed out, their sweat. Women bustled in the kitchen. Any minute, Scott knew, Mac would start to get the jitters and he couldn't bear it. He took all of his pills at once and went outside, pressed his back against the wall under the roof overhang and tried over and over to light one of his joints: the sodden air extinguished the spark before it even existed.

Hell, he thought. What was this? What was he doing? Why was he still there? There had to be something else. But Dr Hoffman had said, when Scott asked her what would happen if he did leave, that Mac would drink himself dead in six months. He hated the bastard, but he loved him too — couldn't do it... If only, he thought, I could light the fucking joint I could stop thinking about this stuff.

An orange helicopter appeared — like some kind of hallucination hanging over the playing field, it hovered above them and then sank down to land. Three figures emerged, ran, laden with luminous plastic-wrapped luggage, towards where he stood. Water streamed over their yellow waterproofs.

'Press—' the tallest one barked. 'Can you find me sockets for these lights, okay?' Limping, Scott dragged wires across the hall while they corralled people into a group. It was something to do and at the end of it, when he pointed at his leg and said he needed to get out, the journalist said Okay, they could take one more. Mac grabbed Scott's arm and begged to come too.

'No,' Scott told him, stuffing his things into the backpack. 'There's no room. Hang in here.'

The machine rose straight up into the rain. And by then the painkillers had started their work. A slow grin spread across Scott's face and he turned to share it with the reporter next to him.

Later, in the hospital in Vancouver, he watched the news: saw himself and Mac beside him, an arm thrown over his shoulder. Different eyes, different hair, different skin tone —

one pure Celt, one part Native, but the same grin, the same stubborn jaw. They were father and son, no way out of it. It was, the reporter's voice said, the story of a Tough Little Community struck by one of the Last Forces Beyond Human Control. The camera panned around the hall, showing huddles of small-town people in layered clothes, the women bravely smiling, the men unwashed and stubbly, drinking soup out of paper cups.

Please, Scott thought, zapping the TV and closing his eyes. Just wash it all away: the whole damn place, everyone in it and everything that's happened in the last ten years. I'll stay here, find a room, work, and start over. But in less than a week Andrea Price from the Baptist's had tracked Scott down, and he returned home to take care of Mac, and then felt even worse than before. And in September, six months after the flood, when Anna Silowski first visited Big Crow, Scott still had his limp. By then, he was taking Prozac and working nights at the Mountain View Hotel. That day he was late again, so Lauren, the owner, checked the party in: Dr Anna Silowski, Prof. Colin Gordon and Prof. Michael Swenson. Archaeologists, something like that. Not at all their usual kind of guest.

2

———— ✦ ————

THE THREE OF THEM SET OUT at first light carrying daypacks, binoculars and cameras. It was a thirty-minute drive to the site. Once there, they kept their eyes to the rock, inched up the gorge, saying little. Occasionally they were startled by the staccato riff of a click bug, or the drumming of a woodpecker's beak on a rotting trunk in the forest above, but mostly they heard only small sounds: their own footsteps, the chirrup of invisible birds. The river huddled in its course, a barely audible trickle, leaving most of the bed exposed.

Anna had a good feeling, a kind of lightness inside.

Prospecting, she explained to Scott later, is not looking in any ordinary sense of the word, but a special kind of seeing. What she did was to read the rock: interpret its patterns and irregularities. She knew how brittle and how dense it was, when and how it was formed and later deformed, where the planes might break apart, what it might contain, how, if need be, it could be removed. At the same time, she pictured what might have lived in the environment the rock implied. She knew from experience the architecture of fossilised bones and their texture, compared to that of this particular rock. She could hold the knowledge of a vanished world in one part of her mind, and at the same time open her eyes to what was there now, in front of her. The two coalesced and she was able to see both what was there and how it had been brought into being.

Listening to her, Scott felt as if he were stone, waiting to be read.

But that day in early September they had not yet met. Anna's gaze passed steadily over the rock. The shale in the Big Crow valley was dark grey, very fissile. It broke in some places into tiny flakes, elsewhere split into broad layers several centimetres thick. On the seams between the layers of rock, the shells of *Sphenoceramus* and *Mytiloides* were everywhere, too common to be worth collecting — and yet the preservation was exquisite and the sheer quantity exciting, suggestive of larger possibilities.

Colin Gordon had recently returned from the Arctic. Mike Swenson, a specialist in the bird–dinosaur link who had taken over Anna's job when she left the university, had just spent three months in the Gobi Desert. Anna was returning from her annual visit to the museum in Tokyo. They were all back from field-work at around the same time, and Colin had come up with the idea of a day's prospecting: since Anna had to stop in Vancouver on her way home, he'd pointed out, why not catch a floatplane to the island and join them in a visit to Big Crow?

Why not, indeed. Soon Anna would have to sit on committees and lobby for her slice of budget and technician time: her least favourite part of the job. But now, she could simply observe the profusion of fauna — flesh and fossil, terrestrial and marine; she could stop to examine a scattering of shiny, blue-black fish scales in a fragment of rock and notice, as she stood, a sunbathing garter snake slithering for cover, a cloud of mosquitoes slow-dancing in a patch of shade. The relics of the past and the creatures of the baking hot now co-existed under the same fierce sun.

An egg-shaped concretion broke open as she touched it to reveal the shiny tooth of a lamnoid shark: perfect, the serrations on its edge crisp, the surface as smooth as the original enamel.

'Anna, over here!' Mike called, and she slipped the tooth unprofessionally into her pocket, smiling at herself for doing so, and picked her way across the riverbed.

'Those plesiosaur fragments turned up here—' Mike showed the other two the spot marked on his map. 'Local amateurs. Ken Rivers is describing it. A flipper almost a metre long. No sign of the rest — could even have been disturbed in that massive flood they had in March. Since then—'

'Enormous ammonites. Crustaceans.' Colin mopped his brow.

The lower part of the cliff had been slightly undercut. Someone had put a marker — a blob of yellow paint — on the cliff above the excavated section, a rather futile gesture, Anna thought, given the rate at which this kind of shale eroded.

'An incredibly rich environment,' Mike said, smiling as he looked back down the rocky valley, as if, Anna couldn't help thinking, he had made it himself. The old awkwardness between them was long gone, and he seemed very easy with himself. Was he fifty-six, now? Despite family life and middle age he'd stayed lean. His once-blond hair was grey, but there was still, when he pushed back his sunglasses, the shock of his eyes, the blue irises sailing in the clearest of white. *See?* Anna thought. *It did work out for the best. And you are a lucky man.* There was a sliver of envy, too — why pretend? But she took a great deal of pleasure in other people's situations, their families and relationships, as well as in her own friendships: *not everyone*, she often had to remind her brother, Vik, *needs to love in exactly the same way.*

In the early afternoon they stopped to rest, sitting on the hot rock to make the most of the treacly September sun. Anna dug in her pack for a bag of nuts, offered them around. Occasionally a fragment of the driest, most fragile shale on the cliffside worked loose, hurled itself down onto the riverbed to land with faint cracking sound as it broke, on impact, into a scattering of tiny flakes. The world is falling to bits, Anna thought, as it is and does, while we, part of it, sit and eat.

'Fantastic paper of yours I read in *Nature*,' she told Colin, who grinned back at her, said nothing. He drank deeply from his water bottle and leaned back into the rock, closing his eyes against the sun. Since she'd seen him last year he had become thin, to the point of haggard; he looked greyer and craggier, as if he were at least part mineral. Clearly, he was not well, but she did not feel she could ask about it, not there and then.

When Mike brushed crumbs from his t-shirt he did it, as he did everything, vigorously, larger than life.

'Three hours back to the car. We two have to get the floater out of here at four-thirty. Guess we'll turn back now, return an-other time?'

The other two had a meeting the next day, but Anna was free and she had a feeling that she should stay a little longer.

'Your cell won't work here,' Colin said. 'Suppose you break your ankle, meet a bear?'

'I probably won't,' she told him, grinning. 'I'll very likely be okay.'

'Bear or no bear, you have to let Anna do what she wants,' Mike said. 'We've all learned that.'

Bursts of loud male laughter faded as they disappeared behind a bend in the river's course. She turned and walked slowly on and up. The landscape was discernibly wilder, as if, within less than a kilometre, she had passed through some invisible boundary. It was fascinating to be somewhere where trees, the enemies of palaeontology, grew with almost insane vigour, where most of what existed, in fossil terms, was concealed. The gradient rose more steeply and the cliffs to either side were increasingly rugged. She examined them through her binoculars: banded with dark grey shales and fawn-coloured sandstone, they reached up perhaps fifteen metres high. At the top, rising out of a thin layer of dry, yellowish soil, the conifers grew denser and older than those in the planted forest closer to town. Two ravens launched themselves noisily from a tree limb far above her, creaked across the valley and then soared into the sky, leaving a third perched on the branch, head cocked, apparently observing their flight.

And then, as she emerged from a slow rightwards bend in the river's course, she saw, as if laid out as a gift, her find: a long line of protruding nodules in the riverbed shale. It could only be the spinal column of some enormous creature long-dead, buried, slowly exposed again, and now ready to be seen.

At first it made no sense: the row of grapefruit-sized nodules veered to the right and then shot back at ninety degrees or so, culminating in a narrow, barely exposed shape pointing back to the left. Perhaps a third of the way down was a confused-looking area, from each side of which a narrow length plunged straight down at an angle of about forty degrees. These two lengths were immense — three or four metres long. They disappeared, reappeared, and then disappeared again, like crude basting stitches in the stone.

It looked, if anything, like a gigantic broken umbrella — and it was only after she had entertained that thought that she realised what she had found. It was not the marine reptile she'd been half hoping for. What she was looking at did not swim, but *flew*: the long bones must be the huge wing fingers of an enormous flying reptile. Not seriously expecting them to hear her, she cupped her hands to her mouth and yelled back downriver:

'Mike! Colin!' She'd already slipped her pack off and was feeling inside it for the camera when the reply came, very faint:

'An-na!' She stood again, yelled:

'Come— here—!' Because now, she could see it all quite clearly: an elongated, pelican-like skull turned to one side, a bend in the neck resulting from the shortening of tendons and ligaments during putrefaction... She could make out the position of some of the bones of the arms, and the extraordinary, extended fourth digit that would have supported the edge of the wing, half open, half folded. Lower down there was at least a suggestion of another pair of much smaller limbs... Whatever was in there was not only very large, but very nearly *complete*.

The concretions were the same dull grey as the rest of the shale, but denser and smoother, less fissile than the rock surrounding them. It was as if each element of the skeleton had been carefully dipped in a protective coating — though what had really happened was a chemical mystery, a serendipitous combination of organic and inorganic chemistry arising out of the process of putrefaction, an accumulation of changes which, for a while, had created atypical strength in the rock. If this protective covering had not formed, the delicate, hollow bones of a flying reptile would have been crushed flat as the mud piled up on top of them. But there it was, and her hands shook as she took the first photographs and then extracted her measuring tape from the pack. She willed herself to wait until it passed, and then set the tape along the spinal column — two metres — and took another photograph. She measured, tried to estimate the wingspan — could not believe the figure she came up with: *ten* metres. She'd forgotten the other two and was shocked to see them hurrying towards her, sweating, red-faced and anxious. She ran to meet them.

'Look! Do you see?' There was silence, and then all three began to laugh and talk at once.

'Lie down, Anna,' Colin said, taking out his camera. 'Next to it, there. Arms out. That's it. Amazing!'

Then they set to work, outlining the nodules with chalk and taking more pictures, from different angles. They sketched a map, measured the distance of each protrusion perpendicular to the cliff. It could be, they all agreed, something like *Pternadon longiceps*, or just as easily, given the scale, the new location and the marine nature of the site, it could be an entirely new species or genus.

It was worth trying to get something out. Anna selected one of the scattering of concretions that lay where the third and the fourth digit emerged, cigar shapes that might contain metacarpals or phalanges. She worked the chisel around the edge of one, teasing away the surrounding rock flake by flake and, when her hand suddenly slipped, cursed herself for being too lazy to put on gloves. Goggles were sensible, too, but she hated them. Blood spread out and dripped with annoying persistence from the wound on the ball of her thumb; she had to hunt in the pack for a bit of bandage. Finally, she chipped through the narrow pedestal remaining and with both hands picked up whatever it was she'd freed. As she grasped it, it broke horizontally in half.

'Brittle!' she warned Mike and Colin who were working behind her, and then she found it had opened almost perfectly, one half containing the fossil, exquisitely preserved; the other its cast.

After that, they were silent, each sitting or squatting on the warm rock and hearing only the thud and ring of the hammer on the chisel. Then Colin cleared his throat and said, 'Hurry up.'

'Why?' Mike said. 'We won't make it in time and obviously, now, we're going to stay the night—'

'Upriver, right by the cliff,' Colin said, pointing. At first all Anna saw was shadow, but then, just emerging from the rock, she made out what could be another long, narrow bone. The three of them looked at each other as if they themselves were discoveries.

Mike eased his concretion out, handed it to Anna and hurried towards the new area. She wrapped all three pieces in the bubble wrap she carried in her pack, and then they set to work all over again, finishing just as the sun slipped behind the trees above them. Cast suddenly into deep shade, they put on sweatshirts and rubbed insect repellent on their hands and faces.

'You've got blood on your chin now,' Mike told Anna. 'Christ!' he said, 'and we thought you'd turned your ankle. What luck! Bastard site though, miles from anywhere.' *Difficult,* Anna thought, *not impossible.* There was history of partnership between their university and the museum when it came to funding applications. And this was something people would want to support.

'I'll get things started,' she said. 'Next summer, we'll be here.' She took Colin's arm, as they set off, not looking anymore, just walking fast. They were all three laughing and talking as they went, though at the same time, in her head, she was bargaining, in a way she tried very hard to avoid, but periodically gave into: 'If I get this one out — and described — it'll be enough.'

Could there ever be enough?

She went to her room while Mike and Colin arranged their extra night and called home, leaving a message for her mother and Janice. Her brother Vik was out too. She set her laptop and cell to charge, showered, dried her hair with the hotel dryer, which seemed to double its volume. Moisturiser, fresh clothes… She leaned into the dimly lit mirror to apply some lipstick, then picked up her jacket and went to the lobby to meet the other two.

✦ ✦ ✦

'What do you want, Scott?' Dr Hoffman had asked Scott in the 'chat' they had before she last renewed his prescription. She was the plainest woman on earth: grey hair, papery skin, grey eyes, thin all over. She was a total pain, but Scott could tell that she meant well — that she wanted him out of the hole he was in, almost more than he did.

'Something big,' he said. 'Different. Exciting. Out of this world.'

'Yes,' she said, smiling for a moment, and then growing serious again. 'Of course.'

✦ ✦ ✦

The mountain that loomed to the west of the town blocked the sun, but indirect light suffused the sky and the air was still warm. They walked the length of the little main street of Big Crow, noting the odd selection of stores that somehow managed to survive: an outdoor activities outfitters cum sports cum general clothing store, a bakery, a tiny library open three days a week. There was a proud, hand-carved sign at the main intersection and a few new buildings but these were outnumbered by the unpainted older ones, many of which looked empty, or, on second glance as if they ought to have been empty, but were not. First the coal mines had closed, and now, it seemed from the protest posters stapled to the hydro poles, the mill had gone too. The setting was spectacular, so there'd be some tourism: outdoor pursuits in summer, good skiing in the winter. Not much else.

Houses began at the town end of the side streets and then petered out as they became country roads. On the way in they had passed a small mall with a gas station, grocery store and hamburger place; they all wanted to avoid that and were glad to push into a dilapidated restaurant, claiming to be genuine Italian.

Now they talked of anything but the find, and thought of nothing else. They had beer, and then a bottle of red wine.

'So,' Mike said at the end of the meal. 'Let's have some dessert between us and another half to go with it.' But Colin got up and put some bills on the table.

'Early start tomorrow. Old man must rest,' he said. Anna

hugged him before he left, and then she and Mike were silent for a while. He offered wine; she nodded to accept. The dessert arrived, a layered confection of sponge cake, alcohol-soaked cherries, custard and cream so rich that they could do no more than taste it from the tips of their spoons.

His family were all well, Mike said. Lily was pregnant with their third. It was tough on her that he was away so much. Tough on him too: they couldn't have proper summer holidays and, one way or another, he wasn't there for most birthdays and family events. There was a great deal that went on which he just didn't know about. Sometimes, he said, rubbing his face briskly with his hands — a gesture she found familiar — he felt like a stranger when he arrived back home, like an important guest of some kind… It wore off soon enough, but then it happened again. Life in two halves wasn't ideal. Still, what is? You had to live with it. He leaned back in his chair, cracked his finger joints and smiled. The waitress brought their bill.

It was thoroughly night when they left. A three-quarter moon hung low in the sky to the east and a scrap of sea, miles away, reflected the light. Away from the streetlights, everything was grey, silver or black. She was thinking about the specimen, what exactly it might turn out to be. How much of the skull would be there? How much of it could they get out unbroken? What a huge undertaking the preparation would be. She was thinking that it would be wonderful if finally the debate over the way the large flying reptiles became airborne could be resolved. If that was something she might do. She was thinking how she must get hold of Rivers, who was writing up the tarsal bones Colin had referred to, and see exactly what he thought those were from. She was thinking about the National Geographic, the Natural Science Foundation, the lesser in-house sources. What the competition for grants might be this year, who to ask to referee, who else it might be beneficial to bring in.

Mike cleared his throat. 'Look,' he said, in a clipped, businesslike tone as they turned into the hotel driveway. The sign: *Mountain View Hotel* was lit with a single lamp; the ugly, low-slung building was set back, beyond some landscaping and a carpark. 'Look, I've got a proposal to make. Let's sit here a minute.' He gestured towards one of the picnic tables set beneath a clump of immature fir trees, and then sat on it. Anna remained standing. She assumed that his thoughts were running on the same lines as hers.

'It's this—' he said. 'I'm still trying to work you out. I used to think you must have gone gay, didn't like men. But it certainly looked to me like you had something on with that Brazilian at the conference last year—.'

What? She almost asked him to say it again to be sure she had heard correctly. Didn't they have other far more important things to talk about? What on earth was he doing, and now of all times? Could he not give up?

'Look, Mike,' she said, keeping her voice as steady as she could, 'let's not go there.' He ignored her, smiled, even.

'It's commitment you don't want, is that it?'

He was right, though she would never tell him so. She stood there, astounded. 'I can't give it,' he continued, 'so, we have a fit. What I think, you see, is why don't you and I have some fun when we meet up like this?' He reached out and ran his hand down her arm from shoulder to wrist, then slipped off the bench and pulled her towards him. 'I've always—' His hands gripped her waist; his erection pressed into the layers of thin fabric that separated their skins and it was odd, very odd, to have her mouth open itself to his and her skin ignite and at least half of her rush to greet the experience, even as another part pulled back, waiting for an opportunity to speak, which clearly was not going to exist unless she made it.

Anna could have said: Okay, Professor Swenson, on your head be it. He was an attractive man offering a simple thing. But leave aside Lily, the kids — he was too close; even as things were, she saw him fairly often and now she'd be working with him on this dig, for heaven's sake! Whatever he thought or said, it would get out of hand and when it ended, he would very likely make a fuss. She pulled away.

'Believe me, this really won't work.'

He grabbed her arm.

'What *is* the matter with you?' he said, and she did half admire him for knowing somehow that he was not getting the whole truth. But it was not as if he had a right to it: since when was there a law that said a person should give a detailed explanation if they decided against fucking someone?

'I thought you were *asking*,' she said. 'Mike, that's my *answer*. No. I want to go in. Let me go!' He did not release her but yanked her closer, grabbed some of her hair with his other hand, and it was then that she hit him. Without thinking, she punched him with her right hand, in the face. His nose buckled, her fist slid into his cheekbone: a noise that was hard and wet at the same time. Pain shot up her arm. He gasped, let go of her. She burst into tears.

'Sorry! Sorry!' she said. Blood was running over his lips and chin. Maybe, Anna thought later, she should have stayed to look after him, found an icepack, wrapped it in a cloth? But at the time, it didn't occur to her: she had never done such a thing before and he was furious — she just wanted to get away.

She pushed into the hotel and the brightness of the lobby and the busy pattern of the carpeting seemed extraordinary, surreal in its vividness after the ghostly moonlight outside, and everything she saw shimmered, because the tears, once started, would not stop.

The flickering of a television set showed through the frosted glass of the partition behind the desk, but thankfully, the receptionist was asleep. A sign next to him said *Scott*. His head rested on his folded arms; all Anna could see of him was a thatch of dark brown hair. His sleep was thick and inert, in all ways oblivious and she took the stairs, let herself into the room, locked the door, and then kicked at it until her toes hurt. Why the hell could Mike not leave well alone? Why must he have everything? Why could he not respect her, even if he thought she was wrong? Why fight? Why now?

3

—————— ✦ ——————

ANNA LIKED MEN, EMOTIONALLY AND PHYSICALLY; she liked the differences, their being in so many ways unlike her. She did not always agree with where it led, but even so, she admired their matter-of-fact single-mindedness, their capacity for work. She liked the way they lived in their skins and — apparently at least — knew who they were without too much introspection or peering into mirrors. She liked their anatomy, their muscle tone, the shoulders, hips, and the textures of their skin — from the velvet of their cocks to the roughness of yesterday's shave. She savoured the animal smell lurking beneath the soap and shampoo, she liked sex very much and as well as that she admired the whole idea of sexual reproduction, the fitting together of sexual parts which, though of common origin had become each other's opposite, in and out, yin and yang. And even though it had served her so very poorly, the scrambling together of two sets of selfish genetic material: the infinite newness that it created, the sheer enormity of its potential, still excited her.

Her life would have been easier if she had *not* liked men, if she had been a nun, or gay. Or both. It would have been easier, too, she sometimes thought (not understanding, or perhaps preferring not to know, how her unavailability made her desirable), if the men she'd met were as eager to avoid ongoing relationships as they are supposed to be... Sex, love, reproduction: none of it was simple. But she had a system: rules that more or less worked, most of the time. Worked *for her*. And the way she approached sex and love, she insisted, was *different*, not lesser, and in any case she was not foisting it on anyone else. Vik had always wanted her to do things the way he did or would do in her position. Perhaps he still felt that way, but he had, thank God, finally stopped saying so.

The rules: theatre, movie, dinner, skiing, etc., yes. Sex, quite likely. Secrets, no. Domesticity, no. As little grief and mess as possible. Absolutely no trying to tell her what to do. *Yes* to people who appreciated the here and now. Who didn't make judgments, or insist upon answers or see their time together as a kind of investment.

No to anyone insistent, greedy or domineering. *No* to anyone too needy, or who might make too much fuss at the end (and the end would come along quickly enough, unless there were very long intervals between meetings). *No* to close colleagues.

No, sadly but absolutely, to anyone who wanted children, or even looked as if they might without knowing it yet: the hardest part. She did want love, *to* love, especially, but the form this took had to be shaped by her circumstances.

And regarding Mike Swenson, despite his obvious attractions, it had always been, and still was, *No*.

Years ago, they had worked together at the university. At a departmental reception once, he'd leaned in, his lips almost touching her ear and said: *Why don't we two leave this idiotic dinner right now and go somewhere where we can take off our clothes?*

A nice thought, she'd said, smiling, *but I just don't have time for affairs. Let's keep things simple, okay?*

Bullshit, he'd replied. He had promised that he wouldn't want to *domesticate* her. That was the word he had used. She noticed, enjoyed even, that he was implying — without irony — the animal in her, the human in him. He was right about *bullshit,* however, and she felt bad about that but it would have been far worse to explain things properly.

After this Mike had sulked, made life difficult: it clearly rankled him that she'd been given the full professorship and in every discussion thereafter he had taken contrary positions over the smallest things, wrestled every possible point. Having to put up with that had been a factor in her making the sideways move to the post at the museum: wonderful in itself, but also a kind of glorious dead end. It had entailed a shift away from her interest in flight towards a more general focus on the Cretaceous reptiles, and eventually a specialty in the Marine.

So *No.* This went way beyond the rules.

How would Mike explain his injury to Lily? she thought as she splashed water over her own face — but perhaps he had a fair bit of experience with excuses? He probably messed her around no end. Didn't he know how lucky he was? That was almost as upsetting as the rest.

She threw herself on the bed, worked at breathing steadily and calming down. It was important, she told herself, very important not to get an incident like this out of perspective and not to leap to conclusions — and that of course was another reason why she was so very angry with Mike Swenson: perspective was something she worked extremely hard for.

If only she had not called out to Mike and Colin! She'd

done it without thinking, because they could so easily have been there, and because in any case she wanted someone to share the discovery with. Perfectly natural, but if she hadn't called them back, Mike Swenson would be home by now.

And now the scar on her forehead, a small crescent of hard white tissue invisible beneath her hair, began to throb. She refused to touch it, but all the same it would not let her ignore it. She did not at all want to think of that particular day, she did not want to think of her father as he was then — a thin man standing in front of her, jerking and muttering as he tried to fasten the buckle on his binoculars case.

Until that moment she had been Daddy's girl — even when, as his symptoms grew worse, he had given up work, things were still good for a while. His books had come home with him, a microscope too, and he would be waiting in the kitchen for her and Vik when they returned from school. He tipped cookies onto a plate, poured them milk. Sometimes he had to concentrate to do it; his arm jerked and white splatters suddenly decorated the waxed wooden table, Jackson Pollock–style — but he'd ignore them, finish the job, and set the bottle down, staring at it as if it were something alive.

'Half out or half in?' he'd joke, sponging the table. He directed, Vik collected, Anna wielded the scalpel. She sliced and stained onion flesh and plant stems blue or pink, prepared slides: hairs, insect wings, their own skin. Peering through the eyepiece, they saw the different kinds of cells, identified their nuclei. They discovered the organisms that swam in even clean-looking river water, a whole other kingdom or creatures who devoured each other, grew, and reproduced.

'Now,' he'd say, 'try this.'

Once Anna brought home from a school field trip a scorpion fossilised in limestone, which he told her was four hundred million years old. She had already seen dinosaur skeletons in the museum, but it was the simple scorpion, its plated body just like that of today's arthropod, that made prehistory real: there in the sunny kitchen with Daddy smiling at her and Vivaldi playing on the radio, she knew for sure that there had been other worlds, as vivid and as complete as the one she herself inhabited; she knew it for sure now, because they had contained not just storybook monsters, but shellfish, plants, insects and tiny organisms completely invisible to the naked eye, just like, but also completely different to, the ones she'd seen with a microscope. All the time, the world was changing into whatever would come next, a thought that was frightening, yet at the same time wonderful. When she looked into her father's face and tried to tell him this, she saw his smile, and she saw two of herself in the pupils of his eyes.

She preferred to remember *that* moment, the smile on her father's face, the two tiny images of herself in the pupils of his eyes. *Not* how the old-fashioned binoculars in their stiff, heavy, leather-clad case had struck her, hard on the temple, *not* blood in her eyes, tinting the world red. Her mother and Vik had gone on ahead and she ran, calling for them, her sleeve pressed into the wound. Her father had vanished when they all returned to the car.

'Daddy didn't do this,' her mother said as she dabbed at Anna's forehead with antiseptic, and then pressed hard with Vik's shirt to staunch the flow. 'He can't help it. He'll say sorry to you tonight.'

Though he never did. He took medicine that made him

even less like himself, and then went to live in The Meadows.

Daddy had been forty-five, only six years older than she was now, when his movements started to show and he gave up work. He was fifty, perhaps, when the irrational outbursts and violence began. Because it happened gradually, it was harder to say when his speech began to slur.

There was a fifty percent chance it would happen to her.

Symptoms could present in any order.

How dare Mike Swenson force her — reduce her — to thinking of things like this? Yet, Anna told herself, she must not blame him for something he had not knowingly done; she simply could not afford to think that way.

Perhaps, in the morning, it could all be forgotten.

Despite the late hour, she called Vik again. Lesley picked up: in bed, she said, but not asleep. Reading *Vogue* and drinking a glass of white wine, as it happened. Vik had missed his plane, was away until sometime tomorrow. The kids were fast asleep.

'Are you all right?' she asked, her voice warm and slow. 'I'll tell him you called. Come for lunch. Next weekend? The one after?' Lesley knew things Anna wished she did not know. She knew that Anna loved her and Vik's two children even more than she naturally would, as their aunt; she knew that there was a longstanding difference between Vik and Anna concerning genetic testing. And Lesley had once said to Anna that she thought Anna expected too much of her brother now that he was married. But that was in the past, and over the years they had grown close.

'Is everything okay?' Lesley asked again, and Anna, very glad of her sister-in-law being there, calm, sitting in a pool of lamplight in the big bedroom of her and Vik's latest house, with her magazine and glass of wine beside her, told her that it was. Lesley stifled a yawn. 'Call again in the morning. Take care, now, and sleep well.'

Anna did not sleep. She downloaded the pictures from her camera, attached a shot of the find to an email and copied it to Maiko and Akira at the Tokyo Institute, and to colleagues at the museum: *Found today. Late Cretaceous, nodular preservation, wingspan circa 10 metres...* They would all know what it meant to find something like this. And since it seemed impossible to record a day that came in two such irreconcilable halves, she did not open *Personal Notes*, the journal file she kept. She got up and stood on the small balcony, gazed at the stars, wished that she smoked.

Scott slept on. He lay in the cot in the windowless room behind the reception area, the alarm on his watch set for five-thirty, when he would wake, switch on the coffee maker in the breakfast room and collect the baked goods from the freezer, the yoghurts, butters and jams from the fridge. He'd pour cream, juice and two kinds of milk into their respective jugs, and then, as Lauren emerged from her Subaru, set off home.

4

---◆---

ANOTHER THING ANNA AVOIDED RECALLING was the winter evening during her third year at university — long after her father's death — when she saw him on TV. She was in her pyjamas eating spaghetti with Julia, her housemate. Both of them had their feet propped on the coffee table. Julia pressed the remote and they were suddenly confronted by the image of a skeletal, middle-aged man strapped into a wheelchair; he was writhing in a kind of perpetual motion and at the same time struggling to bring a child's beaker of liquid to his lips.

Daddy, Anna thought, even though it was clearly another person. She put down the plate, returned her feet to the floor. On-screen, a serene nurse helped the man, guiding his errant arm and a calm voice explained that these wild, uncontrollable movements along with speech problems, cognitive losses, compulsions and mood swings were among the symptoms of a degenerative condition called Huntington's Disease. It was an autosomnal dominant disorder affecting the basal ganglia in the brain, and currently incurable. A sufferer's children each had a fifty percent chance of developing it, usually in middle age. Until now, they had no choice but to wait and see, but a predictive test was about to be launched. It depended on genetic linkage.

On-screen, the man seemed to be choking.

'Do we have to watch this?' Julia said, and in the kitchenette, the phone rang: Vik.

'I'm already watching it,' Anna said.

That weekend, they drove home together. Their mother greeted them, dressed as usual in layers of splendid, intricate knits, but her eyes were deeply shadowed, and Anna realised, as she hung her jacket on the peg by the door, that she already knew why they had come. Part of her wanted to turn back, then, but the other two were already halfway to the kitchen.

Usually there might be a bowl of fruit on the table, or something she had found on one of her walks. Mama had set out a bottle of vodka and three glasses. Vik, his hands cupped together on the table, looked up into their mother's face and asked her what they needed to know.

Yes, she had said, confirming with one word all their fears.

'Mama, we shouldn't have had to find this out from the TV. Why didn't you tell us before?' Vik asked. She said nothing, just looked back at him.

'When did you find out?'

Vik leaned on the table, his long frame hunched over his arms, his large head tilted down. He looked like Daddy, before the disease ravaged him; at the same time, waiting for his answers, he looked like the lawyer he wanted to become.

'Suppose Anna was pregnant?' he'd asked.

'I'm not, Vik!'

'Surely, you could at least have told us the truth when we *left home!*'

Anna hated to remember how her mother's face had stiffened, and then dissolved. She'd crossed to the other side of the table, held her tight, called Vik over. How small mother was, but also how strong, she thought, inhaling the familiar traces of perfume and cigarette smoke, perspiration, lanolin, the faintest whiff of turpentine. And how fiercely she loved them, how very much she had wanted to protect them. That was all it was, Anna explained to Vik. And why know something like this until you had to?

Later that night, Anna and Vik lay a few feet apart in the two guest beds that now occupied what had first been their shared bedroom, and then later, Anna's alone. Outside, caught in the porch light, snow drifted down. Anna listened to Vik outline what he saw ahead, how they should both sign up immediately for the test, how if either of them were positive, they would not be able to have their own children and should ask to be sterilized.

It seemed to her that he was going way too fast.

Suppose one of them was lucky, and one not? And how on earth would Mama cope, if either of them had it? Who would want to go there? And as for children, testing positive would make having them a very difficult choice, not one Anna imagined wanting to make, but it would not mean that you *couldn't have* your own family. She felt the distinction was important, but she knew better than to mention it.

Vik was seeing someone and he felt that he should tell her right away, he said. Was she involved with anyone? Anna felt her brother's eyes on her face, the pressure of his need for her to signal that she'd heard him, that she agreed.

'I think it might be better not to get too involved with anyone in the first place!' she said, finally turning to look at him. She reached out her hand across the gap between the beds.

'Don't you want a life like everyone else?' he asked. It was as if he was angry with *her*, as if *she* had done this to him.

Eventually it all unravelled: for the linkage test, the lab needed samples from their father and his brothers at least, and a family medical history going back two generations. It wasn't there.

'I can't bear it,' Vik told her. 'I don't think I can go on like this.'

Though what Anna felt was the sheer relief, the utter liberation of being again unable to choose to know. Over the next weeks, while his face grew thinner, harder, Anna dug back into her work.

It would be best, she thought, to store the knowledge of her risk at the very back of her mind — and she decided then, it would be easier if no one else knew. It boiled down to what you could bear. Doubt was for some reason easier for her to bear than it was for Vik. If she looked at what had happened carefully enough, if she *decided* — and it was in theory at least a choice — that marriage and a family were likely not for her, then she was free to live an extraordinary life.

Anna immersed herself in her thesis on *Nyctosaurus gracilis*: she inhabited the body, the muscles and membranes, the maths and mechanics of flight; she frightened herself with the intensity of her attachment to the project: the hours, the task of description, comparison, the effort of imagination, the papers to absorb, the striving to make her language exact.

Vik drank and skipped classes. Then he took an overdose of his sleep medication — he called her to apologise and say goodbye; she got him to hospital just in time, sat through it, dropped everything for a week.

Afterwards, she insisted they live together in an attic apartment she found on Dalton Road, dilapidated, but with a huge maple tree to the front.

She tried to explain to him: how doubt could still be hopeful. How it was surely possible to forget the possible future for much of the time. And how in five years, or ten, there might be a treatment, even a cure. Either way, there was actually nothing wrong with him, *now*. She bullied him into studying again, and in return he made her leave her books and go sit with him in a bar. They met each other sometimes after his lectures, walked, saw a movie, ate; at other times they lived their separate lives and came home, pleased to find the other one there.

She liked to look up and see him stretched out on the sofa that had become his, a book in one hand, his forehead tight, and his jaw loose. He had a serious face that changed shape completely when he smiled. There was no need, for now at any rate, to be lonely. There were shaving things on the tiny shelf in the absurd little bathroom. Two empty wineglasses by the sink. She cooked. He did the laundry; he folded her things and left them in a careful pile on the bottom of her bed. They joked that it was a marriage of sorts.

He was proud of her, she of him. They did not talk about it but it seemed that while their risk set them apart from others, there was some kind of compensation because they were closer than before. On New Year's Eve 1986 they found themselves in the middle of a noisy boisterous crowd, hot, half-drunk, turning to each other for the midnight kiss. She reached up, he down, and then Vik's lips suddenly opened to her, hungry, alive, no longer remotely fraternal. His hands settled momentarily on her hips, and then they pulled apart, their hearts battering their chests.

No one had seen, or if they had, thought anything of what they saw: a prank, a parody. And objectively, surely it was nothing? Alcohol was clearly to blame. Yet what had happened became impossible to forget. By the end of the month, Vik had moved out: the best thing, of course, though there was a tiny part of Anna that thought, why not? Who could blame us?

It was very, very hard to remember that New Year, and the lonely months after he'd moved out. He went to counselling, began to study again, and eventually began a successful career. There was a painful reserve between them which never quite melted until in 1993, almost exactly ten years after that visit to their mother's, when the simple test that Vik so much wanted finally became available. Vik was one of the first people in the country to take it, and he came out clear.

'It's the most amazing thing,' he told her. 'I've got my life back, but it's far, far better than before. I feel as if nothing could ever go wrong, again, not ever.' He wanted Anna to have that feeling too and all over again he was trying to persuade her to take the test, wanting to accompany her to the appointment, reminding her how his result had no bearing on hers, that chance was still fifty percent. She would be all right too…he just *knew*.

Sometimes she felt that way too. Sometimes she felt the opposite. Neither feeling, she explained to him, had any basis in fact.

Then Vik met Lesley, the children were born, and finally it seemed that Vik would allow Anna to go her own way.

5

——— ✦ ———

'WE'RE IN OUR PYJAMAS WATCHING *Mulan*!' Frankie's voice was very loud in Anna's ear, and brought with it the entire person, six years old, with blonde braids and huge eyes, greedy for life. 'Daddy's back at three. Mum's painting the bathroom. Did you go shopping in Japan?'

'Maybe.' The children jostled for possession of the phone. Sam, eighteen months younger, was the more serious of the two.

'I made a very exciting discovery yesterday. It must be a secret for now,' she warned them.

'Sam,' Frankie said. 'Promise!'

'Yes,' he said, after a pause. An enormous winged lizard, she told them. One of the biggest ever found.

'*How* big?' Frankie asked.

'Hmm… Its wings would stretch right across your living room and onto the patio. Its body might have been about your size, but lighter.'

'Will you be on TV again? When are you coming to see us? Mum—' Frankie yelled, 'it's Anna!' Then she was gone, but Sam remained on the line, not speaking but breathing heavily into the handset as if at any point he might. Then, suddenly, he dropped it onto the phone table.

Anna felt almost normal as she showered and dressed.

Downstairs, Lauren informed her that Mike and Colin had already checked out and were in what she called the breakfast patio: a bright room with French doors along one wall open onto a deck beyond. A hunched elderly couple sat opposite each other at one inside table; otherwise the room was empty. Mike and Colin were outside. As she stepped into the light Mike turned towards her and it felt as if all the air had been vacuumed from her lungs. As well as the lump across the bridge of his nose, his left eye had puffed up and turned blackish purple overnight; the eye itself was a livid red.

She was going to say how sorry she was, but he cut across:

'I tripped on the stairs,' he said. The mismatched eyes remained fixed on her for several moments before he looked down at his coffee cup. The asymmetry of his gaze made it impossible to read.

Colin grinned and offered her a chair.

'Just how much did you two drink, now?'

'You've both missed your committee,' Anna feigned a smile as she sat down, and noted a grosbeak bobbing about in the new growth at the far edge of the yard. 'But you do have a good excuse.' Colin nodded, mock-solemn.

'Yes. I dare say we won't be fired this time. Just a detention, I expect...'

Mike, unsmiling, stared out at the trees. Even so, she felt her shoulders relax: at least there was to be no scene, no shouting or fists pounding on the table, no spilled coffee or startled elderly guests watching through the French doors. Naturally, Mike was upset. He had come out of it worse than she had and was probably ashamed of himself too. But the important thing was what they'd found: the astounding specimen lying just a few miles from where they sat, which had died, passed through processes of burial, compression, and fossilisation, and then survived the slow collision of tectonic plates, the heaving up of once-submerged layers of the earth's crust. It had lain underground while species became extinct and new ones flourished, while ice ages came and went. A river had carved a bed, revealing it, finally, to whichever human beings might pass by and be able to see what was there: to her, Mike and Colin. It was their luck, their opportunity — their responsibility, too. Forget the rest.

She tried and failed to catch his eye, poured cream into her coffee, sipped. If she did not have any time alone with him before they separated at Vancouver, then she would call him or send a note — something simple suggesting that they had both acted out of character and should put the incident completely behind them.

Out of the corner of her eye, she saw him glance at his watch.

'We'd better go,' he said to Colin.

'Ready?' Colin asked her. 'The cab's due.'

+ + +

'June next year would be the earliest that we could begin a full-scale dig. It'll have to come out with the matrix attached,' she said as they stood waiting on the wooden dock. The sea, a calm, silvery blue, was decorated with webs of mist. 'We'll need a helicopter. That one close to the bank won't be easy.'

Mike, as if deaf, stared out to sea.

'Then, in terms of preparation, it'll really cost,' Colin said.

'Yes,' she grinned at him. 'So?' It was a running joke that he did not have to cope with these kinds of problems, could bring what he wanted home in his pocket, more or less and keep an entire library of specimens on his office shelves.

'We were so lucky!' she told him. 'I wasn't looking for it. I was thinking aquatic.' The floatplane, its wingspan only a little larger than that of the creature she'd found, emerged just then from some low cloud on the horizon. Seeing it, they all picked up their bags, even though it would take some minutes to arrive.

They sat wedged next to each other, Mike in the far window, Colin in the middle, Anna on the nearside. The roar of the engine was both deafening and soothing and the vibration and noise together seemed to scour her mind clean. The ocean below looked more than anything like the skin of some enormous animal, though as they progressed its appearance became more complex. Huge quantities of deep green algae formed viridian clouds, shifting and billowing beneath the surface. A school of thirty or so porpoises, dwarfed by distance, leapt and sank back into the water in apparent unison, sewing their path through the sea. The plane passed over forested and rocky islands, harbours cluttered with yachts and docks, and then they were approaching the delta, the water suddenly smooth, shallow, and heavy with reddish sediments.

For a moment Anna let her eyes close, and allowed herself to imagine a huge winged creature, downy with brownish hair, its legs tucked up, its neck folded down, slowly beating its way through the air and tracked by its shadow on the water below. Its sight, far more acute than human vision, allowed it to see beneath the water — warmer back then and far more profuse with life, home to car-sized turtles, enormous squid. For a moment, she saw what it saw — and then the floatplane, rejoining the water with a bounce, jolted her back into the now: they climbed out into a breeze that still smelled faintly of cedar.

Soon they were in Departures, a man-made bubble of re-cycled air and flickering fluorescence, a world of grey furnishings and static electricity filled with a subdued, brain-numbing acoustic of murmuring voices and the turning over of mechanical systems. Meanwhile, outside, dimly visible be-hind UV-filtered glass, the real world — ancient, vast, complex and extradimensional, continued without them. The three of them, marooned there in their dusty boots and practical clothes, could not afford to fall out.

'Mike — wait!' She fell in with him as he made for security. He bent to retie his bootlace and then stood facing her. They examined each other: he'd shaved carelessly. His left eye, in its purple casing, was smaller but somehow far brighter than the right; the pupils of both eyes were small, his lips tight.

'I'm sorry for my part in it. I just reacted... I didn't mean to hurt you.' Ignoring her, he turned away and joined the line into security. Colin appeared, waved, and pausing to raise a hand, followed suit.

Why on earth these playground games? she thought, furious all over again. She could be dwelling on the insult of it: *I notice you screwed someone else so what about me?* But really, who cared? And now what? Would Mike tell Colin on the way home? If so, would Colin tell her he had been told? How far would it all go? How much of her attention was it going to take? She strode out through the automatic doors, back outside.

Cars crawled by, dropping and collecting passengers; she

crossed and made for a bench in a small garden area by the parkade: a square pond, some dwarfed conifers and a box of orange begonias: an odd combination, habitat-wise. A small, vivid green frog, *Hyla regilla*, sat close to the edge of the pond; its whole body, glistening wet, beat with a tiny pulse. She slipped on her sunglasses. Overhead, plane after plane carved up the sky.

Before long, she would be up there, and then down, out and through to the outside world again, breathing real air even if it was thick with fumes, and climbing into her own car.

✦ ✦ ✦

Once Calgary was behind her, she stopped for gas and called home. Soon she was on Highway 9; to either side stretched broad, flat fields with their swathes of stubble and rich brown earth, the occasional groups of staring cattle. It appeared to go on forever, but forty minutes later came the familiar surprise: the road's sudden plunge into an increasingly arid, meandering canyon. The town itself, a straggle of dino-themed hotels, malls and campsites was an irrelevance soon left behind and she drove on and out into a windswept landscape where low grasses and sages had bleached to silvery green and beige, studded here and there with yellow flowers. Prickly pear still bloomed, and on each side of the river was a narrow but lush strip of cottonwood and alder, their foliage just on the turn.

Home, Anna thought, finally forgetting everything else, and soon she was on the driveway and approaching the cream clapboard house. Her mother had chosen and then decorated it when finally she'd agreed that life would be more pleasant for her (she refused to say easier) — if they lived together again.

The door was unlocked and the smell of good food cooking filled the house. A note from Janice, their careworker cum housekeeper, mentioned lasagne and that salad dressing needed to be made. Anna found her mother dozing on the back porch, her face in shadow beneath a huge straw-brimmed hat. After all the places she had been, it was sweet to pull up the other wicker chair and sit there a few moments, watching the gentle movement of her mother's breath. Stuffed between her leg and the chair was a sketchbook, and to the side on the table were a pile of magazines, a jar of pencils, water, pills, the wind-up radio she insisted on using, the phone and one of the photograph albums from her room. Between the hat and her white-framed Jackie O sunglasses her face was more or less invisible. She was wearing a paisley print blouse in blue and turquoise, and a pair of the stretchy pants she had taken to of late because they were easy to deal with in the bathroom. She seemed smaller than ever, though her hands, which lay curled in her lap, were too big for the rest of her and, with their swollen, shiny knuckles and curled fingers seemed almost to belong to some other kind of being. Despite her own ingenious attempts to escape and the mercies of technology, she was increasingly trapped in her body. Yet she never complained. For some reason which was not simple pity, Anna found herself in tears as she leaned in under the hat to kiss her mother on the cheek.

6

————— ✦ —————

GLASS AND TINTED CONCRETE: part warehouse, part church, the museum was a place like nowhere else on earth. Its staggered shape and ochre walls deliberately echoed the landforms surrounding it, but, as Mama had once pointed out, you could also think of it as a ship voyaging on the vanished Cretaceous seas, a kind of modern-day ark, huge and well-equipped, its storerooms filled with plaster-wrapped life forms awaiting preparation and, eventually, resurrection.

The public carparks were empty; even the staff parking, tucked away behind the landscaping to either side of the main entrance contained only a dozen vehicles this early in the day. Anna slipped her pass into the reader and, inside, felt herself relax into the particular hum — almost, but not quite, silence — that was the sound of the working part of the museum.

Anna wedged her office door open. Light filtered through the Venetian blinds in the farthest of the two rooms, illuminating, just, the closer, larger room where she kept equipment and specimens in use. Waiting on the workbench was the long skull of the mosasaur, *Clidastes liodontus*, right there where she had left it six weeks ago.

The electric lights threw everything into sharp relief and showed up the dust. She dug into her daypack and unwrapped the fossils. The air seemed to stiffen as she set the exposed phalanx under the binocular microscope, steadied it with miniature sandbags, adjusted the focus and, there — suddenly clear — was the porous pattern of the ultrathin bone, a bubbled effect almost, like batter made with self-raising flour. The texture was exquisitely detailed at the joint end, where the top layer had adhered to the other side of the concretion and partially detached when the nodule split. And there, where the border between fossil and rock had been disrupted, she caught the faintest hint of something gold: pyrites, which must have been formed right at the beginning of the fossilisation process.

'What have you there, then?' Peter Grace, aka Wings, stood in the doorway waiting to be invited in. After months of fieldwork, his iron grey hair was especially shaggy.

'Vancouver Island?' he asked, as she stood to let him look. A thin man, he bent awkwardly at the knees before giving in and using the chair.

'It's quite something. The scale—'

'Yes. Two of them. Maybe more.' Later, when Brian Hogarth took his turn at the microscope, she and Peter watched him, knowing what he would see, waiting for him to see it. When he looked up, grinning, you could see the boy in him, Anna thought, despite his baldness and weathered skin.

By ten o'clock, everyone was in the staff lounge. Brian and Pete, Dave, Jan, Ken and Ray: Dinosaurs, Birds, Fish, Mammals, Arthropods, Pollen. Squat, bushy-haired, lanky, unshaven, pop-eyed, dusty-looking, as various as the creatures they studied and all gathered together in an odd, coffee-smelling, windowless, leftover box of a room. This was her other family, her kinship group. It was good to share her luck.

'So, next year?' Pete was applying for co-funding for a trip to the Arctic and so now they would be looking to the same sources, but then, she reasoned, so would several hundred others. It was a matter of the project itself; the various committees would decide.

'Yes,' she told him. 'It's very fragile. I'm aiming for next year.'

'Pressure's on, then,' he said. 'Better get started. Let me know if I can help.' She wanted to hug him, but he'd turned away to fill his cup.

In the preparation lab, a crane lifted a two-metre hadrosaur femur onto a bench; the sound of the machinery, the bench tools and the ventilation system merged into a rhythmic blur of grey noise. Huge metal tubes from the extraction system snaked up from each bench and reached towards the ceiling that towered above them. None of the half-dozen masked and goggled technicians bent over their benches had noticed her enter and Anna waited at Ai Lin's bench until the other woman became aware of her and removed her safety glasses and dust mask.

'You can have him very soon!' she said, gesturing at the row of vertebrae on her bench. How to say she had something better now? And the fact was, she had barely three weeks to prepare a sixty-page application: permissions, outline, significance, context, budget, benefits to local community, referees, maps, pictures, timeline.

She leaned in and unwrapped the fist-sized nodule that Mike had dug out.

'Just look at this, Lin. Very fragile bone in rather tough but also terribly brittle shale—' She watched Lin turn the nodule over in her gloved hands. 'Hopefully, we'll extract it next summer — and hopefully you'll get out of here and join us? Anyway, it's urgent. Funding application. I can't wait until the next committee.'

'No paperwork?' Lin's face with its dark eyes, its stillness, was hard for Anna to read, but she leaned closer as she spoke. 'Not even a *number*?'

'Not yet. But I need fantastic pictures by the end of the month.'

'Two weeks, maybe,' Ai Lin said, and reached for her eye protection. Eighty million years it had lain in the ground: it was, Anna knew, absurd to have these deadlines and agendas, this huge impatience inside her. Later, separating the new specimen from its matrix and reassembling it would proceed micron by micron and take three technicians at least four years.

Physically large, technically challenging, and of the utmost scientific importance, she wrote to Andrew Bellavance at CanCo, the logging company which owned not just the adjacent land but also that section of the riverbed itself. The Ministry of the Environment had said that designation as a Special Heritage Site would take at least three months: there had to be a way around that.

> ... *Although it is too early to know the exact timing of any possible excavation, we are hoping for the summer of next year, and I am writing at this stage to obtain in a general sense the permission of CanCo to extract these fossils (which would of course take place with full consultation*

and in co-operation with yourselves) and indeed to invite
you to enter into partnership with us and our possibly other
sponsors in what will be a hugely exciting enterprise
attracting international attention...

Anna made lists, proceeded with what she needed to do and
tried very hard to ignore completely what had happened with
Mike that night in Big Crow — but it came down to this: the
museum was not a teaching institution and in terms of grants,
it could not go it alone. Nothing would progress without collaboration with a university. It was best to use a tried-and-tested
partnership, and that meant dealing with Mike Swenson, who
was already involved. Surely, he wasn't prepared to jeopardize
the entire excavation out of a mixture of anger and pride? She
certainly was not.

All her instincts told her not to make a fuss. To move on, not
dwell, to bury rather than confront. She hadn't told Vik about
what had happened, and she hadn't told her mother. She
hadn't told Janice (had she told anyone at that point, it would
probably have been her), and she certainly had no intention of
telling anyone at the museum. She would make the incident
go away, and take with it, too, the fears, memories and anxieties it had provoked. This was not the time for them. She
would ignore the man, and make contact with the scientist
inside. And if what was needed was for her to swallow the very
last shreds of her pride and offer him a way back that involved
absolutely no loss of face, not even a mutual apology, well, yes,
she could do that, too.

She looked at what she had written to Mike and deleted *my
part*, replaced *incident* with *misunderstanding*.

I'm deeply sorry about the misunderstanding last week. Let's put it behind us, and begin a new collaboration between our two institutions... She explained that she aimed to commence in June and would like them to put in joint applications to National Geographic, NFS and CFS as a matter of urgency; she was preparing the application and would be able to send him a draft for his input very soon. *Please, Mike,* she concluded, *contact me at your very earliest convenience so that we can agree upon the details of the approach.*

As she left her office, Greta, one of the year's volunteers, emerged from the library. Dressed in sun-bleached clothes and scuffed field boots she looked like the spirit of the place, but, she said, it was her last day.

'Come back next year,' Anna told her as they shook hands, and she added that it would be a very good one: though this was not the way, later, that she would think of it. Neither good nor bad could encompass the experience: it was like one of the vanished creatures she studied come to life, an amalgam of teeth, wings, scales, claws, a huge beast that materialised suddenly ahead of her in a woodland clearing, both magnificent and terrifying. But at this point, life was still more or less normal, and that evening she drove her mother up and out of the canyon to one of their favourite viewing spots. They sat in the last of the sun's brightness and ate still-warm deli chicken, while with each mouthful the earth tones in the valley below grew deeper. A breath of air caught the wisps of hair around her mother's face.

'Gorgeous, darling,' Grace said, waving at the view. The way things looked — that they should be interesting, if not beautiful, mattered very much to Grace. Because of her hands, she could no longer paint the way she wanted to and her career, just as it had taken off, was at an end, even though paintings themselves changed hands at ever-increasing prices. She still thought in pictures; she exclaimed over colours, pointed out contrasts, drew her daughter's attention to the exact way light changed. Recently, she had taken up photography. When Anna talked to her mother about the find, she took pains to give the right kind of visual detail.

'Covered in gold! How wonderful.'

'Pyrites. But you know, we'll have to remove it during preparation, so we can see the structure of the bone. That's beautiful too. More so, even. Like bubbles, or honeycomb. And, of course, that's where the information lies. The thing is, once it's exposed to the air, pyrites can cause the specimen to degenerate. And, you see, it tells us nothing about the—'

'The trouble with science is that so much destruction seems to be involved, and all in the name of *information*.' Familiar territory, this: *Why not leave things as they are? Does one need to know about something's insides in order to love it for what it is or does?*

Smiling, Anna took her mother's hand.

'You'll love it when it is articulated.'

'I expect so,' she said, 'but, darling, imagine it *gold as well*. Gold leaf. Even spray paint. Why not?'

They heard the yowl of coyotes somewhere in the distance and when the sun finally disappeared, the whole town, the entire valley, was for a moment or two, empty of human noise.

Please, Anna had written in her email. But Mike did not reply.

Andrew Bellavance, on the other hand, was very forthcoming. His company was always happy, he said, to be associated with projects that brought positive benefits to the local community and showcased the company as a responsible part of it. They could grant outline permission, had no objection to Special Heritage status for the riverbed area, and were keen to consider to help further. He could put her in touch with a contractor they used for airlifting who might also like to be involved. What kind of payload would they need? He would see what he could do.

Perhaps Mike had some family or personal problems: it would explain everything. Why hadn't she thought of that before? Cursing herself for being so self-centred, she called him again to express her concern, but stopped short of leaving a message on the voicemail. Instead, she called Colin, and asked *his* voicemail if he knew what was going on, if there was something the matter?

Neither of them replied.

How many helicopter trips? Andrew Bellavance asked.

Eight, she said, though she thought they'd get by with four.

I'll approach them for you on the basis of the higher number, he said.

The budget: staff, insurance, vehicles, travel, accommodation, helicopter, materials, equipment, return transportation of the specimens, contribution, donations, shortfall. Supplements: maps, drawings, topographic and stratigraphical analyses. Permissions and consultation: a search turned up several quotes from Alan Coxtis, the leader of the First Nation band that held the lands adjacent to CanCo's property: the Stallquakseen, or, as they wrote it themselves, St'alkwextsihn. Most of these articles concerned their ongoing treaty negotiations and their objections to pollution of the lower reaches of the Big Crow River caused by the now defunct mill; she added to her list the need to contact Alan Coxtis, explain how the specimen was close to, but not on, the reserve, and that the site would be treated sensitively, and ask for input from the band.

Regarding Mike Swenson, she abandoned the personal crisis theory, and could feel her heartbeat gear up when she thought of him. *If you don't answer by tomorrow morning,* she wrote, *I shall be forced to seek another partner for this project.* It would not be hard to find one, given the nature of the find, and it was a relief to declare something and be prepared to stick to it, move on.

The next afternoon, she called Ben Morris, who had been working for years on a huge pterosaur rookery in Brazil. His expertise, she told him, would be a huge asset, and since she had already done most of the donkey work, and was quite willing to do the rest of it, she hoped collaboration would be an attractive proposition.

'I think this is going be astounding, and it would be wonderful to have you as a partner,' she concluded.

'Big Crow?' Morris said. 'Yes. Of course. I think it has excellent chances of support. And, as I said before, it's all dependent on other commitments, but I'm totally behind you guys and I'll do my utmost be there at some point during the excavation.'

'As you said before? Said to whom?'

'Swenson, of course,' she heard him say. 'I'm his referee for this.'

Anna became stone, grafted to her chair, the abandoned mosasaur gathering dust in the lab behind her, the landscape it had been extracted from glaring in the sunshine outside. A hawk hovered in the middle distance.

'What's your involvement?' Morris asked her.

'There's been a misunderstanding,' she said and put the phone down.

Immediately, it rang: Colin.

'Yes,' he admitted. 'He has applied. It's gone in already. He had two of his post-docs working on it...' He sighed. 'Of course I don't condone this, Anna. But at this particular time, I don't think there's anything I can do. And I stepped down as chair last week. I think you two need to sort it out between you. I can't say more, but I believe Mike is under a fair bit of pressure right now.'

'You were *there*!'

'Well,' he said, 'yes. And I should remind you that it was I who noticed the second specimen. But yes, I know... The thing is, Anna, I wanted to respond to your message, but there's nothing that I, personally, can do'

'Are you all right, Col?'

'Let's say I'm doing okay,' Colin said, and then wished her all the best and ended the call.

But surely, Mike couldn't expect to get away with it?

His voice, professionally warm, invited her to leave a number so he could call back. *Are you there?* she wanted to say. *Pick up the damn phone! How dare you do this? How do you think you can punish me for something that you began?* She managed to hold back, say nothing, strode out of the too-quiet office, her hands fisted, the sound of her blood hissing in her ears. *Please, someone tell me this isn't real, or, failing that, to take the matter right out of my hands and tell me what to do.*

Brian, the obvious candidate, waved at a worn typist's chair, an antique almost, he said.

'Extraordinary,' he told her when she'd finished. 'He's always been very professional in my dealings with him.'

'I took all the photographs; Colin was *there*. How can he even think of saying it's *his*? Does he really expect to get away with it?' Brian's shoulders hunched. His blunt fingers dug into the remains of his hair. 'I suppose you'd have to apprise the funding bodies of the situation, put in your own claim... Let them arbitrate. If the evidence is on your side, well... You've got to get the institution behind you. Talk to Sheila.'

Sheila was away on a course.

At home, she left Mama and Janice talking while she looked up Mike's home number. Lily answered.

'I don't know,' she said. 'Let me see.' For several minutes there was total silence on the line, then Mike's voice, very loud in her ear, right in her head it seemed.

'Hello!'

'Mike—'

'How dare you call me at home!'

'I can't get you at work.' She forced her voice to remain steady. 'I know what you are doing. It's outrageous... You know as well as I do how this began.'

'Are you making some kind of allegation?'

'No— I don't want to make allegations. I want to find a way to—'

'This is a *professional* matter,' he said just before he hung up. 'Never, ever call me at home again.'

Professional? Did he actually believe his own lies? Was his behaviour calculated or compulsive? Was it possible that people would in fact believe him, or rather, be unable to believe that he was actually doing what he was doing? Could all this be real?

Downstairs, her red-gold hair recently cut short, her eyes bright, Janice lounged on the sofa, midway through an account of the summer's main events: her eldest son's first job, her mother's visit, how Ken sold some sculptural pieces as well as masses of the tourist lines of mugs and pots, and now had prospects for shows next year. How good the garden had been. The Lester place next door had sold at last, to a family with a web design business who looked as if they might make a go of things.

Anna refilled their glasses, and sat down carefully next to her mother. The room with its honey-gold walls and her mother's large ochre-and-cream abstract over the fireplace was the same as ever; the thick evening light beyond the windows and the sounds outside were just as they should be. But all of a sudden, she was living two lives: she kept slipping or being dragged out of the one she'd made and into its opposite.

Later, when Janice had gone home, she turned on the lamp and opened the bed for her mother.

'Are you all right, darling?'

'Just a bit of trouble with a man,' Anna said as she bent to help her mother swing her legs in. 'It'll blow over,' she told her, leaning over for a kiss. 'It's not important.' Her mother gripped her arm. Her eyes seemed huge and very dark in the soft light of the bedroom.

'I wouldn't have had anything different,' her mother said. 'You know, I never wished I'd met another man instead of Leo.' This was something Grace had often said, and which part of Anna resisted. *But if you had known right at the beginning? What then?* — though she had come to accept it as what her mother felt to be true.

'I know, I know.' She patted her mother's arm, kissed the warm, dry skin of her cheek. Her mother's face was owlish, now that the wild hair was thinner and kept short, in wisps around her face.

'I wish you could have what we had—' her mother said, meaning, Anna knew, family: a communal love that warped and twisted, but never disappeared. Yet how much of that, really, had there been?

'Mama. Everything's fine. This is the best way. I love you,' she said, and turned out the light.

In her bathroom upstairs, Anna searched her image in the mirror: no glassy stare, no discernible facial twitch. Her face was more severe in its lines than that of the wiry child who appeared, holding Vik's hand, or with him sitting on her lap, in the pre-diagnosis family photos her mother displayed on every available surface downstairs, but she looked out from beneath the same unstyleable mass of hair and she had the same tilt to her chin. There was the beginning of a smile, the familiar mixture of impatience and curiosity in her eyes, and, there on her left temple, hidden under the hair, the faint gleam of the scar.

Her mother had been right and wrong, true and false, when she'd said it was not Daddy who had thrown the binoculars at her. The cause of his irritability and his increasing violence was organic, utterly beyond his control. In one way, the violence was not him as he had historically been, but in another way it was, because he had changed at the cellular level and become a new, difficult-to-like man wearing the same skin, a person who despite everything, and perhaps partly out of loyalty to her memories, her mother still loved.

7

————— ✦ —————

ENSCONCED AT THE DESK OF THE MOUNTAIN VIEW and awake long after he needed to be, Scott zoomed in and studied the on-screen raven image part by part: the sharp beak, the huge eyes and stylised claws. You could see the cracks in the wood, the places where the paint was beginning to lift. In real life, he knew, the carving would never be retouched: it would slowly fade and rot and in a couple of centuries, vanish entirely into the soil. And so he should probably leave it alone, too, though it was tempting to fix things, to make them look better than they were, which was exactly what Lauren would want.

'Tourism's all we have now,' she'd told him, her eyes wide with outrage. 'No one's coming here on business anymore. So, better get out there.' At this time of the year, once the schools were back, but before the snow came, no one at all was stopping at Big Crow, though trucks loaded with raw logs still shuddered down the hill. How long could even that last? Some people, Scott knew, might ask how long *should* it last? Did the people of Big Crow want the planet to burn up, the climate to go haywire, the seas to rise, just so they could pay their bills? But no one here mentioned that way of looking at things. The town, like Mac, could think of nothing but its immediate needs; it was in a kind of permanent daze.

Earlier in the day, through the slatted blind on Dr Hoffman's window, Scott had a good view of the main street, half of it boarded up. Hardly any cars about. Thirty families had left since the flood, but Dr Hoffman said that while there were far fewer people in town since the flood and CanCo closing down its mill, those who had stayed seemed to be sick far more often. Well, she'd asked, how was he? He could feel her pale grey eyes all over him, taking things in: how he hadn't done his leg exercises, or been to the gym, for weeks. He still had the limp; he was gaining weight.

He had mixed feelings about the pills. They made him feel as if he wasn't quite in his own life, though then again, did he want to be?

A temporary solution, according to Dr Hoffman. A way of breaking the vicious cycle. Right now, things would be worse without them. Hopefully, he'd make some changes in his life, and then they would become unnecessary.

'You'd find far more facilities for your father in a city,' she'd said, 'and more opportunities for you to fulfil your potential. It's not too late. Why stay here?'

'He won't go. Says he'll die here, where Mum died.'

'Don't tell him. When he sobers up, present it as a *fait accompli*.' Fate what? He couldn't. Why? He didn't know. He couldn't pull a trick like that.

Co-dependency was the other phrase she'd used. Meaning, he depended on his father wrecking his life so he wouldn't have to actually live it?

'Something like that,' she'd said.

'Like it's my fault?'

'I am trying to help,' she said.

Lauren, sole proprietor of the Mountain View, was also the president of the Chamber of Commerce. She had known Scott's mother, hence his job, hence her tolerance of his poor time-keeping, her willingness to overlook the times when some emergency of Mac's meant Scott had to leave, and even the time Mac had turned up and passed out on the picnic bench out front. Recently, Lauren had persuaded the Chamber to hire Scott to create a website.

Two hundred dollars was about a tenth of the going rate — but he'd gone beyond money, way beyond what was normal, what the people you saw on TV or passed on the road looked to be getting, what statistics said people earned and lived on. It was *something*, it might lead to bigger things. He was free to work on the website while on duty (which now included cleaning reception and the breakfast room) so long as there was absolutely nothing else to do.

Lauren had sent Scott out with her camera to get pictures: of the forest, the mountain, water rushing over stones in the river, sunrise over the ocean, of the old post office and these, the carvings that marked the edge of the reserve. Ravens, or crows, depending whom you spoke to. Big beaks, either way.

'They should put events on up there in the reserve,' Lauren had told him. 'Drumming or dancing or pole-carving, something.'

'Why?' he grinned at her, 'just so we can list it under *Attractions*?'

'Yes,' she'd said. 'Why not? Bring people in. We're all in the same boat, except they don't pay tax.' Not exactly willing pas-sengers, Scott thought, though what he'd said, with a slow grin, was *Jealous?* and she'd said no, far from it, but how come *they* wanted it both ways?' Then she'd blushed, and said of course, she had no intention to give offence. She wasn't prejudiced, she took people as she found them and she really admired how his mother had tried to make a different life, and what had hap-pened to their little family was just a tragedy all round.

Tragedy? The word made him uncomfortable. And even if she hadn't been *taken from us*, as Mac put it, his mother must have known, by the time her story came to its sudden end, that she'd married someone from a culture that had its own prob-lems, just as bad, and also someone very like her father — that her bid to escape the rough side of reserve life had failed. If she'd had more time, would she have returned home? Escaped again? Gone elsewhere? Or would she have continued to wait, endlessly, for the right moment? There were worse possibilities, too.

Scott resized the image of the raven carving, cropped out some of the trees, but left it as it was.

Fuck the big questions, he thought. Do they help any? The Door to the Universe had survived the flood and he could go anywhere a webcam went, from some kid's bedroom in Nebraska to the Great Barrier Reef and he could have e-sex with a person called Chryssie Liz (even though he didn't know who the hell she or he or it really was) and he could know any fucking useless factoid there was to know and be part of the craziest things without getting off his chair: a group on the Net — crazies who believed that some people would soon have chips in their brains and skeletons made out of titanium, and they would be the ones that lasted when the planet started to cook. It was fun to think that way for a change instead of just feeling scared about how the icecaps were melting and the sea levels rising and the prairies turning to dust and the forests being cut down or eaten by beetles and the fish having weird babies and cancer being endemic because of all the chemicals, and how before long there wouldn't be enough food to go around and now there was a whole new load of shit in the Middle East and how awful it all was — but there was nothing to be done about any of it because the multinationals who ran the planet didn't give a fuck and had the governments completely in their hands... It must make a change to feel almost on top of things, to look at a normal person, Lauren, say, and have all that going on in the back of your head while you spoke to them and think, *but I will survive.*

8

────── ✦ ──────

ANNA HAD WOKEN FROM A DREAM about Mike: they were outside a
hotel that was the Mountain View but even more run down;
she'd hit him and he'd fallen, crumpled to the ground and he
lay there, not moving, eyes closed, blood gushing out of his
nose. She was on her knees beside him, saying his name and
trying to take his pulse when his eyes sprang open and he
reared up, grabbing her arm... And now the darkness and terror of that moment floated somewhere between her and the
calm, orderly room she sat in, and the sound of her own voice
tearing at its edges made her feel more desperate still.

'I already know,' Sheila said. A tiny woman, the complete
physical opposite of her husband, Ray, the pollen specialist,
she was impeccably put together in shades of dark red and
cream, her hair freshly tinted and styled. She set her coffee
down on a mat on her desk.

'We'll support you fully, of course. Now,' Sheila said, 'let's
talk around this. Is there any background, anything that you
could think of which might have precipitated all this?'

Anna bent to pick a paperclip from the floor; wanted to cry,
did she have to explain and justify heself to anyone who asked?

I hit him: she did not want to say that. The whole of her resisted it, that bit in particular.

Sheila waited.

'We did have a disagreement after the find. But it was absolutely nothing to do with the find itself.' Sheila waited.

'In confidence,' Anna told her, 'he was bothering me. And I said no, but he grabbed hold of me. And so, in the heat of the moment, I — struck him in the face, and I made a real mess of it.' Her own face was a mess too, now, flushed, wet: she hid it in her hands. Sheila's touch on her shoulder made her jump.

'Did you report it?' Sheila said as she squatted down next to Anna.

'Did I *what*? I've tried to apologise, but he won't accept it.'

'Apologise? It sounds as if there was kind of a sexual assault. So — well, that's something that should be reported.' A *sexual assault*? For the first time Anna looked properly at Sheila, who had not said *only a very sick person would hit a man like that*, who peered back at her, her mouth soft, her neatly shaped eyebrows raised in concern.

'Even now,' Sheila said, 'you should make a statement to the RCMP.'

'But it was a misunderstanding. It may even have nothing to do with what's happening with the specimen... Well, it's connected, in that he's angry, but I don't want to blow it up out of proportion, not more than it already is.'

Sheila stood and went back to her chair.

'Things are already rather out of hand, don't you think? It looks to me as if you're being punished in a big way. Look, you've got him three times. You have a great profile for your work here. You have found something of enormous significance, *in his field*, which, because you are female, is unacceptable, but, if he has you, then maybe it can become his. But, you say *no*.'

Their eyes met, pushed against each other. To explain to Sheila why she could not quite accept this account, why she could not dismiss a lingering sense of guilt, Anna would have had to say more, go deeper, further. She couldn't.

'Didn't you once work on flight? There's a territorial element, for sure.

'How's this?' Sheila said. 'I set up a meeting of the research and funding committees. We'll approach the university, alert them to the problem and seek a solution. Meanwhile, it's been a huge shock. Go home now, get some rest.'

'Sheila—' Anna was on her feet, glaring into the other woman's face, 'How am I supposed to get on with my work?'

'Go home,' Sheila told her. 'I'll call you.'

Anna ran. She cut through a tangle of tracks and disused minor roads and then back a mile or so to the east. The ground was flat, but on either side rose the sheer walls of the meandering canyon, gouged out by glacial meltwater and then ever since blown and washed away at a rate of four millimetres a year, showed the ochre, rust and charcoal sediments of a vast alluvial flood plain and the remnants of a long-vanished sea; a landscape full of revelation. She was out of practice; her legs leaden, her chest tight but she slackened off and then, when she came back to the run, it was easier.

Her breath found its rhythm; slowly, the biochemical consolation for her efforts trickled in, lifting her mood a little. Marsh, she reminded herself, who had discovered *inter alia*, some of the first North American pterosaurs, had dealt with wolves, buffalo stampedes, sandstorms; his team lived under a constant fear of Indian attack. Back then, you returned from fieldwork glad to be alive. Surely that put her problems in perspective.

Though perhaps the human enemy was worse than the beastly one, and frank hostilities were different — preferable — to betrayal.

Did Mike believe his own lies, or somehow forget that he was telling them? What did he say to himself about this?

The sky lowered, overcast, its greys melding seamlessly with the mud and iron tints of the landscape below, and finally the rain came, smearing slippery, clayey dust over the road and forcing her to walk.

✦ ✦ ✦

Two days later, two weeks after the find itself, they convened in the boardroom, three abstract canvases behind them, and the blinds down against the late September sun: Sheila, Peter, Brian and Anna, at one end of the long polished table.

From the university: a faxed letter, offering a version of events according to Mike: how he saw the larger of the specimens first, and Anna had acknowledged (as he was sure any committee would agree) that he was better qualified and equipped to deal with a find of this kind and magnitude, and had given him her blessing to lead the excavation. But perhaps she had mixed feelings, because later that evening he'd become concerned because of her reluctance to hand over two small parts of the specimen which he had extracted. He felt her response was extreme, as had been her behaviour ever since. He was more convinced than ever that the university must insist on complete control of the find.

From the museum, the draft of a letter saying that they did not accept this account, would like to resolve; but if not, would take the matter further by making the funding bodies aware of the dispute and its origins.

'It has to be said, all this is going to make a lot of ripples and cause bad feeling,' Pete said. 'Are you ready for that?'

'I have to ask— where are you coming from when you say that?' Sheila asked, and he looked at her, baffled.

'I'm just flagging it up.'

Anna knew Pete was right. She had experimented briefly with the thought that she could walk away, let Mike have Big Crow, tell herself that the important thing was that it was excavated and prepared and who exactly did these things was irrelevant. But at the thought, the familiar surge of rage pushed through her: no, he's not having *this*.

'Anna?'

'I think we have to go ahead. And I think the letter's good.'

Sheila, Anna knew, wanted her to share the whole story, to at least hint at it. But she avoided Sheila's gaze, looked around the table at the rest of them as they studied the museum's ultimatum, their faces variously furrowed and contorted. Jan's pen clicked in and out. Pete yawned, pulled at his ear. It was as if, suddenly, they were back in grade one, struggling with the fundamentals

'Well,' Brian said in his deep, slightly hoarse voice, 'not my department but it seems straightforwardly put. Let's hope it works.'

9

$\qquad\qquad\blacklozenge\qquad\qquad$

ANNA WAS IN THE BASEMENT WITH THE KIDS, watching first Frankie, in a tutu, and then Sam, as himself, walking along the back of a sofa and then leaping onto a beanbag that had to be moved farther away each time, when Vik appeared in the doorway and invited her to see his new toy. He led her to the garage with its polished cement floor and track lighting — large enough, the joke was, for an ordinary family to live in — and revealed a silver BMW, just weeks old and his alone, just for going to and from work. The very first of Vik's fancy cars, Anna remembered had been a black Camaro bought to celebrate his negative test.

They sat inside the car, inhaling the scent of its newness: leather, plastics, polish, pine. Vik demonstrated the seat adjustments, the computerised navigation system, the speakers; he flicked the lights on and off for good measure and then gave a summary of the vehicle's vital statistics and performance data.

'Want to drive?' he asked.

The garage doors slid up. Anna eased out of the driveway, put her foot down once they hit some straight road. It was easy to slip over the limit; they both liked speed. Vik gave directions. The road rose towards the foothills, beyond which the peaks of the Rockies glowed violet white.

They parked at the viewing point, gazed back down and across the flat expanse that stretched east to the city, fading now in a haze of dusty light. Vik touched her arm.

'What's the matter?' he'd asked, and she was grateful that he had seen through her, that he still knew her better than anyone in the world.

She told him: what Mike had done, what she had done, what Sheila thought of it, the dispute over the find: it came out easily enough.

'It's driving me insane,' she said, and then waited a few seconds for him to weigh up what he had been told.

'Yes,' he told her, 'it is a shame you didn't report it.' But there was no blame in his voice. No sense that she'd brought this upon herself, had been unreasonable — above all, no sense that he thought she was possibly suffering from increased aggressive impulses, irrationality, mood swings and impaired cognitive faculties. If anyone other than her would think that, it would be him, but there he was, perfectly matter of fact. Already, she felt stronger.

'I'd say find a way to go for him,' he said. 'At the very least fire a shot across his bow: might send him packing. Not my field. But I know someone—' He hunted through his cell phone directory for the number, wrote it on the back of one of his own cards. 'Here.'

'I don't want to be aggressive about this,' Anna said. He laughed, and a split second later, she joined him.

'You'll talk to her?'

Anna put the card on the dashboard. 'I'm not sure. Now don't get bossy on me, Vik.' He picked up the card and gave it to her again.

'You don't have to act on her advice, just hear it.'

'I do have to act on yours?'

'You could try that out, for once.'

'I am grateful, Vik, really.'

Frankie ripped the exquisite Japanese wrapping paper from her gifts, and then helped Sam. They tossed aside the t-shirts featuring gorgeous, incomprehensible writing, yelled their delight as they came to the heart of the matter: robotic pets that walked stiffly across the room, communicated in a series of electronic warbles, beeps, whirs and squeaks and had to be cared for by pressing buttons in order to feed or soothe them.

Frankie slotted batteries into their bellies and remotes.

'Point!' she yelled at her brother. Lights flashed; the creatures' plastic feet clacked across the wooden floor.

'I'm sorry,' Anna told Lesley, 'but they asked. They'll soon get bored with them and then you can use them as an example next time they want something dreadful.' Lesley handed her some glasses for the table.

'You better be right,' she said, 'or I'll send them to stay with you.'

'Please! But after I've done this application—'

Lesley forgave Anna for the robots when her own gift slipped from the tissue paper it was wrapped in: a length of blue-grey slubbed silk that felt smooth and rough at the same time. The fabric, she said, was perfect. It would make a duvet cover and then a Roman blind... Anna did not care much about decorations, but she recognised the passion. Lesley had some similarities with Mama, and it was easy to see how Vik enjoyed providing for her: her pleasure in the physical surfaces of her life, in the tastes and smells and kinds of things was intense, and so, presumably, was her pleasure in him.

Vik grilled the fish. The low light streamed through the open doors, caught in the polished glasses and the coloured and colourless liquids they contained; it bounced around the table, lightly touching the knives and forks, the edges of plates, and burnishing the grain of the wood. Everything had a great depth and richness, and peoples' skin and clothes looked somehow more than themselves, as if it all were part of a painting, and Mama herself, her cheeks flushed, her white hair electrified, her upper body wrapped in an intricately crocheted purple cardigan, was likewise crying out to be made into a picture. They passed the camera around the table until Vik carried in the salmon, perfectly charred, and used the last scrap of memory for a picture of that. Sam settled on Anna's lap and soon her shirt was damp with sweat, his or hers or both, she had no idea. His head knocked periodically into her chin as she ate, using her fork only, the other hand holding him tight.

Later, when the kids tired of their robot pets and ran outside to play in the last of the light, Lesley closed the doors to the deck and Vik lit the stove; propane flames danced around the coals.

'I'm really hoping we'll have one more,' Lesley told Anna as they cleared up, 'once Sam's done preschool.'

Mama slept in the car on the way home from Vik's. Anna, driving under a sky clotted with stars, felt lighter. It seemed to her that she had let things get on top of her, but now she had support, a perspective on what was happening, and life would eventually return to how it used to be.

10

---◆---

THE EIGHTH-FLOOR OFFICE OFFERED A VIEW through Venetian
blinds and tinted glass of other office blocks; the street between
rose very gently into the distance and bore a steady stream of
afternoon traffic, though no sounds from the outside penetrated
the room. There was a scent of synthetic fibres and cologne.

'May I call you by your first name?' Pamela Schott asked, as
they took their places across a low glass table. Anna nodded,
sipped the coffee the receptionist had poured for her, noticed
the shake was with her again and carefully put down her cup.

'Anna,' Pamela said, removing from the file on the table the
faxed copies of the various letters, emails and photographs,
'what I think would be useful is a full account of what happened in as much detail as you can.'

In the solid, corporate room, she felt that the events of that
night weeks ago sounded especially idiotic and unbelievable. Who
on earth would behave like this? Why would anyone take it seriously? Yet Pamela, dressed in dark grey relieved by various pieces
of delicate, conventional, gold jewellery, sat straight-backed with
her feet side by side and her legs parallel. Her face, though, was
open and responsive. She waited for each answer, nodded when
it came, made occasional notes, frequent interruptions.

'Were you surprised when he made this suggestion?'

'Very.'

'How well did you know Dr Swenson?'

'We worked together for about four years. I went to his wedding.'

'I have to ask — were you two *involved* at any time, or was it a possibility?'

'Well, he was interested, years ago. And when I said no, it caused some trouble. But nothing like this, and as I said, that was many years ago.'

'Not interested?'

'No, I didn't think it would be worth the trouble it would create.' A brief smile of acknowledgment, and then twenty minutes later, they emerged from a thicket of dates and times to more general questions:

'I'd like to know a little more about you, Anna. Are you married? Do you have children?'

'No.'

'Do you live with someone?'

'No.' Anna found herself trying to stare Pamela Schott down and though the other woman did look away eventually, it was not because she'd succeeded.

'How old are you?' she asked, looking up from her notepad.

'Thirty-nine. Nearly forty.'

'How are things otherwise, at work? Your relationships with colleagues, that sort of thing.'

'Excellent.'

'Anna,' Pamela Schott said after another long pause. 'The professional organisations will make their own decisions based on the evidence presented to them, but they are not courts of law and the outcome isn't certain. So there's a choice here for you between a passive or defensive stance and a more proactive one. You were the victim of a sexual assault and I think you can make a complaint about sexual harassment. Universities are very aware of their duties in this respect. But we would have to overcome absence of witnesses, and deal with the fact and that you didn't make your complaint immediately.

'I feel that you could explain your reluctance to report the matter in a convincing manner. I think you could also consider seeking reparation for the damage done to your well-being and your reputation by the comments reportedly made by Dr Swenson and quoted in this letter from the university.' Pamela Schott leaned back a little in her chair and waited for a response.

'I'm not sure. I'd much prefer to just— move on. Find a solution. But—'

'Naturally. But Dr Swenson has taken it further. If you do make any accusations, he'll counter. You need to be prepared for that.'

Anna pushed her hair out of her face. Her hands were damp.

'There's something—' she began, 'something which complicates things. I'm in a *difficult situation*,' she heard herself say and then her voice shrivelled up and she had to clear her throat. *Stop*, she told herself, ignored the order, continued: 'I have some potential health problems. I'm not sure whether this is relevant. I didn't plan to discuss it today. But there is a possibility that there's an organic reason for my lashing out—' Over by the desk, a low tone sounded. 'I think this is what inhibits me, somehow.' Pamela Schott nodded.

'People do sometimes lash out. I don't see what you did as

beyond the pale, under the circumstances. But can you tell me more? What is this possible medical condition? Or would you prefer to make another appointment?'

The elevator plummeted to the marble-lined lobby and Anna turned her back on the mirror so as not to see her face, contorted with the effort to avoid tears. And in the sudden din of the street, the outside air bitter with exhaust fumes, she struggled to orient herself. Her chest tightened. Blindly, she followed the traffic, took the next right into a slightly quieter street and walked, scarcely aware of where she was or of the intersections crossed.

She strode on, shaking her head at panhandlers and at a middle-aged woman in a beige coat who asked was she all right? And at last found herself in a shady pedestrian street with boxed evergreen shrubs down the middle and a sculpture of a horse at one end. There was a café opposite a bookstore and she washed her face in their bathroom before taking a seat at one of the tables. She knew, as from a great distance, that she was hungry.

She could scarcely believe what she had said, or how much she had wanted to say it. Who would she tell her secrets to next? Mike Swenson? It was horrifying to realise that part of her wanted to do just that, to explain herself to her enemy, who sat safe and healthy in his office in the university, to beg him to understand what was going on for her.

A young woman with plum-dark lips and a piercing in the side of her nose came to take her order.

Everyone, Vik once told her, lied to their lawyer, even if they don't realise they are doing it. Guilty or innocent, he said, it was just a matter of degree. On the other hand, there was an urge to confess or to be found out: criminals risked their lives to evade justice but later told an unreliable acquaintance the whole story; adulterous partners left the scrawled phone number of their lover where it would be found, failed to wash the scent of sex from their skin before they slipped back into the marital bed. Everyone wanted to be known. More than to know, perhaps.

Until her knuckles had made contact with Mike Swenson's face, she'd worn her silence like a second skin. And because of it, she had not so far been seen as a possibly-doomed-to-be-sick person, but as Dr Anna Silowski. She could, for the most part, control her own thinking about the future. Reticence about her risk had made it easier to cope with since she was the only one who might raise the subject.

But now, as she sat stirring her coffee and half-watching customers emerge from the bookstore opposite, she still could feel the urge to tell, the way it had flooded through her: it was an almost physical thing.

Vik had his own agenda, well-meaning, but an agenda, nonetheless. Mama knew, and she must at all costs be protected. But there was no one else. No one — and then she had found herself telling a professional, a stranger, who had expressed her sympathy and then concluded:

'I'll think it over, but I really don't feel it is relevant. After all, whatever your medical condition or risk, there was an assault.'

Outside the café, dusk was falling. Anna pushed aside her plate, paid, took a deep breath and made her way back to the parkade, the beaded lines of lights that led her out of the city.

Her skin seemed to feel every breath of air. She put her foot on the gas, slipped the *Goldberg Variations* into the CD player and let its impartial pulse fill the car.

Darkness, twenty-first-century darkness, rushed by outside her hurtling metal box; her headlamps were reflected, for a moment, in the eyes of a roadside coyote, there — then gone. She turned up the music, drove on, towards home. So, she thought, she must fight. She would not let Mike Swenson elbow her out of her part in the collective attempt to know something of the enormous, intricate story of life on earth: those lost moments found again, sometimes almost whole. She wanted those glimpses — just as she wanted to know the present-day flora and fauna: to identify the blue beardtongue and anemone, hear the horned owl at night and know what it hunted. This was who she was, what she was for, and the find was hers. It was her calling. She could strip away her own assumptions and see what was there; she could entertain hypotheses without becoming too attached. And so, if she had to be— what was it Pamela Schott said? *Proactive*, then she would be.

The town was bathed in yellow streetlight. In the park, presided over by an anatomically incorrect *Apatosaurus*, a few teenagers skateboarded in the floodlit area of the park close to the tennis courts. Night surrounded her again until she arrived outside the house. All the lights were on downstairs. She walked straight through to the kitchen; there on the counter-top where she and Janice always left messages was a one-word note: *Hospital*.

11

SHE FOLLOWED THE NURSE TO A TINY ROOM at the end of a long corridor.

Vik rose from a chair by the wall.

'Anna—' he began, but she did not hear the rest.

Her mother was a tiny shape beneath the covers, her cheeks flattened, her mouth agape, flecks of dried saliva in the corners. She didn't react to touch, or sound; there was no sense that she heard when Anna bent down low to kiss her forehead and say that she was here. There was only the electronic beeping that marked the rhythm of her heart. Her hand was cool and dry.

Vik began in a soft voice to describe the damage wrought by a stroke: both sides paralysed, swallow reflex gone, a risk of heart failure — and even without that the prognosis was poor. It had happened around lunchtime. Why did they not try to contact her? They had, but with no luck. He'd got there as soon as he could. Her jacket, Anna realised, with the phone in its pocket, must still be hanging by the door of the lawyer's office.

'I came right away. Janice was there. She was fantastic. There was nothing you could have done,' he told her. They spoke very quietly, although, they would have given anything to wake their mother up.

'They're doing their best,' he said later.

'You've seen Mama's will? I'm not sure she wants them to do their best.'

'Thing is, it has no force in law,' Vik said. 'The fact is—'

'What do you mean? She's made herself very clear.' He leaned forwards, rubbing his forehead with his fingers. 'I agree with you, of course,' Vik said, 'or I think I do. But—' and first his jaw and then his whole face unravelled and hers followed; they clung to each other, pulling tissues from the box.

The room was very warm. The sockets of Mama's eyes deepened and the soft bulges beneath the lids were utterly motionless. Her cheekbones grew more prominent. There was a complete lack of tension in her flesh, just the shallow rise of her chest, and her heart, beating on: Mama, mama, mama.

When Vik went for coffee, Anna took her mother's hand and hummed a lullaby, wanted to feel an answering pressure, a tiny squeeze, to see her eyes flutter, trying even, to open, but nothing happened; things continued as they were and she dozed off, only to be awakened when a buzzer sounded. Staff pushed into the room.

'I'm sorry,' they told her half an hour later.

Vik did not want to see her body but she did.

Grace lay orderly on her back, her arms to her sides. A shocking absence filled the room, and, Anna thought, how she would have hated that icy blue hospital gown.

But aesthetics apart, this, she later tried to explain to Dr Eriksson, was exactly the kind of sudden death that their mother would have wanted. Grace had been very clear: she didn't care if she lost her memory, or if she said embarrassing things, but so long as she lived, she must be able to see, eat and talk, and if this was not possible she'd prefer to sign out. She would rather be shot than cared for by strangers in an institution, and so on. She'd asked Anna to type all this out, then signed it, and stapled it to her will.

'May I give you something to help you through?' Dr Eriksson asked, putting her hand on Anna's arm, and it was then that Anna stopped talking and began to howl.

12

———— ✦ ————

THE TRAILER DOOR OPENED right into the kitchen. To the left, bedrooms, to the right, the living area, the oat-coloured drapes permanently drawn, a TV at the far end. This was where Scott and Mac ate, rather than at the camping table in the kitchen where junk mail and empties piled up.

Mac was awake, upright and uptight when Scott came in. It was as if he could smell the two hundred dollars in cash that Lauren had paid Scott that morning, could sense that some of it was already spent and beyond his reach.

'I can think of easier ways to make two hundred bucks,' Matt had said, leaning his seat back and grinning across at Scott. Matt's dog, Tiger, at least half ridgeback, stood stiff-legged in the back of the truck. They were in the playground parking area with the engine still running.

'Sure.'

'I could set you up with an agricultural project. Rentals are rock bottom right now.' They were friends of a sort. They had both dropped out of high school the same year, despite, as the principal put it to Scott in the last phone call, having *the capacity to succeed.* He'd used the same words to Matt.

'I don't do gardening,' Scott told Matt, though the real reasons were: one, that he knew he'd smoke himself sick, and two, Mac—hardly discreet. They'd been through it all before. Smiling, Matt slipped the banknotes into the pocket inside his jacket, and put the baggie next to the gearshift for Scott to pick up.

'I'm gonna retire at thirty-five,' he said, fixing Scott with his clear, untroubled gaze. 'Properties, the whole damn thing.' Matt imagined things, and then made them happen, though often the cost to others was high.

'Have you got something?' Mac asked as soon as Scott was in the door.

'Hungry?' Scott countered and set to work: he unpacked the groceries, measured out water and rice, and attacked the accumulated dishes. Mac offered to help, which was all very well but he had the beginning of the shakes so there was no point handing him a knife.

'Sweep the floor. Maybe empty the ashtrays first?' Scott opened a jar of Thai sauce, studied the serving-suggestion label on the back. He chopped an onion and a green pepper, sliced the chicken breasts, washed the knife. Since he was twelve he'd been cooking, on bad days to start with, and then pretty much all the time. There had been fires, there had been things cooked and then forgotten, there had been things too disgusting to eat; there had been semi-raw meat and a lot of sandwiches but both of them had survived until this point. Now it was convenience food, or meat in a bun with lettuce on the side for health, and just occasionally something new.

The oil hissed as he threw in the onion and meanwhile Mac

grunted and puffed, reaching out with the brush, groping for the dustpan. Soon his face was running with sweat; forget it, Scott said, and brought him a mug of water.

'Drink up, Dad.' Mac looked at the water as if it were poison. 'Good for you.'

The rice had gone dry. Scott rescued it, added the sauce to the other pan, stirred; remembered vitamin pills, one each, watched Mac swallow his, and then took the two trays over and sat down.

'Chicken,' he announced. It was not bad at all, he thought, but it could be *more* how it was aiming to be. He watched the news without the sound: Israel. Men in suits. A woman who survived a cougar attack. Someone shot outside a bar.

Mac had set down his fork after a mouthful or two, but Scott ignored the ruined eyes fixed on him, following each mouthful from plate to lips; he ignored the fact that a shave was overdue and a haircut likewise and neither would happen unless he took it in hand. *Does a shave really matter?* To his father not at all. To him, just somewhat. To some members of the community, quite a lot.

Scott, it's not good to let your father out looking like that.

On-screen, a Native girl in a photograph, perhaps four years old. A woman breaking down as she spoke. He got up and carried his plate to the sink.

'Hey,' said Mac as he returned, and then reached for the glass of water he'd been given earlier, sloshing some over the food on his plate as he brought his face down to meet it, and then drank: one swallow, two, three, and then opened his eyes wide to suggest its life-giving effects. On the TV, a boatful of windblown tourists in lifejackets, Vancouver in the background.

'What about a top-up?' Mac asked, his chin wet, and Scott told him no. He closed his eyes so as not to see the reaction and because it was so fucking impossible to do a right thing: you give him the money, he likes you for a moment, but drinks, and you're contributing to liver meltdown. You don't give, he hates you, suffers longer, finally goes out and somehow or other gets the drinks, possibly more than he would have anyhow: you personally haven't contributed to liver meltdown, but hell, it's happening anyway. You still see a sick man feel pretty bad and on top of that you're a hypocrite, considering how desperate you are to lighten up and chill out, though of course it doesn't wreck you in such an obvious way.

'You're supposed to be levelling off.'

Mac looked at him and drank the rest of his glass of water. *Go on then*, Scott could ask: *drink another.* How about you eat half your dinner, drink two more waters and have a shave: ten bucks. He'd done that before now. Compromise. Easy to criticize, but when your father cries like a baby — an ugly, old, broken baby — and tells you how every bit of him hurts, and just one drink would fix it, you tend to think *what the hell, it's his fucking life,* forget that it is yours too and give it to him, and feel good momentarily just because the conversation's over for now.

Mostly, then, Scott gave in, gave Mac just enough to get the first drink, but this time, he intended to spend the remaining one hundred and fifty bucks on some more memory for the Door to the Universe and he said no. He said it and began to assemble a joint, the gum on the papers sweet against his lips.

'You cunt,' Mac said, watching every move.

You can't blame him, was what Andrea Price always said. A woman approaching middle age who tried to look as if she wasn't wearing makeup by wearing only the most natural shades, applied rather thickly, she cornered Scott every time he went to the grocery store lineup and asked how things were, and then argued with him about the way he described it.

I can't, Scott remembered his mother saying, how she shook her head but smiled at the same time when he'd suggested that the two of them should run away together. Off into the sunset. *You'll understand one day — I can't.* He'd been only nine then. He still didn't understand, but he'd seen how things were and over time he'd become very familiar with the *c* word and even used it himself a fair amount.

Andrea Price always said how they were all praying for both of them at the church and would he like to come along? .

Well, thank you. Maybe another time.

'You can share this,' Scott told Mac when he had finished making the joint. 'Then I'm going online, okay?'

There was this thing he'd stumbled across, totally amazing: a group of three guys in what looked like bat suits base-jumping off a towering cliff in Norway. They stood on the edge looking down thousands of feet and then leapt, turned a few casual-looking somersaults as they fell through the air; seconds later, reaching terminal velocity, they straightened themselves, flung their arms out wide and hurtled horizontally through the air. The suits, made from some rubbery stuff, had a flap that joined hand to hip. Going at a hundred miles an hour, they steered with tiny movements of their heads. Their fingers all but brushed the cliff; they swooped, turned more somersaults, plummeted, and rose again at will. One of them sank to within metres of the ground, skimmed it, following the course of winding road, and then rose up again. All the time you could hear a strange rushing, flapping sound, like wind in their ears. It looked like Superman, not real, but it was. At the end, you saw them wild-eyed, laughing together: *It's like a dream*, one of them said. *You just look where you want to go and you're there.*

13

WRAPPED IN THEIR COATS AND JACKETS, on a sunny but chilly day, the memorial guests stood or sat in the rows of borrowed auditorium chairs alongside Anna's colleagues, Janice and the handful of new friends Grace had made since she moved. A surprising number had flown in from the East, friends and contemporaries but younger people too: Eileen Hudson, from her gallery, Chuck Tennyson who had collected the best of the work she had done since Leo's death, other artists, their partners, former neighbours, the children of old friends.

Anna wore one of her mother's hand-knit sweaters in oranges, browns and golds. Most of the women and a few of the men had complied with the request she had made in her will: they wore brightly decorated hats and colourful scarves, had draped shawls over their winter coats, so that the garden looked as if it was host to a flock of huge clumsy birds, some of which became human and spoke about her mother: a remarkable woman. Cared for her husband. Raised her children. Painter. Photographer. Optimist. A fantastic mother, Vik said, the best in the world.

Not long ago her mother had stood naked in the bathroom and asked Anna to photograph the mottled skin of her belly because the colours were so complicated and interesting, then laughed at the thought of those who would find it weird.

Oh, darling. Forgive me, she whispered now, real and not real in Anna's ear. *Press Play now.* The music too had been specified — an eclectic mix. To the strains of gypsy fiddle music, the flock of bird-people struggled out of their chairs and made for the warmth of the house. Anna slipped Mama's camera out of her pocket and took a photograph. Vik looked appalled; Janice, beside her, linked arms.

It was impossible, when she returned to her office, to relate to the outlandish task of painstakingly extracting a winged lizard the size of a floatplane from the Cretaceous shale, still less to the notion that a man wanted to fight her for it. As for whether she was developing or would develop HD or not, she had no opinion and no longer cared.

The nights were extraordinarily long.

On weekends, and then increasingly during the week as well, she borrowed Janice's dog, Roger: knee-high, black and brown, bristly, perk-eared and of indeterminate breed, he was the perfect antidote to melancholy. He was keen, but well trained, sat with his tail thumping on the floor; he followed her from room to room, watched her eat and wash. If she closed the door, he waited on the other side until she opened it. He saw her weep, curse, sleep; he watched her sit on the floor in her mother's bedroom, so full of her things, so empty of her.

No one said anything against her occasionally taking him in to work, and she found herself taking him more and more. He was her dog, except that he couldn't be, because she was away so often. He listened to her phone calls, to her reading aloud her description of the skull of *Clidastes liodontus.*

Roger listened to everything, but was not in favour of self-indulgence. And he was a one-answer dog. His nails clickety-clacked across the floor and he waited for her by the door. Out! Out of this house, now! Out into the fresh snow, where white rabbits hide. She could still laugh at herself: a woman, a scientist, who talked to a dog.

After Christmas Vik took everyone to the Yucatan — a low-rise hotel with cabanas strung out along the beach, lush grounds populated by huge, dazzling butterflies and equally brilliant parrots, and turquoise pools.

In the rooms were white lizards that could drop their tails and bizarre flying insects as big as a fist, which took off almost vertically.

Lesley was pretty sure that she was pregnant. So to let her rest in the mornings, Vik and Anna took charge of Frankie and Sam, smothering them in sunblock and then getting them sweaty and covered in sand, and then rinsing them in the pool or the ocean, and doing it all over again. In the afternoons, Anna read in the shade, left the family more to itself, though once, she and Vik joined a diving trip.

Flying fish burst out of the water, then vanished again, leaving it a glistening, undulating sheet stretching right to the sky. When the boat moored, Anna strapped on the tank and checked the mask, waved to Vik; she slipped into the water, was immediately absorbed into a reality far more vivid than anything she had imagined on the way out: the otherness of the sea, its layered blue-green light, the weight of it, the intricacies of the reef, its impossible colour, the quivering shoals of striped and glistening fish. A clever octopus wedged into an impossible crack and peered out, just one eye visible. *Hello,* Anna could not but think at it. *What is it like to be you?*

When the letter came in March, she knew, because of the thickness of the envelope, that it must be good news: acceptance papers to sign. The word pleasure was in the first sentence: *Dear Dr Silowski, It is with great pleasure that I write concerning your application for funding the excavation of the pterosaur remains at the Big Crow River.* Wings sprouted on her back — she felt weightless, could fly there right now! Yet the body of the letter, longer than usual, evoked more complex feelings:

> *Since the circumstances of this discovery are unusual and more than one competent party has expressed an interest in excavating the site, the Society has decided to divide our support for this project between, on the one hand, yourself and Dr Maiko Yamaguchi of the University of Tokyo, and on the other, Dr Michael Swenson. The area surrounding the fully exposed specimen known as Crow River A will be your and Dr Yamaguchi's responsibility, and the larger specimen, Crow River B, partially beneath the cliff, will be Dr Swenson's. The two expeditions will be under separate control but are likely to be simultaneous; we hope you will find many opportunities for co-operation and economies of scale during this excavation and subsequent preparation and description of the finds...*

'We get one, he gets one,' Brian said, as they sat again around the big table in the meeting room. 'The judgment of Solomon. I guess they didn't want either of you, or either institution, up in arms. Trying to smooth things over.'

Sheila hissed out a breath, tapped her notepad with her pen.

'What do you think?' Anna did not usually ask other people how to proceed and everyone in the room stared silently back at her.

'I think you know where I stand,' Sheila said.

'It's still good,' Dave said. 'I mean, if you put your feelings aside, then the fact is it's more or less how it would have been if the problem had never occurred. You and he would have been working together on this, right? So you still are, with the boundaries more defined. Okay, meantime you have fallen out. Okay, he gets to write his own paper. That's what he wanted out of it, if you ask me. Granted, the man's a shit, but you're still in there and that's the main thing. Compromise. I think you should look at it as a success.'

'Yes,' said Brian, 'could have been worse. But if you don't want to go ahead, given the importance of this find, we must consider who else—'

Someone else?

'Of course I will do it,' she said; there were smiles and congratulations all round.

'So should I be pleased,' she asked Roger, 'that I've almost got something like what I wanted? Yes? No?'

✦ ✦ ✦

'I have to advise you that if you are going to voluntarily work with Dr Swenson,' Pamela Schott told her, 'it can only weaken any case you try to make.'

'*Voluntarily?* The committee split the find between us, fifty-fifty.'

'I don't think you understood me, Anna. Leaving aside whether it's wise to work with a man like Dr Swenson, look at it from the other side's point of view. A gift! And how will it seem to a third party, given that there are already weaknesses in your case, and that yet more time has elapsed before you start to disclose what happened?

'Anna, you have to choose what's most important to you here: the find itself or the dispute with Dr Swenson.'

Put that way, it was very clear.

14

---✦---

TWO TECHNICIANS LOADED THE SKULL of *Clidastes liodontus* onto a gurney and steered it towards the door.

'Had enough of this guy?'

'I need some space for this!' she pointed at the caudal vertebra from Big Crow which Ai Lin had prepared for the application.

'Size doesn't matter, then!' The two men's guffaws were suddenly muffled as the door swung behind them. Freed from the matrix, the fossil perched on a sheet of glass. A vestigial neural spine, little thicker than an envelope, jutted up and back: it was a simple, perfect, almost weightless structure, suggesting, if you looked at it carefully enough, an entire architecture, a skeleton that supported the muscles and tendons which flight demanded.

Anna switched on her bench light. She settled herself on the padded stool, adjusted the light, reached out.

'No!' she yelled as Roger shot out from under the bench. *'No! Lie down!'* He obeyed, cowering, and then began to sound the alarm: a low growl, a loud bark, repeated. *'Quiet, Roger!'* she hissed at him, but already there was knocking on the door:

'Are you all right?' Brian.

'No.'

'What's up?' The barking stopped as he approached.

'Don't tread on it!' Brian's eyes widened, searched the floor. Fragments everywhere. Somehow, the vertebra had skittered to the edge of the bench, flown over it, hurtled towards the floor and then, even though it was so very light, burst apart.

They looked at the pieces. The movie did not rewind.

'I hadn't even looked at it,' she said. 'How can I face Ai Lin?'

They knelt and collected the pieces. Brian's square hands and blunt fingers and Anna's small-boned digits were equally deft. Brian puffed unapologetically as he bent and reached; Anna's breath scarcely existed.

'Well, you've got more of them? And it can be fixed. Lots of time and a bit of glue... But, Anna, I think you're going to have to reconsider the dog!' he said as they each placed their fragments into the lid of a storage box.

'Okay now?' Brian asked at the door.

'Yes, thanks, Brian.'

Roger? Casters over the laminate floor, action and reaction as she reached across? Involuntary movement? She did not know exactly what had happened. She would never know.

When she called him Roger came over, sat panting and looking up at her. He seemed to watch her as closely as she was watching him. She rubbed the back of his neck, and then clipped the lead onto his collar.

15

——◆——

IT WAS SPRING; THE WIND WAS WARMER, brought occasional blasts of white-gold light between showers. Scott had just finished making a site for a band called DDT. At least, he thought as he drove home, he had made them *look* like they might be okay. He hoped Chryssie would be online and hot when he got in.

The front door was ajar.

'Dad?' he called, standing a moment in the kitchen, where the light showed the dust and everything seemed unnaturally still. There was a CD lying face down on the floor: one of his system discs.

He knew already then, but strode to his room to confirm: all that remained of the Door to the Universe were two shadows in the dust on the desk. Gone: every last lead, cable and bit of it, even the mouse and its mat. Liquefied. He grabbed the paperweight, a mango-shaped rock he'd found by the river, smashed it experimentally into the wall. The thin panelling cracked, splintered — but it did not feel like enough.

At the liquor store, Fraser confirmed that indeed, Mac was there the night before, along with two guys from out of town. Scott bought whisky of his own. He waited in the lounge with the TV mute, the rock close by; he drank slowly, waiting, and thinking what he might say, the perfect, bitter one-liners: *So, I guess you didn't feel you'd had enough out of me? Look, there's something I've wanted to do for a long time.* He did not imagine what might happen afterwards, or care. When a car door slammed outside, he jumped up, the rock clenched tight in his hand, crossed to the kitchen. There was coughing outside, the sound of the key stabbing unsuccessfully at the lock.

He resisted the urge to yell, or to spring to the door and yank it open, because once he did that the whole thing would happen at once and he wanted Mac to realise what was happening, and why, to know what was hitting him. It seemed to take forever for the key to slide home, the door to crash open. Mac lurched in.

'Scott?' he struggled to focus, and at the same time, to stand. Scott watched his father, bearded, his jeans buttoned but not zipped, register the unusual quality of the situation, sniff at the hostility in the air, and in slow motion, and divine the reason for it. A lopsided, hopeless grin spread itself on his face and he reached into his pants pocket and pulled out a crisp new twenty.

'Take it. Yours.'

'Aren't you even *sorry*?' Scott's voice broke. He hurled the rock at the window, not at the old man with his flies undone who'd once lain with his mother in bed and started a life, his life, this one, his. 'Look after your own fucking-self!' he yelled and then he was in his truck fumbling with *his* key, couldn't even see it, or what was beyond the windscreen.

Finally he pulled out of town. Go, go and go. You've been through all this before! he told himself. So what. Damn, fucking, pissing rain. Spring? It never stops here, he thought, as the wipers smeared dust and pollen across the screen.

He drove without thinking left and up, towards the reserve trail to the lookout on the cliff. *Your place too*, his mother used to say, *if you want it to be.* Never mind, she told him, the judgments about her leaving. There was family there still, a distant cousin or two. He'd seldom visited since her death, but he did feel something for the place, a pull.

Like mother, like son: loyal, stuck, screwed. Her time ran out: the aneurism. Over in minutes. *Scott Macleod, please come to the principal's office* (life as you know it is about to end).

A lesson there, no doubt about it.

Fucking rain. No jacket. Had enough.

He got out and jogged through the forest towards the cliff, feeling the rain again as he emerged from the trees into the weather and the roar of the water below. The last of the melt was coming off the mountain; the muddy water crashed down the falls upriver and then churned and raced past the cliff. It was a year since the flood.

Can't leave, he thought, staring down at the water skittering over the rocks on the other side, can't *stay*. Can't go back to that stinking trailer and live In Real Life with Mac going under and no chat rooms or MOOs, no weird and wonderful facts at my fingertips. No credit. Still owe the bank. What else did he have? Chryssie — a person never actually touched, who'd send a photo of her (or someone's) slit and tell you what she'd like you to do, type in real time how thinking about that made her feel, but wouldn't step into your actual existence: not much of a tie. And irrelevant, given lack of hardware at home. *Can't leave. Can't stay.*

The water churned below. Fast, not so very deep. Here and there you could still see rock. He thought of the men in wing suits, jumping off their cliff. His heart pounded inside him and the rain beat on his skin. *Can't go on—*

'Hello,' a voice said, right next to him. A person about shoulder height wearing bright blue raingear had appeared out of nowhere and was standing right beside him. Hairs rose on his arms and neck at the shock of it, yet she was real enough. Female, with brown eyes was about all he could tell. She held out a hand gloved in Gore-Tex.

'Mr Bellavance? Anna Silowski.'

'No,' he told her, his hands jammed in his pockets.

'But I'm supposed to be meeting him here right now. Does that truck on the road belong to you?' she asked. 'Have you been here long? What are you doing here?'

Mindyourownfuckingbusiness.

'What are *you* doing here?' he asked, and at that, she looked away, down at the water. 'If you're from CanCo,' he said, 'don't tell anyone in this town.'

'Well, no—' She looked back down the trail, and then took out a cell phone: it wouldn't work, but he let her go through with it. He started to shiver, remembered a half-joint in the truck; nodded in the direction of the road and set off, the rain beating on his back, his shoes soaked.

'I guess there is no point in me waiting there,' she said, when she caught him up. They took the trail back together in silence. Her white Corolla was parked behind his truck. Hired: no one sane would buy white.

'You're soaked,' she said, as if she'd just noticed him properly for the first time. 'Are you all right?'

'Just great, thanks,' he told her, and slammed the door shut.

He fired the engine, turned up the heat, stripped off his

t-shirt and wiped his hands dry on the other seat. The lighter and half-smoke were right where he thought he'd left them; he found music, pushed the seat back and lit up.

He started up on the old script about Mac not being able to help himself because it was a disease. Though, of course, if he hadn't ever started drinking, it wouldn't have shown itself. It was a kind of potential that had to be activated. Ironic, of course, that Mum saw him as a way out of the kind of life she had as she grew up. He was just fine when she met him, she'd said. And maybe his inner alcoholic was just waiting for a good wife to come along so he could safely let rip. And now here he was, picking up where she'd been forced to leave off. It was almost funny, really… Scott was warm all over and just beginning to relax when a knocking on the window jerked him right up in the seat. He wiped the window and there she was again, the Woman in Blue.

'My car won't start. But I've got lights. Maybe it's the alternator, or something? My cell phone *still* won't pick up.'

So she stood next to him holding an umbrella while he checked what he could under the hood. Nothing to be done without parts. He began to see the funny side: her, the umbrella, him stoned with no shirt. He hunted for the tow rope in the back of the truck but it was gone.

'I'll drive you to town,' he said.

'I really appreciate this,' she told him as she shoved her laptop case under the seat. *Hell, everyone but me*, he thought, seeing it, and then turned up the fan, got the wipers up to speed. But he was alive, at least.

'Scott,' he told her, as he heaved the truck into a U-turn; he couldn't see through the back, but hardly anything ever came that way. 'So, what were you doing up there?' *Oh, come on,* he thought, watching her hesitate, *I've been half-naked with my arm in your engine. Don't I deserve to know?* Besides, it could only be Forestry, Mines or Tourism, and who cares?

He had no shirt on and the car smelled of marijuana. They were avoiding publicity. She didn't know what to say, but couldn't not answer. She was good at avoidance, at keeping quiet, but not at outright lies.

'I'm a palaeontologist,' she told him.

'Dinosaurs?' he asked, turning to her, and then back to the road, 'Here?' She hesitated again. 'Well,' she said. 'Not *exactly* dinosaurs. Winged lizards. A different part of the evolutionary tree.' She wiped the window with her sleeve and then pushed back the hood of the blue jacket. A huge amount of dark hair, still dry, sprung out to either side. How old was she? He couldn't tell. But it was interesting: until now, palaeontologists had been wind-tanned men with big beards mumbling long words on TV, not women with huge eyes and wild hair.

'We're hoping to excavate them this summer.'

'Cool!' he said. *Stop there,* Anna advised herself. But he was very kindly driving her and she returned his smile.

'Yes. Exciting,' she said, 'though there are issues. It's actually going to be extremely challenging—' and then she found herself telling him about the bone, and how it was only millimetres thick and honeycombed with air pockets, yet strong enough to bear the huge strains imposed by flight muscles, and how the creature had a fused section of backbone in its chest area, and wings that were built from membrane stretched onto an enormously long finger and that this was nothing like a bat's wing or a bird's… And that scientists did not yet agree as to whether the pterosaurs had evolved from the thecodonts or were a separate offshoot of the diapsid archosaurs, but certainly they were not at all related to the Cretaceous or Jurassic birds, and that flying in all its forms, which included gliding, active flying and soaring, had evolved separately several times and that it was an ability that could also be lost (likewise, sea-dwelling animals had moved to the land and then back again, the whale being an example). Air, Anna told Scott — and it was something that stuck in his mind afterwards — was basically a thin fluid. They could think of themselves as standing — or now, driving — on the very bottom of an ocean of air. Flying, she said, was really a kind of swimming — by this point they had arrived at the Mountain View, where she was staying and he worked.

'I'm on shift in ten minutes' time,' he told her. The handle on her side of the truck had seized up. He got out and opened the door for her, saw her properly for the first time as she emerged: thought how she was like some strange kind of creature herself, with that springy hair and those eyes that looked as if they might jump out of their sockets, and the whole of her somehow emitting a high-pitched kind of vibration, a sort of hum. .

She dived back in to retrieve her laptop, thanked him. They shook hands. He rushed home to change.

I should not have told him all that, she thought, still waiting for Bellavance's call while an overall-clad man from Roadside Assistance drove her back up to the Corolla. I'll have to sort that out somehow. Just as Bellavance finally picked up, the phone beeped and went dead again.

✦ ✦ ✦

All that day, Scott clung to the strangeness of the woman he'd met on the cliff, used it to keep his mind away from his lost computer and the thing he'd almost done. He discovered that she had stayed at the hotel for two nights last September. He Googled her, skimmed through snaps of her outdoors, arm in arm with a group of people in what looked like a desert in Mexico (actually, Alberta), wearing dusty boots, shorts and cool shades, her head tilted back, laughing: curator of marine reptiles, two degrees, forty years old: a life as different to his as could be.

There was also a photo of her in which she posed with her hand resting on a monstrous skull on the table next to her, striped light coming in through the Venetian blinds to the side: more like a painting than a photograph. A portrait. You met her gaze and she looked right back at you, completely herself, like: *yes, and you?*

When Anna walked into the lobby shortly after ten that night, looking just like her photograph, he startled both of them by saying *Good evening,* as if they were characters in a black-and-white movie, or at least in a better kind of place.

'Good evening. Did you get your vehicle fixed?' His name plate was right there on the cedar and tile counter he stood behind, and he saw her take it in.

'Scott—' she said. 'I did, and thanks for all your help.' Either she didn't really want to talk, he thought, or was shy but overcoming it. She ran her fingers through her hair. It was between ringlets and waves, seemed to him a vast twisting mass. Her face was bony, her eyes almost black; she wore a muddy red lipstick and looked even more sci-fi now in the double-bright lobby lighting that made everyone pale: she looked part animal, part android — some kind of being from another planet. Weird, and almost wonderful. A palaeontologist.

'You find that Mr Bellydance, then?' he asked. There was a twitch of a smile and then a gasp as she turned her face away. A sneeze, he thought as she reached for the box on the counter, pulled out a tissue and blew her nose.

'I spoke to him. He's going to fall some trees up by the road so we'll have a bit of space for the chopper. A Sikorsky 61,' she said, still not turning right back. Her voice was muffled. 'We're going to need that.'

She grabbed more tissue. Her eyes were welling over, and she saw that he'd seen it.

'Excuse me. I've had an exceptionally difficult day. I need sleep.' She glanced at the stairs to her right, but didn't take them: she couldn't get there. Instead, she put her arms on the counter and her head on top of them. Her shoulders shook; she tried to swallow back the sound. He had no idea what to do.

'It's okay,' he told her, and her head jerked up.

'It is *not*!' she came back at him, her voice tearing, and her face seemed to be nothing but eyes, drilling right into his, as if there was a huge history between them and some really terrible thing had just happened and it was all his fault. They both stood there, frozen. Then she looked away.

'I'm sorry,' she said. 'Very sorry.'

'No problem.' He shifted his stance, moved the bell on the counter a little to one side. 'Anything you need? Otherwise—'

But she stayed there, waiting, as if she had just arrived.

Go upstairs, she told herself. Don't make it worse.

'It's been an incredibly stressful day. Is the bar open?' she asked and he had to tell her it had been closed for nine months.

'I could really do with a drink,' she said.

There was Joe's, across the way, he told her. But she didn't move.

There might be something left still, he said, knowing that there was a half-bottle, or less, of vodka. He unlocked the bar, flipped back the hatch and found the bottle in the fridge. He was intending to pour her a double to take to her room, but she followed him and sat right down in the empty bar. Bluish light came in from the sign outside but otherwise it was dark. Well, you couldn't see the dust. He rinsed out a glass. Just vodka, he told her. No ice, no mixers.

'Thanks.'

'No problem.'

'Please, join me,' she said, sipping already. 'That really wasn't me out there,' she told him. 'I'm not like that. I don't yell.'

'I almost went for my father this morning,' Scott said. 'That's not me either.' They both gave a quick laugh. 'He stole my f-ing computer and sold it for booze,' he added. 'Who needs enemies. Cheers!' They drank. 'What happened to you, then?' he asked.

There was a dispute, she explained, over who had discovered the fossils she had told him about. To put it bluntly, someone else was trying to steal her discovery and what had happened today was that Mr Bellavance had been talking to that other person as well, and he had mistakenly assumed she was just some kind of assistant — and then, when he changed the date of the meeting the email had gone to the wrong person, and she hadn't been informed. She'd had to chase the man down and make the whole ridiculous, embarrassing situation clear to him.

'Even though it worked out in the end, it was very upsetting—'

'Sounds totally extreme.' They had both, Scott thought, had something stolen from them. He refilled the glasses, wondered about lighting up, and then didn't quite dare. 'Stormy weather,' he said. 'Has to change sometime, I guess.' They sat in silence, and he was starting to feel loose, though still on the good side of drunk. It was a pleasure to hear about someone else's troubles, and an opportunity to offload some of his own: he mentioned the flood, losing the house, the fact they'd let the insurance lapse. The move into the trailer. Mac's decline.

'Won't work. Does anything to get a drink. And… sure, it was only a machine—' he tipped the last of the bottle into her glass, 'but I was very connected to it.'

'It's hard when you don't know how much you can really blame someone. Or, when you know you can't,' she said, looking him in the face — examining him, it seemed. When she leaned forwards, the light from the sign outside gilded her skin, made her hair glisten. She looked, for a moment until she moved again, as if she were made of metal.

'I certainly know about that,' she said. Already she half-knew where she was going and that she would get there this time, lay the whole thing out, not just a couple of facts. There was something about him, she thought. It would be all right.

'You okay?' he asked.

'Do you mind if I tell you something?' she asked. Scott shook his head. What did he expect? Maybe she owed money. Perhaps she was a gambler, something like that. Or maybe she'd left her husband, walked out after years. Maybe she'd killed the bastard, was on the run—

'Do you know anything about genetics?' she began.

'What?'

It did not take her very long to explain and his first reaction was that it was way too bad to be true: the brain clotting up with this out-of-control protein, the jerking, staggering, and slurring, not being able to swallow, the thing she called 'cognitive decline,' the turning into someone else, the whole idea of the fifty percent chance hanging over you for forty years. It was *exactly* like something someone very cruel had made up to scare you.

His second thought was that maybe this woman was some kind of compulsive liar? It was possible, he thought, that *none* of what she had told him that day was real.

'So the way I snapped like that earlier could be a symptom,' she said. 'Do you see? Temper. Loss of impulse control. Mood swings. I feel I sometimes can't tell anymore what is me and what's not. I'm thinking about this kind of thing more and more. All the time. I drop my fork and I don't know: was it just nerves or an accident, or was it a symptom?'

'Shit happens,' he said. Whether he believed her or not, his heart was racing again.

'You can know. I could find out. There's a test.' She drained her glass. 'You can know, but there's nothing you can do to stop it. Would you take it?'

Yes, he thought and nearly said so but a second later, he thought, no, of course not! Forget it! Crazy. She was crazy. Or was she? In any case, the way she looked at him seemed far too intense and he wanted out of that unlit room.

'Don't answer that,' she said. 'It wasn't fair.' He shrugged.

'Do you need anything else? Otherwise, I've got to lock up

now.' He sloshed the glasses clean and came out from behind the bar.

'Thanks,' she said when they were back in the brightness of the lobby, and offered her hand, as if they had concluded some kind of deal. Watching her climb the stairs and vanish at the top of them, Scott had a feeling of being pulled by some new kind of gravity into a parallel universe.

Either she was sane, he decided in the morning, or she was a clever kind of crazy because his first search threw up thousands of hits and everything she said fitted. The Hellish Disease even had its own abbreviation, HD. A doctor called Huntington: not much fun having a thing like that named after you. But as for whether she was at risk or whether she had it or not, there was no way to tell.

✦ ✦ ✦

Waking in the beige-painted room, with its brown velveteen curtains — 201, at the far end of the corridor from the one she'd had before — Anna felt better than she had for many weeks, clearer, more capable. Then it washed over her: she'd drunk more than her empty stomach could take and told everything — not just a little, but everything — to a stranger, a young man, not a professional of any kind, who already had quite enough to deal with on his own account. It appalled her, and yet she did feel different. Better. It was like being at the end of a long dive, the sheer relief of pulling off the suit. She lay there a few moments more, enjoying that feeling.

No harm had been done. Not yet, anyway — she clung to that and a little later, when she was up, she wrote his name on

one of the envelopes from the folder in the room and under-
lined it. She got out her chequebook, dithered over the amount,
deciding eventually to err on the side of generosity. A line had
to be drawn.

Downstairs, she folded the receipt he gave her into four and
put it carefully in the pocket on the side of her laptop case.
From the same place, she extracted the envelope and placed it
between them on the counter.

'Thank you for last night. I'm sure you understand that I'd
like you to keep the find and the other, personal things I told
you completely confidential.' She pushed the envelope towards
him. 'Something towards your new computer. I hope everything works out with your father.'

Scott was broke. He was curious as to the amount. He did
want whatever was in there — but at the same time, something
in him held back. He wasn't sure what taking it *meant*.

'No need,' he said, looking back at her. One of the first
signs, he'd read, was something subtly wrong with the small
movements of the eyes. He could see nothing of that kind, just
a mixture of deep gold and dark brown. Despite the craziness,
he liked Anna Silowski. He liked there being giant winged
lizards in his hometown. He liked standing on the bottom of
an ocean of air, his mind filled with things that might or might
not be, and he even liked having to make up his mind what he
believed to be true.

'Please,' she said, 'take it. Thank you, and goodbye.' She
reached for the bag she'd left on the chair, and a moment later,
was gone.

16

━━━━━━ ✦ ━━━━━━

HE WAS AMAZED BY THE FIGURE on the cheque, which worked out
at over a hundred dollars an hour. Even so, there was no way
to raise the rest of what a new machine would cost. Chryssie
Liz had dumped him: *You're not there when I want you.* Lauren was
perpetually on his case about time-keeping and attitude: *It's time
to take some responsibility.* He was punishing Mac for being the
cause of all this: not long ago he'd seen him passed out under
a bush on the bit of scrubby ground by the filling-station sign;
he'd slowed down to check he was breathing, and then driven
on past. Later that night, Constable Sutherland (Baz, who grad-
uated from Big Crow 'High' the year Scott and Matt dropped
out) had called and suggested that if he picked his father up
and took him home they would turn a blind eye to the small fire
he'd started on Creek Road. *I'm at work, Baz,* Scott had said,
and hung up. He didn't tell Dr Hoffman how he felt about all
that, or how, to justify himself, he was digging up memories
he normally preferred to forget: the few occasions when as a
boy he'd actually seen his father lash out at his mother and
worse still, the days following the outbursts when Mac would
weep and beg for forgiveness, call her, of all things, his *Indian
Princess.* He would promise her the earth and then, gripping

Scott's shoulders too hard, push his forehead onto his son's as if he could press his thoughts through the two layers of bone right into his brain, tell him what a saint his mother was and how Scott should always treat her well. Remembering these things made it easier to be hard on Mac, but even so he knew it was shit, and it made him feel worse than before. At the same time, he couldn't stop doing it. But he mentioned none of this; he just shrugged, and said he thought maybe he was building up a tolerance to the medication. He needed more of it, or something far stronger.

'Scott,' Dr Hoffman said, 'it's not possible to build up a tolerance to the type of antidepressant you're taking.' What did she know about it? Scott thought. You could build up a tolerance to anything. And then suddenly he felt he would give way. He wanted to hit her. What would she think of that?

'We'll review things at the end of the prescription. But there is something else...'

How long, Dr Hoffman asked, had Mac been out of work? She was asking because a brand-new facility had opened up near Nanaimo and there was a possibility Mac would be eligible for a funded treatment program — and near the top of the list too, if she referred him and they acted fast.

'He has to want to do it,' she said. Want? His father would not want to do anything, ever, but Scott kept that to himself.

'You owe me this,' he told Mac. 'And you'll do it. Tell her you want to do it.'

17

WAS SHE THE PERSON WHO ENDLESSLY replayed a minor accident anyone else would put behind them, the person who had drunk warm vodka and then chosen to confide in a stranger? Was she the person who called to make an appointment to explore the possibility of taking the test she had been opposed to ever since she first heard of it, and then, less than an hour later, called again to cancel? Was she the person who finally agreed to making the appointment again only on the understanding that she probably would not turn up?

'Yes,' she had told Juliette on the phone, 'on a no-commitment basis, I'll make an appointment. But—'

'That's absolutely fine,' Juliette said.

I'm going to go in, she told Roger now, opening the window a crack and then getting out of the car, *but I might come right back*. And was the whole noncommittal thing a kind of trap, a way to reel her in? But even so, and partly because she could still turn back, Anna gave the receptionist her name and then sat to wait for Juliette, who arrived suddenly, before she could leave: a tall, Modigliani-type of woman in flowing clothes. She had a hint of grey in her hair, a warm, firm handshake.

'Shall we go to my office? Or would you like some coffee?'

They sat in a small, rose-painted room, its window covered by a dusty Venetian blind that hung slightly askew.

'I'm sorry. It's hardly the Ritz. We're moving to a new building, but not there yet.'

Anna didn't so much mind the room. She liked it being plain and empty, insignificant. The problem was not thinking straight. She should leave. No: it was the right thing to do. She was not sure. Yet somehow she was here.

Juliette's face was calm, her eyes alert.

'So,' she began, 'what led you to contact us now? Why are you gathering information about the test at this point?'

I'm not. This is a mistake.

But Anna stayed in the chair. Words came out of her mouth.

'I have constant feelings that this or that thing might be a symptom. Only last week, after a couple of drinks, I told a complete stranger about the situation I'm in. It was a huge relief, and he was extremely good about it, but it seems like an odd thing to do—'

People closer to home often had an interest in the matter, Juliette said. Perhaps, she suggested, Anna wanted to confide in someone, but also to be able to escape from the person she had told?

Possibly. But — she didn't say this — she also wanted the opposite of escape. She wanted more. Several times since the trip to Big Crow she caught herself feeling as if there were a connection between her and the twentysomething man who had stared back at her from the other side of the bar. He had pulled her back from the edge that night. He had qualities:

steadiness, tolerance, kindness. A kind of straightforward intelligence. Though really, she knew nothing about him, and probably he had forgotten the incident by now.

The test, Juliette explained, had a protocol which involved a series of appointments and would take several months. It was important to make clear that it could be halted or paused at any point, and might take far longer.

'What we are trying to do is be sure that you really want the information we can give you, good or bad, and that you have support to cope with it. So, if you wanted to continue after today, or after we have finished, however long that takes,' Juliette said, 'you would complete some psychological tests which I send to Dr Hutz. He would see you next for a psychological assessment, at least once, possibly more. That appointment would be at least a month away. And from there, you would make an appointment to see the neurologist, Dr Persaud, and after that, you can book your results appointment, which would be with Dr Persaud and me. And at some point during that process, you would give your blood sample, which takes about a month or so to process. So we find it takes sixteen weeks as a minimum. At any point in the process, of course, you are free to put things on hold, or simply slow it down...'

There were flow charts to explain the protocol, diagrams to explain the transmission of disease, which Juliette quickly put away: they had more time, then, for everything else. They moved on to family history. A brief questionnaire, which, if Anna did want to go ahead, would be sent to the psychiatrist.

Rate yourself on a scale of one to five for suicidal thoughts.
Optimism. Anxiety.
Complete the following with a word of your choice.

Juliette left Anna to complete these and when she returned with coffee, put the questionnaires in an envelope and sealed them. She could send them along or not, she said. Dr Hutz could be asked not to open them if Anna changed her mind, or, if he already had, would be requested to destroy his notes.

'This is your information,' she said. 'But you must ask yourself, are you in the best possible position to receive it? Do you have support? Is this the best time? What else is happening in your life right now?

'I do think you should wait,' she said a little later on.

At the end of the interview, they walked back down the corridor, into the hum and bustle of the hospital, past the cafeteria and the mothers and babies and play space and finally, to the way out.

'I like people. I want to help,' Juliette told Anna when she thanked her. 'Take care.'

She was glad to wait. Was not. Was in tears by the time she reached the car.

Was she this person?

18

---◆---

SCOTT FED THE BLINDING WHITE, plastic-smelling trainers on to his father's feet, pushed down to feel where his toe was. A few aisles away, he held the sweatpants against him to check for length. Phoenix House had sent a list: shaving equipment, toiletries, so many pants and shirts and underwear, shoes, and — mind-blowing, Scott thought — swimwear and gym kit. They had stopped on the way there to buy what they could.

'Looking good.'

'Why are you doing this?' Mac asked as Scott steered him towards the checkout. 'Jackie wouldn't like what you're doing to me—' he said, tearing up. The vast jelly of a woman at the till, and a bleached blonde and her teenage daughter behind them in the line, were staring hard.

'Leave Mum out of this, okay? You're going so they can make you better. So you can stay alive.'

At Phoenix House, Mac had been assigned a third-floor room with brand-new furniture and a strong smell of paint, to be shared with one other man who hadn't yet arrived. The window was small, but you could see the jumble of the city, and beyond it, the sea.

Scott unpacked Mac's things while Mac sat down on the

bed, began to light a cigarette, then remembered the 'not in the bedrooms' rule. Scott began to realise, then, how huge this was, how he himself, in the same position, might not be able to come through. He rested his hand on his father's shoulder.

'There's a patio, remember?' They went to find it, settled into two chairs with an ashtray between them.

'I might go away for a while. But I'll keep in touch, okay? There are always the Prices in an emergency. Their numbers are written in the book I gave you.' Scott's heart thumped in his chest. He had, he felt, to offer something more. 'I'm a hundred percent behind you.'

'I'm not feeling so good,' Mac said, coughing, shaking his head.

'There's a doctor right here. You're already booked in, okay? They'll fix you up.'

He'd have liked a blessing. A good luck, a wink, even from this wreck of a parent. A wave of the hand, saying: yes, go. But, nothing. Mac said nothing and ash fell on his chest as he sucked on the cigarette. His eyes watered, and his hands shook as he put the cigarette down and made as if to pick up a drink that wasn't there, then closed his eyes in despair. Skin, teeth, eyes, hair, fingernails, every bit of him that Scott could see looked broken and you didn't want to imagine the insides. He felt the tears building.

'Behave yourself now. Good luck.' He got to his feet, and then bent down and kissed the top of his father's head.

The air outside smelled of summer coming. He was free, now, he could take off — right now, even — though probably he owed it to Lauren to give notice. He could get himself to Vancouver, set up a job, a place. Insist, after Phoenix House, that this was their home. Better himself, bit by bit. He could, as Matt had been telling him to, just vanish with no forwarding address, nothing — drive south until the truck died, just believe something would turn up. Travel, seek his fortune, have incredible adventures, wheel, deal, make tax-free money and end up somewhere like in Rio or Cancun where stunning women lay naked on beaches fingering themselves and just waiting for him to come along and help them out. Matt would give him a deal on an ounce or two of his best to get him going and it would be better than money in the bank... The danger, there, was of ending up in a Mexican jail... Perhaps, he was thinking, perhaps — insane as it sounded — he would try and avoid weed completely for a while? If Mac could do it, perhaps he could, should? It was then, just as he was about to open the driver's side door, that his phone rang.

'Who?' he asked, pressing his hand over his free ear to cut out the traffic noise.

'Anna Silowski. How are you?' He remembered the cheque then. How it must still be in the back pocket of his black jeans. 'I'm calling,' Anna told Scott, 'because there's an opportunity that might interest you.' Though the truth, or another part of it, was that minutes before she had picked up the phone and called the Mountain View to obtain Scott's number, Anna had been on the verge of explaining everything to them at work and withdrawing herself from the dig. *You must do whatever you need to do to get through*, she had told herself, and then she had picked up the phone.

'Is this a good time? Do you have a few minutes?' The tightness in her voice took him right back to that night in the bar.

'I thought you might be interested in joining the dig as a community volunteer. We start June sixth.'

'Hey, thanks.' He frowned at the phone in his hand, 'But I'm thinking of travelling,' he told her, 'and I don't know anything about palaeontology.'

'You'd learn,' she said, 'and we do need a local volunteer, and also someone in charge of the food. And as well as that, what I really need,' she said, and gradually her voice became hers again, 'what I do need is a particular kind of personal assistant. I told you about my... circumstances. And you dealt with things very well that night and I feel you could help keep me on track during the dig. I know it's a lot to ask,' she said. 'You'll want to think it over.'

It was the way she said *It's a lot to ask* that made him decide he would go: the way she had asked him for this enormous thing, acknowledged the scale of her request, yet refused to beg.

Just over a week later, Scott found himself carrying a sixty-pound pack and at the same time dragging a cart loaded with canned foodstuffs and many litres of liquid up five kilometres of riverbed which, Anna Silowski said, was once a tidal flat covered with mussel beds, crabs and something rather like kelp.

19

———— ✦ ————

ALL I WANT, ANNA WROTE IN HER PERSONAL notes the night before the dig began, *is to bring her (I shouldn't think of the specimen this way, but I do) safely out of the rock. I will not go to pieces. I may have done a crazy thing asking Scott to join us, but the fact is I already feel better because of it. It's as if I had handed the most difficult part of my life, the endless questioning, over to him, and I need not think of it now.*

'I had hoped to arrive before Dr Swenson,' she said to him as they climbed out of their white van in the carpark next to the river access and saw, from the two other vans already parked, that the other half of the excavation was already there.

'Dr Swenson will be excavating the other specimen,' she explained to the team as they prepared to unload, 'the larger one partly buried under the cliff — and quite how he will do so I don't yet know. It's fair to say that he and I do not get on. This is not an ideal situation, but we all have to make the best of it, okay?'

Scott divided the catering supplies between two carts, and took one of them, dragging it behind him as he followed Anna along the trail that led to the river.

The rest of the team: confident, handsome Jason; Felix, oval-faced, his head shaved a few days ago to save on effort and shampoo; Ai Lin (who, Scott thought, could at first glance be either a very delicate, rather female kind of male or a slightly masculine woman) and Greta (blonde, Californian, very definitely female) chatted away in a language Scott did not understand:

'What functional morphology tells us isn't always clear.'

'What really interests me is the taphonomy—'

Jason, in baggy cord shorts and oatmeal t-shirt with a T. rex skeleton printed on the front, took turns with Felix to drag the second cart. Jason was doing something called a post-doc and, Scott calculated, had been studying, if you counted grade school, for twenty-eight years. Jason had known from age six what he wanted to be and now he was there, right at the beginning of a brilliant career.

'So,' Jason turned briefly to Scott, 'Anna said you were a member of the local community?'

That, then, was her translation for completely unqualified, ignorant, acting camp cook, unofficial minder, if/as/when required?

'Quite the opportunity!'

'I'm looking forward to it.'

His t-shirt was stuck to him.

Downstream were the swimming holes where his mother had watched him play when he was a kid; older, he went there on his own to join the daredevils jumping from the cliff above: Thompson, Jay and Walker from the reserve, skinny Carl and Matt from town. There was a thin path that took you almost to the top, and from there, you had to climb across to one of the ledges, turn around and then stand, clinging to the rock behind while you psyched up: that could take three minutes or half an hour, the sweat running down your sides and your spine, but once you were up, everyone was watching and there was only one way to go. The minutes went by until some combination of boredom and terror tipped the balance and you stepped into the air — plummeted down, hands to sides, straight as a needle, in. The time under the water wasn't time at all; it was some kind of extra, other thing. The water swallowed your speed; silver bubbles of air ballooned above your head as you pushed back towards the light, suddenly very much alive.

The pool was warm but not so very deep; towards the end of July their feet would start to touch the rock at the bottom and by mid-August they couldn't jump anymore. And once you were past sixteen you just didn't do it anyhow. Skinny Carl died in a crash but the rest of them were still around, and now he travelled in the opposite direction, pulling the cart. It took two hours to get there. If nothing else, he would be fit, he thought, at the end of this.

Anna had outlined the main parts of the specimen in chalk, and now the team spent time on their hands and knees, familiarising themselves. It was bigger than all of them, Scott thought, and that was just the collapsed bones, not the thing as it would have been, the wings spread wide, soaring.

'I aim for this to be totally intact,' she told them, smiling.

'Move over, *Quetzalcoatlus*,' Jason grinned back at her. It was hard not be very aware that opposite and only slightly upstream the Swenson team had already unpacked and were more or less ready to go, but Anna kept her back firmly to them while she spoke.

They might, she said, be able to drill some holes in the shale tomorrow; meanwhile, they should collect rocks to hold their guy ropes and put up with the sag.

'The helicopter will bring in heavy equipment,' she explained, 'more chemical toilets, supplies and so on first thing tomorrow. Meanwhile, please do your best to minimize impact. Not too much washing, please! Every three or four days someone gets to go back to town, shower at the room we're retaining in the hotel, and bring back fresh supplies. Scott has kindly agreed to co-ordinate...'

'Listen,' she said, looking carefully into each face, 'I'd very much prefer it if we keep the details of our approach to ourselves. This two-team thing is crazy, but the reason for it is something that might have legal repercussions so I'm not at liberty to explain in detail.'

'Big fight,' Scott heard Jason whisper theatrically as they broke up, 'Bone Queen versus Stone Man.'

For ten minutes in the middle of that first afternoon, Scott escaped and lay in the greenish glow of his tent, the book he had found in the library unopened on his chest. The title, *Reading Fate*, bugged him and besides, he was not used to reading much. He tucked the book back under his sleeping bag, fantasised instead about rolling a joint: an amazing thing to do in such a confined space, even though the label inside the tent warned against smoking. Me in a tent, he thought, Mac in his brand-new, paint-smelling room. Who would crack first?

He had enough of Matt's best left for an emergency, but aching limbs and the feeling of being a different species to the rest of them and there on false pretences didn't quite qualify. He was just a few miles away from home, and within spitting distance of ancestral territory; if he ran, he could be back at the carpark in an hour and a half.

He wished there was something better than thin foam and polyester fibres between him and the riverbed. Someone, rather than something. Someone real — for example, Greta, another surprising palaeontologist. He could see she would be in demand. Ai Lin, then. Both — they appeared behind his closed eyes in thongs, total opposites. He had better not, something warned him, go too far along this route, and it was fortunate he did not:

'Scott?' Anna was right there, just outside the tent. 'Are you there?'

'We'll talk later,' she told him as he emerged, 'meanwhile, come and meet Dr Swenson and his team, please.'

Swenson reminded Scott of the Marlboro Man — the firm jaw and stubble thing. Kevin was pale, with thick mouse-coloured hair that needed a wash. The twins, Gunnar and Joe, gangly, crested with identical blond manes. Marc, heavyset, monosyllabic. After the hand shaking, the two teams stood around, welded to their beers. Most of them, Scott realised, had met before, online at least, and normally they would get on like a house on fire, but in this situation, they were uncertain what was allowed or required of them.

Later, when he cooked burgers on the barbecue, one of Swenson's team called out, 'Smells good over there!'

'*Is* good,' Greta yelled back.

They sat in the failing light, listening as the bickering of the ravens gradually thinned, and then, without them noticing, stopped. Swenson's team erupted now and then into laughter. Ai Lin told Scott to call her Lin.

'It's so good, to get out of the museum, away from the desert,' she told him, waving at the deepening blue above them and the trees, minute by minute becoming silhouettes. 'And my life here is so different to what it would have been if we'd stayed in Hong Kong. Sometimes I can hardly believe all that still exists.' How come they made the move? How old was she? Scott was going to ask, but Greta decided to have a campfire, and Lin got up to help find fuel.

'Come on, before it gets totally dark. There's stuff down here we can use.'

Anna stayed, working on her laptop. Light from the screen lit up the planes of her cheeks, the underside of her eyebrows.

'Scott, I'm making it very clear to everyone that you're here to learn and help me out, and if it does create any problems we'll just have to deal with them in a professional manner as they arise.'

'Sure,' he said into the growing darkness. He could hear the hum of the fan on her laptop, the voices of the others on the other side and his own team calling out and laughing as they followed Greta downstream.

'I guess you might feel somewhat stranded in amongst the rest of us palaeos?' she asked.

'Somewhat,' he said, feeling, and enjoying, the odd sound of the word in his mouth.

It was the weirdest job: a mixture of the very basic and to-tally subtle. The extra, important part of it — warning her if she behaved badly, reassuring her — had been discussed, but even that was not quite it, not quite all that she wanted of him and there was no sense, even now as he sat there across from her of *how* he was supposed to do what she'd asked for, no contract, nothing. And, another thing, which he'd realised at dinnertime, was that he had forgotten to bring his pills: all sorts of bad things from psychosis to suicide to mass murder were supposed to happen if he stopped them suddenly, though so far, although he felt different — too aware of things, not sure how they fitted together — it was okay.

She gestured at the rock beside her, 'Why not sit down?' He was becoming familiar with the way in which Anna could command and beg at the same time.

'So this is where you grew up? Your mother was from around here, too?'

'She was from the reserve.' He pointed at the cliff behind her. 'Left it to marry. Hoping for better things. Qualifications. Job. Nice house. Sober husband. Got some of them.' He shrugged. 'It was okay to start with, I think.' Though that side of things had always puzzled him: how did you get from the wedding photos to the fist in the face? Was the way it ended somehow waiting in the beginning?

'I'm sorry,' she said, 'if I—'

'It's totally fine,' he told her, 'but I need to sleep, now.' More than anything he needed to be alone, unseen and unremarkable, and he could hear the others returning. Later, inside his tent, he smelled smoke, heard the spit and crackle of damp wood and Anna saying goodnight, then her footsteps as she passed by.

He lay in the darkness and tried to imagine his parents as they once had been. They'd met at a dance in the community hall. Mac was new to town, and also ten years older than her. Maybe he was growing weary of life on his own, just the days in the mill and evenings in the bar. Lonely. She was sitting outside with her friend, watching who went in. She'd come down to the town for a night out — and maybe she was looking: she wanted to escape the future lined up for her: the housing, the kind of life her mother had, the feeling of being separated off from the bigger world. She wanted things on her own terms, but they weren't that extreme: a second chance at education, some kind of qualification. A child or two, not too many.

At that point, Mac's drinking was likely nothing compared to what she was used to and maybe he got a grip on it while he was seeing her. Didn't feel the need. And he wasn't prejudiced, at least not if it was a good-looking woman you were talking about. He never did care what people thought.

They drove out at weekends. Visited Vancouver. Borrowed a friend's boat and pottered along the coast, married soon, the reception in the old Community Hall. Ten years later, it had got pretty bad, but surely everything *began* well, with the house and her getting her early childhood educator qualification and work in the daycare on Smith Street. When he was born, she took him there with her.

He could remember coming down the yellow slide in the yard there on a bright winter's day with her watching him. Her hands were stuffed in her pockets, one of granny's knitted hats with the dangling pom-poms covered her hair and ears; other kids milled around. She had to watch everyone, but she watched him especially.

'You just slipped out,' she'd tell him back then, when he asked about being born. 'No trouble. Perfect!' He made her happy. He made up for a lot, she said.

Feeling trapped was the worst thing. The computer was the last straw, but being trapped was what had stoked the anger that nearly drove him to smash a rock into his father's head. Did Mac too feel trapped? Trapped in himself, his drinking, his thoughts about what his wife might be doing when he wasn't there?

Wind blew through the trees above the camp, rustling leaves, rubbing branches together. He liked the dark, the feeling of everything outside being so close: he thought he could listen all night and yet before long, slept, and then woke half-numb, at first not knowing where he was, then slowly remembering. He liked hearing the other tents unzipped and deciding which person it was that struggled out of it. He liked hearing Anna walk past and call out 'Scott? Early start,' and then the coolness, the half-light of outside and the tang of their coffee in the air, the warmth of its steam on his face and the sweet, scalding liquid on his tongue.

Anna smiled, sat there at the wobbly plastic table, combing her hair with her fingers. Everyone was pale and rumpled from sleep; the men whiskery, the women soft-faced. They waited in near silence for the helicopter, first a mere vibration in the frames of their chairs, concentric rings in the cups, then the throb of it hammering across the gorge, shaking their bones; the machine itself was suddenly there, hanging above the gorge, churning leaves and grit from the ground and whipping it into their eyes. Amid a skittering of shale chips, the load inched down, touched, and then collapsed onto the ground. Felix and Scott in hard hats and ear protectors ran out to undo the hitch and then the machine lifted away, leaving a shocked silence behind it. Bodies and minds slowly returned to each other, somehow new.

'Ours!' Anna yelled across to Swenson. They set to breaking open the crate. An audience had arrived: Gus and Garth, Camera and Sound, ready to document the unpacking of two-by-fours, a generator, an air compressor, drills, jackhammer, angle grinder, box on box of smaller tools and fixings. Hammers. Goggles. Gloves. Masks. Sacks of plaster, rolls of sacking.

'Dr Swenson is over there,' Anna said, to get Gus and Garth out of the way, but soon they were back, instructing everyone to forget they were there.

'That burlap should be under cover,' Jason told Scott, 'along with the plaster.' *Burlap?* he had to ask, and soon Felix, his long face calm and attentive, like that of a nun or a monk, was explaining how the technology hadn't changed much since the nineteenth century: it was a kind of sacking and each piece of the fossil would be wrapped in lengths that had been soaked in plaster and then later reinforced with two-by-fours and more plaster-soaked burlap to make a jacket that would protect it from shocks on the way to the museum.

'I have a colleague,' Jason interrupted, 'who wanted in on this dig so bad, but didn't get picked.'

'I guess you'll have to tell him all about it,' Scott said, turning away as the helicopter returned with Swenson's gear. The third time it came it brought more jacketing supplies for each team and two blue portable toilets that dangled above their heads like a pair of outsize castanets.

A central axis, and then a grid of metre squares had to be set up over the entire site, covering both specimens, and numbered at each corner for easy reference. Each metre could be divided further when detail was required. Both teams stood amid a jungle of equipment and waited while Swenson and Anna discussed the placing of the axis and then numbering systems each preferred to use: letters and numbers, just letters, lower, upper? Swenson let out a hiss of breath to show when he tired of the discussion. Scott noted that Swenson didn't look Anna in the eye, but sent his pale blue gaze out and away, at the other people, at the specimen. When she let him have his choice, Swenson relaxed and grinned; she came back tight-faced.

'Hey, who cares,' Scott said.

She bent down to pick up two small hammers, handed him one of them.

'Please. Here. Greta will show you what to do.'

They drilled and then drove in slender pins to mark the main axis, which ran between the two specimens on their side of the river, stretched a line across and then another north to south. From there, they measured parallel, marking each inter-section with a dot of white paint, and writing the co-ordinates on the rock. He had to check and double-check that the lines were parallel, call out to Greta, mark the spot.

'Don't trip over it when you stand up!'

Anna photographed each square. Greta's skin burned pink even though she wore sunblock and a hat. All of them were sweating hard and their smells emerged: nothing too bad, Scott thought, just individual variants of smoky and pepperish, blended with a variety of disintegrating perfumes, and in the case of Anna, cut grass, blood, rain after a dry spell; it was like the trace of some unseen animal passing in the woods. Maybe he was hallucinating from lack of drugs and the heat.

He and Felix taped off the area surrounding Specimen A, and after that, Swenson's team had to walk around it to get to 'their' Specimen B ('None of these specimens are *anyone's*,' Anna said), though at least twice already Mike ducked under the tape — its existence, it being put up by someone else's hand, let alone hers, too much to bear.

'We're working on the tail.' Greta handed Scott a slender chisel, a dusty pair of safety glasses and some brand-new gloves, and then crouched down next to him. One section has already been removed: the bit Anna had dropped and broken: she had still not told anyone about that.

'Like so.' Scott copied her movements, splintering off tiny flakes of rock. She ran her fingers through the debris.

'Look at every piece. There might be something—'

'Like what?' Moisture condensed inside his goggles and mingled with the dust there to make mud; he pushed the goggles back on his forehead.

'Fragments of our specimen. Or of something else — a tooth, or fish scale, an arthropod...we're trying to go underneath, see? Better safe than sorry,' Greta said. 'They can take excess matrix off in the lab.' Her buglike safety glasses were jammed under the hat which shaded her face and neck; her breasts, encased in a pale blue stretchy sports top were in full sun — and then, looking up again, Scott realised that this time they were on camera: who could resist such a shot? Garth, hunched over his camera, zoomed right in.

Periodically, Scott visited the different points of the excavation and filled the wheelbarrow by the dustpanful, watching all over again for any kind of irregularity, while the others covertly watched to see that he was taking the right amount of trouble.

It was on the way back from the dumpsite that Swenson fell into step with Scott, bringing with him a new variant of the human smell, a blend of hot skin, DEET and fabric conditioner.

'Where are you from, then? Local? You got the short straw there,' he said, turning his face to look into Scott's, but not taking off his Ray-Bans. 'Fantastic experience though. Camp cook too?'

'Kinda.' The barrow bounced along.

'Might make sense to pool our resources in that department.'

'You'd have to ask Anna.'

'I won't be doing that,' Swenson said with a twitch of a grin, a sideways nod towards the site, where Anna crouched with Felix, Lin and Jason in the skull area, her finger brushing the rock as if she were reading Braille. 'She chewed you over yet? Be warned, that one bites. Come take a look at what we're doing. We're going to have to cut right in under the cliff...exciting stuff... So what's in it for you?' he asked.

'What?'

Mike grinned. 'As for me—' he said as they splashed through what was left of the river, 'I think this part of the world is really going to start to open up. If there are two of these, then there will be others, that's how it goes. Some kind of nesting site, an offshore island. I think the only viable explanation for this kind of preservation, is some kind of toxicity during a period of volcanism and seismic activity. There's a life's work here, and a chance to get a few things settled: I don't think that in ten years' time anyone will still be thinking that these larger species actually *flew* — not actively. That whole line of thought has been a diversion: how does an animal this size *take off*? I've never been persuaded. At this scale, *gliding* is far more plausible. A completely different thing, and of course it has implications for every aspect of their behaviour and ecology.'

Swenson grinned, rubbed his hands together. They had reached the cliff, the shale layer at the base of it a fissured background that seemed almost ready to burst apart. The camera was on him now:

'We'll take what's out here, and then go in for the rest. This is the jaw—' he crouched beside it, looked up into the lens 'The head in its entirety would be almost as long as I'm tall.' He stood. 'And there's a lot of information inside that skull about the brain, of course, and the diet. We'll take the cliff back just here—'

'How will you do that?'

'A little bit of drilling and a lot of elbow grease,' Swenson smiled, folded his arms across his chest. 'Watch this space.'

Scott found Anna in the office area outside her tent: two folding chairs, a white plastic table with a sun umbrella, which cast the table in shade. The laptop was plugged into a solar panel that she had propped up in front of the table, and she was entering the grid data, a long job. Her hands already felt stiff, she said.

'What did Dr Swenson have to say?' she asked. 'No, don't tell me...' Though at the same time, she needed to know and wanted to know, and also, what had Scott made of the man? But she could not ask that.

'Important questions,' she said of Swenson's gliding theory. 'But on the other hand, flight is certainly *possible*. Absolutely. Because we mustn't be dazzled by scale: it doesn't matter nearly so much as the wing area to weight ratio, the flexibility of the wing, and the ways in which it can be moved, angled and adjusted. The wing-loading and aspect ratio would be very similar to that of some of today's large sea birds, like the albatross. I think we could imagine short bursts of active flight, interspersed with long periods of gliding and soaring on thermals.

Manoeuvrability would be excellent and stalling speed low...

'We have to keep our minds open. There might be some answers, on flight, say if there was some soft-tissue preservation — attachments to the bone which allowed us to have a better picture of the actual musculature. Then again, there might not. And there might be some other information entirely that we're not even thinking to actively look for, so the more possibilities we can entertain the better. From now on, it's a process,' she told him, sitting there in the canvas chair, straight-backed, hair loose and wild. 'Not a moment of illumination. Areas of relative clarity, a few pieces of hard evidence. If we find a fish inside its stomach, then we know what it ate. But mostly, it's not like that. The scale of an eye socket suggests either the importance of vision, or the darkness of the environment, or something you haven't thought of yet; the flexibility of an assemblage of neck vertebrae implies an ability to scan behind itself and to preen. But it is,' she smiled, 'a kind of supereducated guess. We can't do experiments, the way they can in physics or even psychology. I hope I haven't bored you? You can use this if you want,' she waved at the laptop. 'No Net, of course, but there are some useful programs and a couple of games, if you'd like.'

He remembered her calling flight *swimming in air*. He'd never knowingly seen an albatross, but he could imagine a huge heron flapping lazily above them. Branches would sway, leaves flutter on the ground as it passed.

His eyes were the colour of the forest, she thought; it was not a terribly useful thought and she turned quickly back to the screen.

✦ ✦ ✦

He made chilli with rice and afterwards walked upriver thinking how his father would be in the worst of it now, and how
good it was to be away; when he returned, scruffy Kevin and
the twins from Swenson's team had joined the others around
the fire, and everyone was lying on their backs so they could
stargaze without hurting their necks.

'Ursa Major and Minor, the two bears,' Felix said, quietly, as
if the stars might overhear them, 'and over there, the swan, the
eagle.' No one could see the swan or the eagle, and they argued
over what they did see. Scott, silent, peered into the swirling
mass of stars above him: it was like a thick liquid boiling, and
eventually, by hanging on to what Felix said, he thought he
could make out Draco, the dragon, towards the north.

'Thousands of years ago, it *was* the north,' Felix said. 'One
of its stars was the polestar, and the dragon used to spin over
our heads. Since then, the world has shifted on its axis.'

'What do you mean, *shifted?*' Scott asked, sitting up. Everyone laughed, but it still felt more or less okay.

'Bit by bit, Scott,' Greta said, 'not so you'd notice.'

'Actually,' Felix corrected her, 'some people think the axis
has shifted very dramatically in the past and will do so again.
The magnetic pole, on the other hand, is wandering all the
time, and there's clear evidence of big shifts back in the
Cambrian.'

The world was full of boiling iron, Felix told him, which
surged and sloshed around inside and responded to external
forces too.

'Of course, it could be tied in to climate change, or vice
versa. Don't get me started on that one...my family's in Alaska.
Enjoy the stars.'

Scott's smoke tin was digging into his thigh, but he ignored it. If you looked at the stars long enough, it made you feel as if you were vanishing, becoming smaller than one of those pricks of light, at the same time as your mind spread open, taking them all in. Did what Felix said about the magnetic north mean that all the measuring they did would be different another day, or next year? He wanted to know, but didn't want to ask, and he wished, suddenly, that he'd not given up school. At the time it had been the obvious and only thing to do, after months of taunts: *half 'n' half, loser*, to which he could not back then reply as he later wished he had: Okay, so there's no mum driving me to soccer and Dad is not showing me how to fish or use the workshop tools, and I'd be scared to let him if he tried — yes, I'm not like you. What the hell?

The attack behind the gym was broken up by Mr Myers, and the ringleader, Barry Sutherland, eventually penned a letter of apology which was published in the *Echo*. Barry became very religious (and was now the local constable). Still, Scott had not felt like returning to school, not even to show, as the principal suggested, that he wasn't intimidated. Why go there where he didn't fit in? Right to an education? Learning what, exactly? By then, he had the Internet, the electronic tit, which offered endless information and virtual everything, and fit better around life with Mac... Now, abruptly weaned, Scott lay on his back in actual darkness, saw the stars, listened to the night — human footsteps, and laughter, unidentifiable rustlings, a sudden, animal shriek — while the pole wandered, and the earth boiled inside.

'Thanks for the education,' he said to Felix when he finally got up to leave.

'Who *is* he?' he heard Kevin ask as he made his way to his tent.

'We're all asking,' Jason said.

'Let it go, Jayce,' Greta said then. 'I like him.'

I should not find it astounding, Anna typed, sitting only six metres away from Scott in her tent, *that two such opposites as Mike Swenson and Scott Macleod can co-exist, but I do. If I ignore Swenson and focus on Scott I feel stronger. The important thing is the work itself, which is why he is here in the first place. I need to remain calm and patient, and take the longer view...*

✦ ✦ ✦

Scott turned on his flashlight, opened his book at random, stumbled over *deoxyribonucleic acid, nucleotides, cytosine, guanine, thymine, adenine* — somehow, he gathered, these words translated themselves into proteins: flesh, blood, bones. Skipping, he found a chapter with actual people, scientists in laboratory in Massachusetts, thirty years ago, trying to discover which part of the enormously long sequence of code correlated with the disease. They needed a sign, a marker; to find that, they needed blood samples from several generations of an affected family — a large family or else the result would be inconclusive. They worked for years, getting nowhere except better at the technical side of things. But they were unable to give up because they wanted so badly to find their answer, knew it was right there, hidden, invisible, but there in the test tubes of blood they could pick up and hold in their hands.

20

———— ✦ ————

JASON AND FELIX WERE JACKHAMMERING — *jackhammering* — a trench a metre away from the skull area.

'I thought we did everything with a paintbrush!'

'Later! When they're done, we'll hand-cut through the layers closer to the concretion…lever them off.' Anna was shouting, her voice tinny in Scott's ear. Even with ear protectors on, everyone could hear and feel the sound of metal on rock, its echo, the pulses of the generator and compressors. Over by the cliff, the same thing was happening; if one team was quiet, the other was not.

When at last the noise did stop echoing from the cliffs, the silence following it seemed unreal: a weird, Zenish, cloudlike thing that descended on them: a happy nothing happeningness, just the buzz of crickets and other bugs while they studied the ground, tapped and pried, brushed, scraped and sifted.

They had knee protectors, although not everyone wore them. They squatted or knelt on the rock, looking down at what was before them, trying to see how it was made and how it would break. No one said much; no one took an extra break, even when the sun hung right above them, burning up the shade.

Tap, tap and tap: the shale held out once, twice, three times or more and then shattered, perhaps into countless pieces, perhaps into two thick layers, then a thin one, and then a hard lump that might or might not be of significance. Steadily, they worked towards the specimen itself, invisibly wrapped in its own especially dense stone: compacted clay, Felix explained, in which the spaces between the grains of sediment had been filled with a mineral deposit.

'It's like working blind,' Scott said. They'd gathered for lunch under the canopy rigged up for shade, and were drinking water that was tepid but nonetheless wonderful to drink, and eating folded-over slices of bread and cheese. 'But the rest of you, you've a clear picture in your minds of what you're looking for?'

Anna said that sometimes what you saw outside and what you pictured in your head could come together and reveal what was really there. What you saw outside could alter the image you carried in your mind and likewise the picture in your mind could open up what was in front of you — or blind you to it: that was how you read the rock.

She put her food down and fetched a book, tapped her finger on the drawing inside.

'Ours,' she said, 'is going to be *something* like this, not exactly the same, of course: it may or may not have had tooth sockets like this one,' she explained, brushing crumbs from the page, 'or it could be a toothless with a kind of cartilaginous filtering system, like the baleen plates of a whale. Then again, it might have a beak, though I tend to feel... Come, let me show you,' she told him, and leaving the others to finish their food, they squatted on the safe side of the trench in the rock by the skull area.

Her hands moved between book and rock. There might or might not be a crest on the top of the head, here. There would be upper and lower *temporal fenestrae*, openings in the skull something like this, and also pre-orbital openings, nostrils and rings of bony plates around the sockets of the eyes.

'If we're lucky, there will be a cast of the *inside* of the brain-case. Hereabouts, in the ventral position, beneath the braincase, will be the *occipital condyle*. It's a ball and socket articulation with the first vertebra... You know I'm going in a little closer than I'd like,' she told him, 'because I really want the skull to come out in one piece. The rock is dense, and then you add in the plaster and so on — we just could end up with something too heavy to be lifted out, and have to cut it in two after all the trouble we've gone through. It's a juggling act.'

She pointed out the position of the elongated cervical vertebrae. The dorsal vertebrae she expected to be fused together to make a *notarium* with a *superneural* plate to support various moving parts... Ribs, of course. 'Underneath the notarium we'll likely find a sternum—' her hand migrated briefly to the centre of her chest, 'to which the flight muscles attach...broad, with a kind of keel, do you see?'

He saw how much she saw.

But who invented all these words? And how many more were there? Words for all the parts of everything that were normally invisible, for the insides of bodies, the layers of the earth, the kinds of rock, words for the invisible parts of things that first had to be seen or guessed about, and then given names.

They moved around and down. She spoke of extra ribs, *gastralia*, the position of the sacrum and the pelvis, the caudal vertebrae: the tail.

'My territory!' Scott joked, and she grinned at him from behind her sunglasses, her skin lightly varnished with sweat. A damselfly with huge turquoise eyes darted between them.

'Actually, the tail plays a very important role in flight. So, do you have more of a picture of it now? The limbs are straightforward enough: femur, fibula and tibia, tarsus, metatarsals, humerus—' and here she pointed to her own arm, opened her hand: 'Radius, ulna, carpals, metacarpals, phalanges.'

Her hands were small with square palms, the fingers proportionately long. There would be a word for that, too, he thought and found himself opening his own hand.

'Not so different, then,' he began.

'Different to what?'

'Humans!' he said. 'Apart from that fourth finger.' He pointed to the picture in the book, looked back at her, frowned as if making a serious comparison — and then they were both laughing and the rest of the team looked up from their lunch. Lin smiled; Jason and Greta, sitting shoulder to shoulder, stared. Felix chewed steadily on, studying them as if they were some mildly interesting kind of wildlife.

'There are some very significant structural differences! But, really, you're absolutely right,' she told him. 'The vertebrate skeleton really is remarkably similar throughout the subphylum.' The *what?* From above came a sudden burst of deep, throaty calls: the raven, *Corvus corax*, she had told him earlier, after which his hometown was likely misnamed. Ravens, she'd said, had very large brains, proportional to their size, and they showed some highly intelligent, almost scientific behaviour.

'That was the female call, I think.' It was a strange, lovely sound and they both fell silent until it was done.

'The avian skeleton, too, has many similarities with our own.' She smiled. 'And with that of the pterosaur — but the differences are what matters.'

When he looked up to see where Anna was, often he'd see her checking on him too: sometimes their eyes would veer away; at other times, she might give a nod, the twitch of a smile.

Her naming of things seemed to make them more alive — he wanted more of it, but at times it was almost too much to bear that every part of the world about him, and of himself, was so much more than it seemed.

✦ ✦ ✦

Scott took his turn in town. He drove their garbage to the dump and arrived at the Mountain View just as night fell: why not stay where once he worked? He did not want to go home, and the room would be paid for whether he used it or not.

Marilyn Jensen was working what used to be his job.

'Hey, star,' she said, raising her eyebrows as she handed over the key with its worn cedar tag. 'Saw you on TV! But Lauren's still mad about you dumping the job. She'll just flay you.'

'I'll skip the breakfast tomorrow, then.' He smiled back at Marilyn, appreciating what there was to like: the plumpness of her cheeks, the full breasts. She was three years older than him, and already a mother twice.

He threw himself on the double mattress, appreciating the foam and springs as if they'd just been invented, and called Phoenix House. Minutes stretched out, slowly passed and passed again while someone went to fetch his father: he could hear footsteps

and voices, their TV, in the background, and over it all, someone loudly complaining about someone else being out of order.

'Son? That you?'

'You doing okay?'

'Why don't you try it? The world hurts,' Mac said, his voice
slow. 'It hurts, like every sound and every ray of light is made
to torture you. Whose fucking idea was this?'

'You're nearly through the worst.' Mac didn't respond to
this, but almost a week had passed, and he was *still there*. The
doctor there had scared him to death, Mac said. *At last*, Scott
thought.

'You've never got this far before. Hang in. I'm proud of you.'
A few minutes after they hung up, Scott's cell rang.

'You're right. I'm over the hump. But Scotty, come and get
me. They're such cruel bastards here. I can do this better at home.'

'I *can't*,' Scott told him and pressed End, wished he could
keep pressing it over and over, wiping out all the crap that ever
was: *end, end, end, end*.

He had Anna's laptop so he could download her email for
her. He put it on the shelf in the closet and hid it beneath the
spare pillow before setting out to meet Matt at Joe's.

'So what's it like up there with that blonde with the awe-
some boobs: you getting what you deserve or are those nerds
top of the food chain?' Matt nodded at the TV above the bar,
and there it was: the dig. Himself, kneeling on the rock. Greta
in her tight top. Jason and Felix carrying a sack of plaster over
to the storage area. Anna photographing the grid. Mike
Swenson supervising his team.

'Scientists at Big Crow hope to settle a dispute as to whether
these animals could actually fly, or had to launch themselves

from clifftops and glide. Dr Swenson, an expert in flight, is a long-time champion of the gliding theory—'

'That something this big could fly, as opposed to glide, is just a fashionable new theory. It's gained momentum of late. But I'm not convinced. I'm hoping we can finally settle the matter. Some very exciting things will emerge I'm sure. This site is comparable to recent finds in Brazil...'

'It may be the Brazil of the North, but the scientists at Big Crow sure have a difficult job ahead of them and a big one, too.'

Matt, clean-shaven, almost straight-looking, apart from the multiple earrings, leaned back in his chair, interlaced his fingers and then pushed his arms up and back, palms turned out, for a stretch. It was ironic, Scott often thought, that his dealer friend looked so much like the type that mothers liked their girls to bring home: clean-shaven, a good provider.

'So what goes on up there?'

'Work, work, work. No pay, though.'

'I'd like to help out,' Matt said, sitting a little straighter, 'but this is business.'

'No, I didn't mean that. I'm thinking of cleaning up a bit.'

'Think away,' Matt said, laughing. But later, when he drove Scott back to the Mountain View, they sat in the carpark with the radio, lights and engine on.

'You want to sample? It's very good.'

'I'm okay, thanks,' Scott said.

'What about the nerds?' Matt asked as Scott made to get out of the vehicle, 'Don't they need to relax? I could come up with a good price, if it was worth my while. Hey, is it true you're going to blast the cliff to get those fossils out? Can people come watch?'

Marilyn finger-waved to him as he came in, and looked as if she'd like to talk, but he went straight up and downloaded email. Anna had 402 new messages. He had 26, deleted them all and then slipped into the Net.

Dr Michael Swenson, he learned, was the Chair of Palaeontology, currently taught Diapsid Anatomy, Foundations of Palaeontology, and Cladistics; he declared an interest in proto-avian species, had a list several screens long of articles with long titles. Students could rate their professors and here Swenson came out average. Some gave him five stars and some none. Comments ranged from *Totally inspiring!!* to KYD, which decoded as *keep your distance.* You liked him or you loathed him. Or liked, then loathed?

Scott turned out the light, dreamed of flying effortlessly through a huge dry canyon, the sides and floor dotted with little camps. He came lower, saw a homely, grey-haired man sitting with a woman and child by a campfire, and knew at once that it was Dr Coneally. Scott had read about him the night before: how a park ranger drove at night through the Grand Canyon to give him the news from his lab — they had found a correlation, a marker, which narrowed the location of the Huntington gene down to somewhere on the short arm of Chromosome 4. It was the culmination of over a decade of work, the high point of his entire life, Coneally said.

✦ ✦ ✦

By eight o'clock the next morning it was already warm; Anna had sent Jason over twice to ask Dr Swenson if he would please ask his crew to turn their music down. Twice, the volume had briefly diminished, and then increased: a thumping beat, wailing guitars, crescendos of percussion: things she'd heard twenty years ago and had not wanted to remember since, music with a brain-scouring, aggressive quality she did not want in her life, least of all here, where she was trying to work. The sound itself was rough-edged, blurred with echo, verging on pure noise. It was impossible to hear each other, or the birds and the insects; even the ring of hammer on chisel was more of a vibration in the hands and arms than an actual sound. She knew it would make things worse if she tried to confront Mike, willed herself to stay on her side of the dividing line, but felt as if she might at any moment burst into tears or scream.

Felix and Greta blotted the sound out with their headphones; she put on ear protectors, started to feel even more deranged, disconnected both from herself and from what she was doing. Dropped her chisel. Lost her train of thought: this was what happened when he, Scott, was not there. Why had she let him leave?

Turning onto Fifth, Scott noticed two beaten-up camper vans parked on the corner lot and four more in the Save on Foods carpark, both plastered with Greenpeace and anarchy stickers, little rainbows, and messages about wild fish not doing drugs and letting the trees live so people could breathe. They'd been parked all night — wispy bits of Indian cloth hung over steamed-up windows. He rapped on the last van as he walked past and heard someone groan.

He pushed into the empty store, filled the cart. Canned ground beef. Bread. Noodles. Crackers. Hard cheese. Soft cheese in a tube. Baked beans. Carrots? Apples? Onions. Nuts. Raisins. What was Mac getting nowadays? High protein? Tuna steaks? Wheatgrass juice? Cereals. Pancake mix.

'Some kind of *Treehuggers*,' Tracy told him at the till. 'Filled up the whole of Shady Acres and more still turning up. All wanting organic fruit! How the hell do they afford it?' Outside, a white woman with mouse-coloured dreadlocks emerged from one of the vans wearing a purple tunic half-transparent in the morning sun.

It was past ten by the time he got back to the dig. He'd been hearing Led Zeppelin for the last half-hour and knew it would not be Anna's favourite. She jerked around angrily when he tapped her shoulder, offering the laptop.

'In the office!' she shouted, unable to hear her own voice. 'Then, Scott, please stop this!'

Hell, he thought.

The sound clarified as he walked towards it. They had an old CD player wired into two external speakers; he unplugged them, and carried the machine over to Swenson.

'You're scaring the birds.' Swenson got to his feet, chisel in hand.

'Bothering you?' he asked.

'I heard it over a mile away.' This, Scott thought, was where a person might drop the player on the ground and, using the hammer by Swenson's foot, destroy it with a couple of well-aimed blows. Or fight, wrestling the chisel out of the other man's hand. But he stood straight and smiled into the Ray-Bans.

'Don't want to have to confiscate your batteries,' he said, and behind him, someone laughed. Mike, too, smiled.

'My hands are shot,' Anna told him. 'I'm making a lot of errors.'

'You use your hands a lot,' he pointed out. He was sitting in the shade, ready to enter data onto Anna's laptop. The screen came to life and he found himself in something called *Personal*: the whole directory was visible and available. Some kind of diary. Folders with dates, others with people's names, and one that caught his eye called *sexrules.doc*. 'You didn't exit properly!' he told her. 'If this is going to be passed around you need to set up passwords for your personal files. Here, look—' He felt his face burn as he pushed the machine back to her.

'I think I'm forgetting more,' she said.

'Everyone forgets. No one else normally uses it, right?' He looked away while she dealt with it.

The work was just data entry: the name and number of the parts of the pterosaur that had been removed and their co-ordinates on the grid. It had to be exact. Her own hands resting in her lap, Anna watched carefully as Scott typed each item into the spreadsheet, double-checked, and moved the ruler down on the paper for the next piece. She felt the slow release of tension in the flexor muscles of her forearms, breathed in deeply. The chatter of the keyboard was oddly soothing and, towards the bottom of the first page, she leaned back a little, allowed herself to close her eyes. She slept, her head tipped back and to one side, her hands on top of each other in her lap.

It was strange to see her with the beam of her attention switched off: she who was always doing, talking, acting, reacting — now still. For a moment Scott's hands fell still and he took in the fine skin on her eyelids, the new shape of her face now that her mouth and jaw were loose, the paleness beneath her chin.

Phalan. L, 1, prox, he typed. *N3.15, W6.6*
Phalan. L, 1, med, N5, W6.6

It felt almost wrong to look, and very hard not to. Weird: like you were suddenly close in a way neither of you might want. Suppose the insect that circled the pair of them landed on her, what would he do then? And what was it? Those big opal-shaped wings, the gangly legs: she'd know, but she was asleep.

He saved everything, moved his chair back carefully, left.

✦ ✦ ✦

She showed him the Cretaceous-Tertiary boundary, a blurred line of pale grey in the darker grey of the cliff, in some places a metre above where they stood, in others less, or invisible. 'Dust and volcanic ash,' she explained. 'So: years of low-light conditions. First the plants go, and then the animals depending on them. Toxic gasses, fires, disease, growth of the insect population... I do tend to feel *all* these things, rather than just one of them. But in any case, you can see that despite what Dr Swenson says, it looks as if our specimens *predate* the mass extinction at the end of the Cretaceous by at least five million years. Perhaps he meant to suggest that there were earlier periods of hostile conditions on smaller scale. That's possible.

'The bones are still associated, so predation is unlikely. Likewise, a sudden event like a mudslide or a flash flood. So, it's a mystery—' She stopped midsentence. Stood there in the gorge, looking him in the face in a way that seemed to suggest that she was somehow seeing beneath his skin, and very likely naming things he did not even know were there. 'A not very scientific word,' she said. 'Something religious about it, compared to say puzzle, conundrum. Maybe I should say *unknown*...

'And what you feel faced with the unknown is a kind of

yearning, like the desire to travel, to set forth in your canoe or your space ship, towards whatever it is that might be out there... I'm thinking more and more that all we can hope to do is *see* it. A glimpse even. That perhaps we'll never be sure of understanding anything. Do I make any sense?' she asked, and then her face changed, seemed to shrink. 'Am I talking too much?'

'No—' She grasped his arm.

'You'll tell me, won't you, if you think I'm symptomatic?'

'Yes,' he said, and she let go. But he knew that he couldn't be sure what he would do in that or any situation and that he was already way out into his own unknown. No one had ever spoken to him like this before, and none of these people were like him.

'Good. Thank you,' she told him, and then set off downriver with the laptop in her backpack; she walked at a brisk pace, not looking back, the pack bouncing a little.

✦ ✦ ✦

Sometimes Anna thought she could see the Native part of Scott quite clearly — in the shape of his jaw, the set of his eyes, in the width of his face — or was it just that now that she knew about his mother she was looking to see it? In any case he was changing: his skin darkening in the sun, his body growing leaner from the work he did. And more than once, at night, Scott had appeared in her mind's eye, smiling and squinting a little in the sun: a strong face, but also one that liked to laugh. A face that could suggest irony, or enquire *How are you?* Or signal *Back off. Let it go, okay? Cool.*

Was she exploiting him?

It was an arrangement — unusual, yes — but one of mutual convenience. Need, even. In six weeks, she reminded herself, the dig would be finished; Scott would move on and find something new, hopefully better than working in the hotel. And as for her own afterwards, she would think of that only when she absolutely had to.

21

—————— ✦ ——————

BECAUSE ANNA WAS AWAY, the Swenson team came over with two litres of red wine. People set their chairs to claim space around the fire, and then stood by Scott's kitchen area with drinks and plates in their hands while he cooked their sausages and sipped wine from an enamel mug.

After the meal, Swenson stretched out, feet reaching to the fire, hands above his head, looked around, and grinned:

'While the cat's way, eh.' People laughed. 'How're you getting on over here?' Everyone waited for Jason, acting director in Anna's absence, to respond:

'It's tough shale, and we're being cautious, but pretty good.'

'I guess you're going to have to make very good time,' Swenson said, 'if you're to get everything out of here before we go back into that cliff. We've got an engineer on the case and he's very positive — there's no overhang. We'll use tiny charges, but there's always a theoretical risk of some degree of collapse. So for health and safety purposes you'll need to be offsite as well when we go in… Has Anna said anything about that?'

'*Charges?*' Lin asked.

'Maybe you could make sure she's fully aware…'

'Sure,' Jason said.

'Good man,' Mike told him. 'Don't forget. And look, there's no need to stay over here. You're welcome any time to come over and see how we're setting it all up.'

He shifted in his chair then and focused his attention on Greta. Scott, opposite, watched them. He knew how Anna would see all this.

'USC?' Swenson was saying. 'You must be working with Alexei Goodman? Old colleague of mine. What's your thesis topic?'

'You're very quiet tonight,' Lin said as she sat down next to Scott. It was almost dark.

'Well, you know, I don't really speak this language,' Scott told her. Her laugh was a tiny rustle, a gasp beside him.

'So you must learn. I learned English at school. This is only vocabulary...'

'I'm more interested in people,' he said.

'Difficult!' she told him. 'Even so, if this is their language, you will have to speak it.'

Mike topped up Greta's glass with the last of the wine. He wrote something down for her, leaned in close as he handed over the scrap of paper. She smiled across at him: nothing too hard to understand there, it seemed to Scott.

Marilyn, Scott's replacement on the reception desk at the Mountain View, looked Anna in the eye and said she was sorry, but there were no other rooms available, just 221, the room Anna had specifically asked *not* to be given. Marilyn placed the key on the counter between them, and waited for Anna to give in.

Just a room, she told herself. It had been used by others since the night she lay there sleepless in the aftermath of hitting Mike. It had been vacuumed and polished, changed. She was avoiding anger (expressing it, at least) and she wanted more than anything to settle on a real bed and call Lesley and Vik. So she took the key and let herself in.

'How's your monster?' Lesley asked. 'Tired,' she said of herself. 'Way bigger than when you last saw me. Way bigger than I ever was with either of the other two. Exhausted, weepy and sentimental. My wits are gone — but actually, it's okay, except for when I look at myself or put on a pair of shoes, so I'm not doing that. Blood pressure's still high, but they are letting me be.'

The nursery was perfect, Lesley said. Buttermilk with stencilled border, jungle-print drapes and high-contrast mobiles dangling above the matching cribs. She didn't think they would make the trip over to the dig. She knew *she* couldn't. Maybe Vik would bring the kids? He was asleep already. She'd suggest it to him in the morning, though he too was very tired.

Anna lay between the hotel sheets and imagined her nieces to be, floating in the amniotic sea: half-knowns. An almost mystery moving towards an ongoing revelation. In the time it had taken to return to Big Crow and begin the excavation, two entirely new people with identical DNA had been made: it was dizzying to think of the replications and divisions, the switching on and off of genes, the differentiation of tissues and organs and limbs, all of it happening two times over and that while it happened, while the twin girls in Lesley's womb quietly created themselves in the darkness, the mundane lives of those already born continued as if nothing was changing: they rushed in and out of cars, made telephone calls, booked flights, made sure there was food in the freezer, wrote papers, argued...

So she lay quite happily in the same room where she'd raged against Mike Swenson and fought against her own memories.

It seemed to her that life was sometimes terrifying, at other times shot through with bliss. So much in it, all at once: the creep of continental plates, the code in your genes, the smell of cooking, the memory of your mother's voice calling you out of your dream. Extinctions and creations. The rush of birdsong at dawn. A woman's belly, tight with the life inside. There were so many discoveries: those you went looking for, yearned for so much that it hurt, and others which lay waiting and which, if you knew of them, you'd do anything to escape, and behind each of them, another. A switchback ride, a dream of flight.

For a moment or two, she allowed herself to imagine Scott Macleod — that he was next to her, dark and solid against the white sheet. She could hear his breath, wanted to lean back into him and at the same time, wanted him to vanish: a twentysomething man whose mother was St'alkwextsiḥn, whose Scottish father had drunk himself almost to death, a high-school dropout getting work experience: a surprising, sweet young man with whom she should not ever get involved, and certainly not at this time of her life.

In the bright white circle of light from the flashlight suspended above him, the real Scott lay on his stomach inside his tent and read how for years after Coneally's good news, fifty-eight people in six different labs collaborated in the hope of finding, in an area of 2.2 million base pairs, the actual piece of code that created a human calamity. How they began to burn out, how they questioned themselves: the code they wanted seemed sometimes to be in one place, sometimes another. Perhaps there were several mutations, and perhaps they had to be present in particular combinations? Or perhaps the cause they sought was not a mutation, but a normal gene that failed to switch on or off at the right time? They wore white coats, had some kind of computers even back then, but they were searching for an invisible needle in a barn full of invisible straw... He turned the pages, aware of Anna's absence, one ear alert to the sounds of the night.

22

—————◆—————

ANNA MUST HAVE LEFT THE HOTEL well before dawn.

'Totally out of order, Jason!' Scott heard her shout. 'Not you. Him. I don't want messages! He must talk to me direct. Will someone tell him that? Scott? Where is Scott?' He struggled into his jeans, shoved feet into boots. Swenson's music was playing already, subdued, yet hard to ignore.

'Hey, what's going on?' She was huge-eyed, her fists clenched, beyond herself, not caring who saw it.

'Just tell him, Scott. Please. Tell him he has to talk to me direct!'

Of course he couldn't say that, it would make her look foolish. He crossed to the other camp and crouched down next to Mike.

'Come and talk to Anna about the cliff, Mike.'

'I'm busy.'

'I'll wait,' Scott said. 'Can I help?' There was no response, so he sat on the rock and watched them work. The Swenson team had most of their vertebrae out in large sections and were jacketing them, their hands and forearms gloved in white. Gus and Garth were setting up to film the process.

In the strengthening light everything grew visibly sharper

as he watched, as if the world was focusing itself. Scott waited almost half an hour until Swenson got to his feet, wiped his hands and said they could go.

'Not much fun,' Swenson said, 'being the messenger boy?' He pitched the question halfway between taunt and sympathy — and it was very simple, Scott thought: in any particular situation, Swenson did as much as he judged he could get away with.

Anna and Swenson lowered themselves into director's chairs, and she indicated that Scott should draw up a third, which Swenson made a point of noticing, though he said nothing.

'You must be aware that I'm aiming to go in under the cliff by the end of July at the latest?'

'You haven't kept me informed, and so naturally I have no idea of your plans. Surely that's a very questionable thing to do, to *remove the bottom section of a cliff*?'

'That may be your opinion. The fact is for health and safety reasons you'll need to be finished over here before work starts.' He made as if to get out of his chair.

'Wait, Mike. You intend to *blast* it away?'

'I always have done,' he said, smiling now, and words deserted her. She noticed how the plaster on his arms and hands had dried to a cracked crust. The silence gathered force and then pushed her out of the chair and onto her feet; she could almost have struck out at him again and instead she strode away in the direction of her tent, her face fighting itself.

'So— we're going at the necessary speed,' Scott filled in. 'We'll keep you posted.'

'Who the hell are you!' Swenson barked. 'The cook? Who exactly is in charge here?' Everyone heard it, and as Swenson made his exit, Felix, running his fingers through a pile of shale chips to check for any kind of pattern or change in texture, for tiny signs of life pressed into being stone, was the only one still at work.

How was he, Scott Macleod, supposed to make this good? Anna was not helping. She was acting oddly. She was *not* sick, but she was acting that way and if he let himself, he'd be thinking that she might be and what he might have to do it. The whole thing was insane, and it was none of his business. But it was his job.

'I better go check on Anna,' he told Jason.

'No,' Jason said. 'Help Felix go through that waste pile, and get it offsite.' That meant that he had to make things between them worse still by ignoring him.

Anna's face, framed by the door of her tent, was colourless and sharp. He knelt on the rock.

'You have to get back out there. You've just got to calm down, back off a bit,' he told her. She clenched her fists, opened her hands. He grabbed them, tried to keep them still, she pulled free, buried her face in them. He was not helping and had absolutely no idea what to say or do next. Finally, she let her hands fall.

'I can't,' she said, letting her hands fall and looking up at him. 'Too angry. I've got to write to the funders, telling them what is going on here and making my position absolutely clear, surely you can see that?' He didn't see and stared back at her, helpless. 'You're meeting the Yamaguchis from the afternoon floatplane,' she said: it was the first he had heard of it. 'So you can go early, print out my letter, send it by fax and email, *both*, do you understand? Will you do that for me?

'Maiko and Akira are lovely people,' she added, before she sealed the tent door. 'Thank you.'

✦ ✦ ✦

Maiko and Akira wore identical glasses with delicate wire frames and rimless lenses. He, Akira, was very slim; she, Maiko, was small but plump, with short, slightly greying hair, expensively styled. Scott introduced himself as a volunteer, picked up their bags.

'My colleague, and also my wife, Maiko.' Akira's smile carved up his face. The lightweight, high-tech clothes they wore rustled all the way back to the van.

'So very exciting!' Maiko said as she climbed in. 'Is it going well? Do we drive far?'

It was their sheer strangeness that made Scott stop and pick up two hitchhikers who were waiting just past the turnoff: a tall man and a woman with a shaved head, the dark stubble just growing through. Heavily pregnant, she had rich blue Celtic tattoos on her chest, arms, and ankles — everywhere that was exposed. The man's green eyes glittered out of the deepest tan Scott had ever seen on a white man. They wanted to use the Internet, he explained, in the library or a café, and then they climbed into the far back of the van and sat silently looking at the road unfold; and until Scott let them out no one else felt that they could speak.

'How is Anna?' Maiko asked, as soon as they were gone.

'Great,' Scott told her.

At nightfall there were two fires and people called across and passed from site to site. A stranger, Scott thought, would not have known that anything but good science and a major flirtation between Greta and Jason was happening. There were jokes, laughter, even cross-teamwork: team Swenson boiled the pasta. Scott, assisted by Lin, made the sauce. They estimated their progress, congratulated themselves on the weather, stoked the flames of the campfires.

Orange light played over faces and hands. There were tales of other discoveries: how, after a week of fruitless prospecting, Felix's supervisor tripped over the edge of the shell of the turtle they were looking for on their way back to the jeep. How hadrosaur trackways had been spotted by a seven-year-old having a birthday flight with his dad in a six-seater; how someone in North Carolina had CT-scanned a dinosaur specimen and was able to see the heart inside; it had four chambers and a single aorta, warm-blooded, just. There was talk of a half-hatched maiasaur with bits of eggshell sticking to its scales. Live young inside an ichthyosaur. And another scientist, a woman from Texas whom Jason had met, had recently discovered fossilised soft tissue attached to the femur of a T. Rex.

'Meat, basically!' he said. 'It's getting very close to actual DNA. We're *almost* in Jurassic Park.'

'That frog in amber, where was that?' asked Gunnar. 'They could surely get DNA there.'

'Private collection, Mexico,' Kevin told him. 'Probably end up as a necklace.'

No one had said not to ask about the discovery of the specimens they were working on, but absolutely everyone knew not to.

'A colleague of ours,' Akira said, 'just found a hadrosaur near Mifune: the first to be found in Asia. Perhaps we too will have our own pterosaur soon.'

All the time, Anna said, they were finding more, and seeing what they found better. Jason and Greta slipped away. Swenson, seated opposite Maiko and Akira, smiled and nodded when they spoke; he held out his hand to each of them when he got up to leave.

'Scott—' Anna held out her hand to him. A shake? A high-five? Something between a grasp and a squeeze.

He sat in his tent, legs akimbo, wrist on knee, book on the floor, read how less than a decade ago, in 1993, they'd found their golden needle. The normal gene: cytosine, adenine, guanine; the abnormal, *just the same* but with extra repeats of the sequence that doubled its size. It was a good place to stop. He closed his eyes; he saw two immensely long tangled strings of beads, a jumble of red, yellow, white, red, yellow, white.

23

——— ✦ ———

GUS MOPPED HIS REDDENED NECK with a scrap of burlap.

'We'll aim to give a sense of time passing,' he said, 'not to make the viewer actually experience it.' They only needed to film when there was some kind of change or result; there would be other footage, a voice-over, interviews with Anna and Dr Swenson, opinions from experts, and so on. He and Garth, he admitted, had had no idea when they first came how very slowly it would go.

'Slower, even, than *psychoanalysis*!' Garth rolled his eyes. Until now, that had been his last assignment: a man lying on a couch! Sighing and rambling to himself while another man sat very still and listened… Every hour had been a month… 'It'll never air, I'm sure of that.'

'We're with Swenson, I must admit: get to the big stuff as soon as possible. Should be exciting when that cliff comes down!' Meanwhile, they said, why not let them help? They could take photographs, push the wheelbarrow, sweep, sift through the waste pile, whatever: 'Just say where you want us.'

One wing-finger concretion broke lengthways into three pieces and one of the pieces had cracked down the length. Jason, who'd been working on it with Felix, was furious with himself, but Anna remained calm and pointed out it was surprising that they had it in just three pieces.

The pieces were laid out on strips of precut three-quarter-inch marine ply and Felix and Scott donned orange latex gloves, slapped on the soaked burlap, then the lumber, then more dripping burlap; tomorrow, when it was cured, they'd fill it in and protect the other side and strap the whole thing together.

Felix, squatting easily, worked fast, pushing the wet cloth in tight, smoothing it with his long strokes, his face perfectly relaxed. He'd never wanted to do anything but this. From boyhood, he told Scott, he had devoured anything about fossils; his dad had encouraged him. He was drawn to the Cretaceous era because of the extinction at the end of it:

'An era of climate change not unlike our own,' he pointed out, 'although arising from natural rather than human activities. Though I guess people are part of nature... Some of them, anyhow.' He had mixed feelings about people: the things they did, especially to children and animals. He liked all animals without reserve and was particularly drawn to the larger marine and airborne creatures in the fossil record.

'Utterly different,' he said, pausing for a moment, lost in his thoughts. 'Hey!' he flung out a skinny arm, pointing: 'Who's that up there? What are *they* doing?' There were people on top of the cliff, standing right where Anna and Scott had stood the day they first met, looking down at the site with what looked like binoculars.

'Hikers,' Scott said. There was a sign at the entrance to the trail telling people to seek permission from the band, but it rarely happened. And with all the media attention people would naturally be curious. Half an hour later, when he returned from

emptying a barrow load of waste, they were still there, still looking. He waved; someone pointed at him, but no one waved back.

'*They* are filming *us*,' Gus said, sounding both shocked and
pleased. He studied them through his own lens, watched the
figures move back from the edge. 'Voyeurs,' he added, with a
nod at Jason and Greta who were no longer crouched side by
side at work, but standing, her face lifted towards his, her
breasts grazing his chest. A pair of safety goggles dangled from
her wrist.

Scott was mixing plaster when he first thought he heard something: a soft wave of sound, like the sea, but not. Singing,
perhaps. 'You have media deprivation syndrome!' Lin suggested
when he asked her if she could hear it too. 'Since you so kindly
lent Anna your CD player.' When Lin smiled, it looked as if
she was sealing her lips together to stop something shocking or
even terrible from coming out, but at the same time, her eyes
sent out sparks.

The music grew clearer: singing. Drums.

'You must be able to hear it!'

'Maybe there is something, yes,' she agreed with a little
nod, just as, behind them, Jason yelled to everyone to come
see: the third cervical vertebra had split and the half of the
concretion could be lifted off, like a lid! They could actually
see the fossilised bone, new-looking except for the slightly
brownish grey colour. Flecks of something that glittered stuck
to it here and there, and Anna was just explaining what it was,
when she too heard the music, which grew louder by the second. Swenson and his team strode up. For a couple of beats
everyone waited as if themselves fossilised — even Felix, once

he had finished the plaster that had been made up, wiped his hands and fell still.

They saw: the beginning of a line of assorted people bearing placards, chanting in a language Scott recognised but could not understand. A few kids, a woman with a baby in a sling, a hundred or more adults and teenagers, some carrying drums or rattles, others just bringing themselves. A huge assortment of hats, a few sun umbrellas. *This Land Is Not Your Land*, one placard read, *Leave our ancestors alone*. Several said 'CanCo, Can GO!' There were people from the reserve, and people Scott knew from town, including Andrea Price's special needs brother and one of her grown-up sons, and several old men who'd once worked with his father at the mill, as well as strangers — young people in loose clothes who looked like peasant extras in a dragon-slaying fantasy movie, their hair dyed and shaved, tousled and teased and braided — almost hip, yet not quite.

Rentamob, CanCo would call them.

'Oh my God,' Anna said. She realised, then, what she had done. *Not* done.

The singing, strong and deep, filled the space completely, like a thick liquid. For a moment, Scott wanted to join in. Mike Swenson broke out and strode towards the oncoming crowd.

'Stop right there!' he called out as he reached the leaders — elders from the reserve, and one tall, pregnant woman: one of the hitchhikers Scott had picked up, now wearing a bandanna over her shaved head. 'This is a site of special scientific interest,' Swenson continued. 'Only authorised people are allowed onsite during the excavation.' He spread his arms wide, but the crowd parted and continued past him; he had to catch up and then fall in beside the leaders as they walked right on past the tents, stepping carefully over the rocks that kept them in place, still singing, and finally arrived at Anna's part of the excavation, where the column came to a halt, and suddenly there was complete silence. They stood with their heads bowed, looking at the earth.

'Scott,' she said in a low voice, 'are these the St'alkwextsihn?' She stood just in front of the tape, between him and Mike Swenson and the twins; Greta and Jason and Lin, Akira and Maiko and the rest were inside the work area.

There was a great aunt of his. And Thompson, a little older than him, very tall, with the main part of his hair gown long and worn in a ponytail, the sides shaved close. He was some distant kind of cousin; he had been at Scott's uncle's funeral, which was the last time he'd visited the reserve, perhaps five years ago. Back then, Thompson's hair was long all over and he'd clearly been wrecked, but now he stood tall. Leading the crowd was Alan Coxtis, the new band leader, a stocky man in jeans and a white t-shirt, neat hair, wire glasses and big watch: there was nothing obviously traditional about him except the shape of his face and the silver pendant he wore on his chest.

Coxtis pulled a piece of paper from his back pocket, glanced at it and then shoved it back where it had come from.

'We, the St'alkwextsihn,' he said, making the sounds not as they had become, *Stallquakseen*, but as they were supposed to be — the explosive *t*, the rough *x*, the abrupt but breathy *h*, the stress on the *i* at the end — and then waiting for the applause from behind him to subside. 'We, the St'alkwextsihn Nation do not recognise the lines drawn on your maps. We are the Big Crow River People, and this valley, and all the creatures living in and buried in it, are part of our lands and our culture. We do not want them disturbed, not by logging, and not by scientists. We do not want our dead, human or animal, dug up. Negotiation with the provincial government is ongoing.'

There was more applause, whoops and catcalls.

'I know who he is—' Anna said.

'Very tough. A good man, they say,' Scott told her.

Garth and Gus roved around the edges of the crowd. The protesters' own crew, up on the cliff, did the same, and members of the crowd, too, were recording things as they took place.

'We and our supporters...' Coxtis coughed, '...the Forest Nation and the people from the town of Big Crow call upon you to stop what you are doing here and leave the land intact until the treaty negotiations are complete. We call on you to show your support for us by severing your relationship with CanCo, whose planted forests occupy many acres of our traditional lands to either side of the river and whose planting practices have severely affected the biodiversity of the area and our traditional way of life.' More applause. 'Thank you,' he concluded.

'Mr Coxtis,' Anna said, holding out her hand, which he did not take, 'Anna Silowski. Please accept my apologies. I believe this is my mistake: I intended to write to you about the excavation, but during a time of great personal difficulty it somehow got missed. I'm very sorry. I hope we can talk.'

Coxtis lowered his head a little. 'We can talk,' he said.

'There's not much to say.' Swenson stepped forwards and stood between them, too close to both. 'We're scientists, doing our job, preserving an amazing find — and on a shoestring, I might add. We have permission from the current landowners and are having an absolutely minimal impact on the site. I don't see what argument there can be and I can't believe what I'm hearing here. If you want to protest, why not pick something worthwhile. Fish farming. Nuclear Energy… This is just bloody *politics*. We're asking you to leave, and if you don't, then we're going to have to call in the RCMP.'

'Who is the leader here?' Coxtis asked, looking between Swenson and Anna.

'Both of us,' Anna told him.

'You must speak with one voice,' Coxtis replied, 'or what is the point?' He took a folding stool handed to him by another of the protestors, opened it and sat down; in semi-unison the rest of the crowd followed suit, some on stools, some on blankets, some right on the rock. *Leave Our Ancestors Alone*, another of the signs read, *Let the Big Bird Sleep. Go Away, Scientists*, a third declared.

Mike Swenson dug his cell phone out of his shorts pocket, handed it to Gunnar: 'Run to the carpark and go call the RCMP, get them to send someone up here immediately. These people are trespassing on a site of special scientific interest. And it's a dangerous workplace.'

'Wait.' Anna reached towards Swenson, and then froze. 'Let's try and sort this out.' But Gunnar was already striding off, picking his way through the seated crowd, who neither helped nor hindered him, but acted as if he simply did not exist.

'No filming!' Swenson yelled at Gus, who ignored him. 'I suggest everyone get back to work!'

Anna turned to Mike again, and this time without realising it, briefly grasped his arm. 'We must talk this through. Maiko, Akira, Scott. Please excuse us, Mr Coxtis.'

They sat under the kitchen awning. There was a tremor in her hands and arms again, but Scott was there and Maiko and

Akira; she was determined not to think of it, and to treat Mike as if he were any other colleague.

'I had it on my list to contact Mr Coxtis, but I forgot to do it. That was a mistake. The application happened in such a rush. We absolutely should have gotten their blessing.' She looked across at Swenson, who did not offer to share the responsibility.

'Well, perhaps,' Swenson said. 'Would they ever give it? And it's really not the point!'

'Yes,' Scott found himself saying, 'You should have asked, both of you. And now—' Swenson turned, glaring.

'Whose side are you on?'

'My mother was from the St'alkwextsihn.'

'So do you have something to do with this?'

'Don't be ridiculous!' Anna said. 'Scott is offering to help us understand the situation. Why did you bring along all this media in the first place is a better question! There'll be more to-morrow. And Mike, suppose the RCMP come; they're not going to drag all these people away, are they? I think we have to talk with them. Apologise properly. Somehow show them that what we're doing.'

'They don't care what we're doing. It's a means to an end. Isn't it?' Mike turned to Scott, who felt his face burn.

'We have to respond,' Anna said. 'We are going to have to take the time to sort this out.' Her hands were vibrating inside, but she kept them pressed to the table. You couldn't see it. She checked, looked back up again.

'How much time do you have?' Swenson got to his feet. 'I have no desire to waste mine talking to people who refuse the evidence of their own eyes, and prefer to believe the earth was made by a raven breaking open a clamshell. They can sit there if they want. You can waste your time if you want. It's a discussion that could take *decades*, so long as someone funds it!' He made to stride off, but stopped and turned to face the others again. 'That's if you've *got* time,' he said to Anna, 'between whatever you're doing with him—' he jabbed his finger at Scott. 'I am going to get on with what I am here for,' he told them.

Akira and Maiko sat straight-backed, conveying by their very stiffness how appalled they were, and for a moment, Anna felt, things were so dreadful that it would not be impossible to laugh.

'I am sorry for this unpleasantness but glad that we have Scott here,' she told them. 'This is a difficult situation, but we have someone with St'alkwe<u>x</u>tsiḥn heritage we can consult.'

Maiko smiled, and turned to Scott as if she expected him to make some kind of speech.

'Wait a moment. I didn't grow up on the reserve. My mother never even applied for status,' Scott told Anna. 'She left—'

'It's really good to have you on the team.' She gestured back at the site, at the people, everywhere, sitting like human rocks. 'There must be some kind of agreement we can come to. All I want is to see what's here.'

She wanted to see what was there, to unwrap the gift in stone. Swenson wanted to get the cliff out of the way, prove his point about gliding, get his name on the find in as big a way as he could. If you knew how far he would go, then he was easy to hate, but *what do I want*, Scott asked himself as he tipped the last drops out of one of their plastic water carriers. He wanted a good time. The best possible out of a shared occasion or situation: it was what had kept him with Mac, wanting it to work out, somehow. He wanted Anna Silowski to have what she wanted, the huge winged lizard freed from the rock, re-assembled and resurrected; he wanted her burdens to be lifted from her, and sometimes he wanted to put his arm round her, but because of what Swenson had said, could not. But at the same time, he wanted the St'alkwextsihn to get *their* way: *we, us, our,* he half-thought as he followed Anna back to the site, and wished there was something in between *theirs* and *ours.*

Anna crouched awkwardly in front of Coxtis' canvas stool. The crowd, bar a couple of kids, fell silent; Swenson's team was still working and the tap of their hammers and the whine of the angle grinder continued as they spoke. She needed him to listen to her, yet why should he?

'May I show you what we are doing and tell you what it means? Just one or two people to begin with, since it's very delicate.'

Alan Coxtis conferred with the elders to either side of him, and then rose and helped them to do likewise, slipping his hand under their elbows, allowing himself to be used as a steadying post once they were up. He ducked under the ribbon, agile despite the beginnings of a pot belly. He held the ribbon up for the two who followed him: John Fleet, a tall, greying man and a more rotund, much older man with a walking stick, Ben Tate. Scott stood behind Anna, she could feel him there; the rest of the team, finding themselves suddenly part of a larger drama, sat like sculptures of themselves: Greta leaned back into Jason. Felix, chisel still in hand, his long legs crossed at the ankle in front of him. Lin sat straight-backed, as if meditating, Akira and Maiko stood solemnly behind her.

She wanted to give them the best picture she could: the warm sea filled with extraordinary life forms. The pterosaur taking off from a cliff riding thermals, swooping to feed, rising again and then circling to land.

She showed them a drawing, explained about the fourth finger supporting the flight membrane. She brought over the piece of exposed bone that Jason had cracked open that morning, took them up to the head area and explained exactly how they were excavating beneath it, trying still, to keep it in one piece and how people are coming from all over the world to see the specimen. She introduced them to Maiko and Akira, all the way from Japan, who smiled and stepped forward to shake hands.

'It's the first pterosaur ever to be found in this bed of rock and that is why it's of huge, international scientific importance.' As if the words coming from her mouth were traffic at an intersection, Alan Coxtis raised a hand to signal *Stop*.

'It is also Big Crow, the bird ancestor,' he said. After a moment or two, the shorter of the two elderly men continued:

'After the flood came, and Big Crow snatched up the last surviving man and his woman who had a child in her belly. He was going to devour them, but the man promised that they would not fish above second bend in the river, and that every time they had a catch, they would leave fish on the stone for Big Crow, and that all their children and their children's children would do the same. Do you remember this?' he asked, with the ghost of a smile, looking over Anna's shoulder to where Scott stood.

'I think so,' Scott said, and stepped forward into the small circle.

'Anna,' he said, 'go on.'

'That's a fascinating story. And what's so very interesting,' she pointed out, 'is that it has a flood in it, because the geological record indicates that this area has indeed been flooded at various times, including during the late Cretaceous — though that was long before people existed, of course. Sea levels were rising then in response to atmospheric conditions. And the other connection is that you see the birds as having ancestors, and maybe that idea is rather like the idea of evolution.

'But you see, if we don't remove it now, it will be destroyed. Water and grit grinds away the softer rock and these concretions here get loosened and then carried away when the river is full and they're soon broken and dispersed and once they're dispersed, we can't—'

Again, the stop sign, the pause.

'Our culture is not very interested in preservation,' Alan Coxtis said. 'We're more interested that things should be where they belong.'

There was applause from the crowd then, a ripple that seemed to spread from front to back. And Anna knew without Scott telling her that she had to go on, find better things to offer.

'Where things belong,' she said, 'is what I'm interested in too! The way I see it, what we have here is a creature that belongs in a piece of deep time which we're trying to illuminate and to learn from, and also one that belongs in a series of relationships to other creatures of the same era, and before and afterwards. And although I found it, it most definitely doesn't belong to me. It belongs to no one and everyone at the same time, and so it seems to me that means that it belongs in the museum, where not just scientists, but anyone who wants to can see it.'

'It belongs where it is. The things in museums are twice

dead,' the taller elder said. 'Even the stories they write on the walls there are no longer alive.'

She wanted to say yes, the pterosaur was very dead, and maybe was dead twice or even three times over — but still it was part of the history of life, and that in its way was a sacred thing. She wanted to say that she felt as if she meant well. But suddenly she could find no more words.

Coxtis smiled; his eyes remained serious, but not, she felt, hostile in a personal kind of way. She could like him, despite the trouble he was bringing her.

'You must understand,' he said, 'artefacts are found in museums, scattered all over the world — things taken without permission, and things many of us no longer know how to make. Cedar baskets, beadwork, ceremonial masks. Museums are where they put the remains of what has been overrun.' It was true, of course. But did she personally have to suffer for it?

'I do see that,' she began, 'but at least, there is a pretty good record.' She realised as she spoke, where the conversation would go: to the general continuous overrunning of everything by time, geology, and the endless random creativity of evolution, versus the specific overrunning of one group of people by another, who were resisting. Who, for good reasons of their own, had picked something she very much wanted to focus that resistance upon. Here quite simply, were a group of people who thought completely differently to her and somehow they must agree.

'I think you see where we are coming from,' Coxtis said just as two RCMP officers, their armpits circled dark grey and their faces running with sweat, ducked under the tape and asked where was Dr Swenson? Jason went to fetch him.

'Hey, Baz,' Scott said to the broadest-shouldered of the two officers, the young one with a shaving cut on his cheek, 'this is quite a situation!' and Baz looked away, at his feet while the other officer pulls out a notebook. He wrote down Coxtis' words:

'This is a non-violent protest against the removal of Big Crow Ancestor from our traditional lands.'

'Big Crow is showing himself to us now, to tell us, *Courage! Stick to your path.*'

'We're doing everything we can to sort this out,' Anna said, and the constable wrote that down too. For a brief moment it seemed to Scott that everything had come to rest briefly in a strange kind of equilibrium out of which anything could arise. His heart was thumping as he put his hand on Anna's shoulder, which for a moment or two, she allowed.

'Please drive me to town, now, Scott.'

There were vans and trucks parked by the river and lining the turn off. All the way back to town they passed makeshift signs directing people back to the Big Crow Protest. Scott parked in the Save On parking lot, bought two ice-cold waters and waited while she made calls. To Mr Bellavance:

'Would you consider talking to them, Andrew? They'd appreciate it, I'm sure. Well, maybe you can think of— I do appreciate that, Andrew. I can see your position.'

To the museum:

'The police got them to move back a little but they're going to be there every day. Brian, I feel it is my fault, because I— No, he didn't. He's taking quite a strong position.' Her voice deepened as she spoke.

'No, they won't. No. Part of their mythology. According to the map and the GPS both of the specimens are on CanCo land, but they disagree with the map. I don't think they'll just tire of it and go away.'

He sat next to her, listening, ready if required but not sure what he could possibly do to help. He thought how he should perhaps call Mac, could get his own cell phone out, but it didn't seem like the moment: the two of them, side by side, each with their own emergency, jabbering into a bit of plastic. He imagined his father sitting in the big, clean meeting room at Phoenix House, wanting a drink but not getting one and having to listen to someone else talk about how low they've sunk...or, white and shivering, being taken in a group to the swimming pool.

'Physically, they aren't doing anything except sit there and I suppose we *can* continue, but— Brian, this really is a very difficult situation— would you consider coming meantime to see for yourself? Of course I can cope, but I think we should. Okay, I'll keep you posted.'

'They'll have a meeting about it *next week*,' she told Scott. 'Next week! And so meantime, I'm on my own with this. We'd better get back.' Scott made the mistake of turning on the radio: 'Big Crow is not just a clash of interpretations,' a female reporter was saying, 'but also a—'

'Clash of interpretations?' Anna turned toward him as if he'd said it. 'Surely there's a difference between science and storytelling?'

'I don't think that matters,' Scott said. 'The St'alkwextsihn have been ripped off. And from their point of view, you're way, way nicer than Dr Swenson, but you're kind of saying the same thing. You wanted my advice— well, I guess you'll have to offer something.'

He felt her looking at him as he drove.

'Brian suggested we could give them some kind of panel on the final museum display!' she said. They both laughed. 'So,' she said, 'this is Big Crow, where you grew up—' and he had a sudden memory of the schoolyard, felt again the awful despair of being there.

When she asked him to pull over, he stopped in a patch of shade. The brush by the roadside was beginning to yellow in the heat, but the conifers were deep green against the sky. It was very quiet without the engine and general clatter of the van moving along.

'About earlier...'Anna said, '...when you— I don't want this to get out of control, and not just because it's work. Look at what Swenson said — that's not going to make life easy. So can you promise not to touch me again? It's not professional. Please don't argue with me.'

'Okay,' he said, and shrugged. He did not want to make things worse. She was utterly impossible, yet at the same time, she made him feel totally woken up.

'Have you thought what you are going to do after this?' she asked as he started up again.

'Guess I'll see how things turn out.'

'Once you know, I'd like to help.'

People were beginning to leave the river parking lot, packing their chairs and banners away, eating at the picnic tables, making use of the pit toilets behind the trees. Barry Sutherland roamed from group to group, pointing out that any vehicles left overnight would be towed away.

'Scott!' Thompson yelled as they climbed out of the van.

'What're you doing on the wrong side?' Scott raised his hand in greeting and yelled: 'Working!' before following Anna through the gap in the trees, down the boardwalk and on to the riverbed.

If he had not met her that day on the top of the cliff he might well be on the other side now, even just for something to do. As it stood, he felt that he was on both sides, and yet whatever he thought about what should happen, this way and that, it was in the end, he realised with a shock, how the outcome affected the woman with the incomprehensible vocabulary walking beside him that mattered to him most of all. But her mouth was tight, her eyes intense; she was not thinking of him at all.

Why not, Scott suggested when they returned, offer food to the half-dozen protesters who had stayed to bed down on the rock? It meant using both sets of cooking equipment, and had an unexpected benefit: Mike Swenson and the twins stayed away. After the plates of beans and rice had been handed round there was silence for a moment or two while people stirred the two foods together, investigated how spicy the meal was.

'Look,' Anna said quietly to Coxtis, 'I've been through so much to get to this point. You can't imagine.'

'It's not personal,' he replied, setting his plate aside, 'simply a matter of justice. And in any case, I *can* imagine. My people have been trying to negotiate an agreement with yours for ninety-six years.

'So,' he explained, 'we know this may take time. Everyone will be back in the morning. If they block the access from the parking lot, there are other ways in.'

A long silence followed this: there was nothing to do but eat. Eventually Spruce, the Forest Nation spokesperson, asked Anna whether or not she had looked into CanCo's environmental record before she approached them for sponsorship?

'They're a logging company. Supporting us is actually one of the better things they do. Without them, their permission and their help, we can't get the specimen out.'

'We don't like that word, *specimen*,' Coxtis said. 'For us, that is not what it is. It is either Big Crow, or Raven.'

'It's very hard for me to call it Crow or Raven,' Anna told him, 'since it's not a bird of any kind. Fossil?'

'Creature,' Greta suggested. Jason, welded to her side, arm around her waist, nodded his approval; his hand, Scott noticed (and so, he thought, must everyone else) had pushed its way deep under the waistband of her low-rise pants.

'Are you saying,' Anna asked, swallowing her etymological objection to *creature* — a thing created — 'that you want the... fossilised creatures...to be left where they are? That to your mind, they can't be touched *at all*?'

'If that *was* the case, what do you think would be the right thing to do?' Coxtis, Scott knew, was talking around things the way the Big Crow people always did; even his mother used to do it, answer a question with a question — it used to drive Mac mad.

'That's really hard for me to say. I think I'd want a third party to make a judgment.'

'But was it a fair question, Alan?' Scott asked, and everyone turned to look at him. He tried to clear his throat: 'Like: there probably isn't a right thing. This side or that side, someone's always pissed. There's only whatever you agree to.' Finally, throat welded together, he looked down at his hands, wishing he could vanish, had never come here at all — and at the same time not caring who Coxtis was, or who they all were, or how many degrees they all had and wanting to cut through the crap, all of it, and wishing he could stop thinking about what was happening opposite between Jason and Greta, what they'd be doing later, what Mike Swenson thought Anna and he might be doing too. The easy way to be rid of all this would have been to get up and do some hard, useful work, but it was dark. He wanted to explode — shoot up like a firework, up above the circle around the fire, the camp and the riverbed and the forest above all their heads and then burst into a million shining pieces.

'We hope you will refrain from digging,' Coxtis said.

'I think,' Anna said, 'that we may have to continue, but I promise to take nothing away.'

'Can you promise not to touch the cliff?'

'That's a very reasonable request, but it's not for me to say. I'll pass it on to Dr Swenson.'

Maiko leaned forwards, smiling gently at the circle of faces: 'This kind of problem,' she said, 'does not arise in Japan.'

24

———— ✦ ————

THE FIRST OF THE PROTESTERS REAPPEARED at dawn, and more arrived steadily as the morning grew bright and hot. By noon, the shale was baking; the work, already painstaking, witnessed by so many people, seemed to go even more slowly than it always did. Yet, because it was such a large task with its own logic and continuous demands, the work had a kind of insulating quality, like ritual, which made it possible to continue while watched.

Lin and Scott finished wrapping the bones of the left arm and hand, began the excavation of the pelvis: a confused lump of hardened rock that likely contained the fused bones of the ilium, sacrum and pubis, along with another bone unique to the species, the prepubis: a kind of sitting-bone, Lin said, as well as a support for the fossilised creature's intestines. From the direction and structure of the hip socket, Lin explained, they might be able to learn something about how it walked and, if there were significant differences in the proportions of the pelvic bones in each specimen, they might be able to assign gender.

The preparation department in the museum was hoping, Lin said, to acquire a CT scanner to help with this specimen, but if it didn't materialise, then it will be down to her and whoever else to find the bones inside the stone, removing the shale a micron at a time with an air scribe. Maybe Scott should visit the museum sometime, see how it was done, what was there, she said as one gloved hand scooped away a handful of broken rock and the other reached for the brush.

Swenson refused to discuss anything unless he and Anna were on their own, *without Scott*, he specified; she agreed to walk a little way upstream with him, making it clear first to the others what she was doing.

'I told Alan Coxtis we'd try to find a solution,' she told him, 'and that I won't remove anything from the site until there's agreement. They want an assurance that you will not take the cliff down without their consent. Would you be prepared to meet with the chairs of our departments and come up with something clear that we can offer?'

'Do you think I'm not aware of what is really going on here! It won't work,' he said. The discussion was already over: he turned his back on her and set off back to the dig.

'He thinks,' Scott explained, 'that *you* have set up this protest to stop him from digging under the cliff, and that I've helped you. I think that's it.'

'What!'

'Maybe it's the kind of thing he might do.'

What might thinking that way lead Mike to do or say next? Things were worse than she had imagined they could be, and yet, immersed in the continuous emergency that the dig had become, she had no time to worry about anything else, certainly not about her life after the dig. She clung to the fact that there would be a meeting at the museum, from which surely, a tangible offer would emerge. She felt, in the midst of it all, a peculiar kind of calm.

'Meanwhile,' she announced, 'back to work.' Scott struck his chisel and the rock split cleanly along the bedding plane, freeing a small concretion.

'Split it,' she told him. Inside was a thumbnail-sized beetle that could almost be alive: they could see some kind of joints in its long antennae, and the fine ridges on its wing cases — the *elytra*, she called them.

'Our first insect!' she said. Watched impassively by the protestors, they took it over to the plank bench, gave it a number and recorded it in the log: *Coleoptera?*

The flight of insects, she said, was another matter entirely to that of pterosaurs, birds or bats, and very imperfectly understood.

That night he sat up after the others had gone. Not so long ago he had spent his nights in the trailer with Mac, arguing about how much was a reasonable amount to spend on alcohol per week, why he never washed dishes, and who the hell was it who left open the door and let in all those damn flies, and how that had felt like the entire possible world. Now, just a few weeks later he was here and Mac was, so far as he knew, still at Phoenix House. Instead of Mac there was Anna: her passion for the deep past, her fear and courage and secrets and silences, all the parts of her that almost no one knew anything about. There was this new world where people spoke in Latin and Greek, read the rock for signs of other, ancient worlds, feuded, made grant applications, dug up monsters, or, as he had read in *Reading Fate*, they spent their days in laboratories measuring things they could not directly see. All this now stood side by

side with the other world of the St'alkwe*x*tsiḫn with its atmosphere of pride and hurt, where stories were as real as
science, and maybe more use.

He slept at last, right there on the rock by the fire.

✦ ✦ ✦

At dawn, Anna went to collect tools and noticed immediately
that parts of the specimen had been moved. She knelt among
the jackets, a jumble of hard, white parcels, checking and double-
checking numbers against the log. The bones of the right hand
and one of the caudal vertebrae were missing.

'Oh, hell, hell, hell!'

'Someone must have gone right past me!' Scott, hollow-
eyed, wanted to check again, but she was already sure, and
threaded her way around the excavation and over to where Alan
Coxtis sat, his back against the rock, the Cretaceaus-Tertiary
boundary passing a metre or so above his head.

'Do you have them?' she asked, her body waist up reflected
in his sunshades. 'The missing pieces, do you have them?'

'Missing pieces?' He looked around him, as if searching. 'I
have nothing,' he said. 'You say these creatures belong to no
one,' he continued, removing the shades, making her image
vanish, 'yet you want them so very badly. I hope that you can
find a way for each of us to get what we badly want.'

'I am going to have to report the missing pieces to the police.'

Coxtis shrugged, looked through her as if she did not exist.

25

―――― ✦ ――――

ALL WORK ON THE DIG WAS SUSPENDED. Fifteen officers were drafted to the site, and the two crews sat waiting on the rock in the midday heat, much like the protestors themselves. Downriver, the entrance to the parking lot had been cordoned off. Police conducted a search of the parking lot, campsites and the riverbed: no one could leave without their bags and vehicle being checked, even though it seemed very likely that whoever had taken the pieces would have hidden them during the night. Vehicles, once searched, were allowed out of the carpark, but not in again. Camera crews and journalists arriving there were turned away and had to make do with interviewing those leaving the site.

'I'd like to conduct a more detailed interview with Scott Macleod,' Constable Sutherland announced towards the end of the day.

'Why?' Scott asked.

'There have been some accusations and so I'd like to be absolutely clear about your movements last night.'

'This is ridiculous!' Scott heard Anna say as he and Barry walked downriver. Once out of earshot, they sat facing each other on a couple of rocks, the constable sweating in his uniform, Scott in his shorts and cap.

'How's your father doing?' he began.

'Suffering. But I think he's still there.'

'Any idea where these bones might be?'

'No,' Scott told him. Though really, he had too many ideas: they could be under a piece of sacking in somebody's garage; buried in the forest, or planted beneath a bush in someone's backyard. They could be wrapped in pieces of tie dye and batik in the back of one of the Forest Nation campers, or packed into someone's deep freeze alongside cuts of meat and frozen blackberry pies. Smashed to pieces and scattered. They could be in a locked drawer in the filing cabinet in Alan Coxtis' office, or carefully packed in a carved cedar chest in the newly built longhouse; they could simply be farther down- or upriver, concealed under a pile of branches and shale. They could even still be onsite, buried, perhaps by one of Swenson's team, in the refuse pile.

'I'd like to know,' Sutherland said, 'about your connections on the reserve these days. Do you see much of the younger people up there, like, say, Thompson Brown?'

No. Nothing at all, really. Did he leave the site during the night on which the fossils were stolen? No. Did he have any way of proving that? Jason and Greta, Scott pointed out, were the only two who could possibly prove anything of that kind, and Constable Sutherland flashed a smile, continued his writing. It was as if he had forgotten the past, but it was surely impossible?

'Some people felt I should check things out with you,' he said, 'but frankly, I see nothing pointing in your direction. I'm not thinking of bringing you in at this point.'

'Good to know that, Baz,' Scott said, getting to his feet. He did not like the way the rest of the team studied him when he returned.

'Swenson,' he told Anna, 'obviously! Thinks it's me in cahoots with the protest. Could just as well be him, wanting to bring things to the boil, get the protesters moved away, or to undermine you by making it look like I'm involved, or any twisted thing, for fuck's sake—'

'Okay, Scott.'

It was, they both realised and saw the other realising, the wrong way around, her calming him down.

'Okay.'

It would be impossible, she thought, not to like his smile.

That night, four officers remained onsite and both teams were to help them keep watch. There was a sliver of crescent moon in the sky, and a light breeze. Even the ravens seemed to be on guard, calling occasionally to each other in the night with a staccato sound halfway between a croak and a bark, and then before dawn beginning a complicated and noisy conversation.

At about ten, the media were allowed to return. Alan Coxtis read a press release announcing that the protest would migrate to the clifftop area, on reserve land, and plant its banners there. Johnny Fleet, the taller of the two elders accompanying him, was asked for his view:

'This is very serious,' he said. 'Very serious. It is dangerous to disturb the spirits of the ancestors. I see only bad things coming from it.'

'We still want to reach a compromise,' Anna said. 'I will be returning to the museum very soon to discuss the possibilities.'

Mike Swenson was not available for comment.

Around lunchtime, two Forest Nation people were badly injured trying to abseil down a crumbling cliff just upriver from the carpark, and CanCo sent Andrew Bellavance to explain that the company would have to withdraw their funding if negative publicity continued.

'I think it will turn around very soon,' Anna told him.

Was there a curse? journalists asked.

No, Anna said. There had been a *misunderstanding* and now there was a *disagreement*, which she hoped would be resolved by means of negotiations. The museum would respond shortly to the demands the Big Crow River People had made.

I feel strong, she had written the night before. *I want to deal with this: I'm prepared to do whatever is necessary.*

So now the dig stumbled along: gloved and padded, watched from above, Anna and her team knelt in the trench that had been dug around the head and began tunnelling well beneath where she had calculated the bottom plane of the head to be. Once through, she explained, they would reinforce and jacket the top in situ, and then cut through the plinth and lever the specimen over onto plywood boards, before manoeuvring it up onto level ground.

'Then we'll jacket the underside.'

'Anna!' Swenson, shaved and cleaned up, stood at the edge of their circle. His cheeks were flat and hard.

He had his specimen's jaw out and jacketed, he said, and was ready to get to work on the cliff, but could not. First, Anna had not finished, and in any case, he could not cut into a cliff with a crowd of people hostile to the entire enterprise and especially his part of it standing close by on what was apparently their land.

'You should know,' he said, 'that I have faxed the funder and made a formal complaint about your unprofessional conduct and mismanagement, and to express my concerns about the resulting delays which are preventing me from progressing.' He tried, then, to hand her a copy of his letter. She stood up without reaching out; let it drift to the ground.

'Get out of this part of the excavation, Mike,' she told him, adding, 'Please.' He didn't move.

'I can't tolerate delays,' he said. 'We have to be ready for when these dammed protesters are finally cleared. My team is free. I'll send them over to help you finish.'

'No,' she said, 'I don't want them here.' She felt it happen, fought it, lost: she knew she should have said *yes*, but it was too late. 'What do you think is going to make the protesters move? Just you wanting it? Why does no one want to engage with the actual problem?'

'Anna,' Scott began, and she caught his gaze for a moment and then pulled herself away. 'In no circumstances,' she told the team, 'are you to work with any of Dr Swenson's team on this part of the site. I hope that's understood?'

'Now,' she said to Swenson, 'leave.'

'You shouldn't be in a position of responsibility,' he told her before he strode away and she thought she could feel them, some of them, silently agreeing.

'Leave me alone!' she told Scott when he called to her from outside the tent she had sealed herself in, hiding from the atmosphere she'd helped to make.

'You asked me to tell you. Everyone's exhausted and thinking why the hell have they come here. You need to come out and be nice to them. And you need to offer the St'alkwextsihn—'

'I can't come out now, I'll make it worse. Go away, please.'

'What a complete fucking mess!' Jason said, poking the fire
and sending up a trail of sparks. It was his turn to keep watch
for the first part of the night. 'Has been from the start.' There
was no beer left.

'I don't get what's happening,' Greta said, 'I've worked with
her before and it was fine.'

'The protest is about history,' Scott told them. 'It's not her
fault. Anna says she will come up with something. She's trying,
for sure. There's this meeting, at the museum...' Felix sighed,
slipped on his headphones. He listened, Scott had discovered
recently, mainly to natural sounds: animal and bird calls, the
jungle, the sea. People stared unspeaking into the flames. Akira
and Maiko, who had gone to bed early, could be heard talking
quietly to each other in Japanese. The winged lizards were becoming a distant memory; the mosquitoes seemed far more
important.

'Can I do anything?' he asked Anna's tent. There was no
light within.

Was she even in there? He could hear nothing, not the
slightest sound.

'Anna?'

No reply. Total failure all round. A muggy, starless night,
the tent stifling. He took his foam mattress and bag and went
downstream to lie in the open air again, staring up at the darkness so dense that he could hardly see where it joined the top
of the trees.

Maybe you couldn't help anyone by trying to? Maybe there
was nothing you could do. Maybe the person you were trying
to help was the one who made it work or not: they took what

they needed, and it might not even be what you think you were offering: look at what had happened with Mac. He felt like crying.

Maybe, as Matt had said, he'd spent too much time on this?

✦ ✦ ✦

'Scott?' A glimmer of light. She was dressed in clean clothes and wearing her backpack; she was *smiling*.

'There you are. Please,' she said, 'drive me to the floater dock. I'm going to the museum. You and Jason will hold the fort for two or three days. Hurry, please.'

She waited while he found his shoes and jacket: a different woman. *Not me*, he remembered her saying when he first met her. *That was not me.*

'I do know how it could work,' she told him as they set off, almost at a jog. The birds were well away by then: a huge noisy conversation between ravens, subtle tapestry of other songs. 'It came to me last night that all we need ask for is to *borrow* what is here, and then return it. And we must pay for that loan with something magnificent.'

'Depends on what that is,' Scott said. She did not tell him that, although she could actually see it in her mind's eye: a long building in the forest, built in cedar or rammed earth, beautiful, imposing.

'We must learn from what has happened in archaeology. It's obvious, but I need to persuade the others,' she told him as they climbed into the van.

Could he help? He had, she said. It was because of him being there that she could think straight at all.

'Hurry!' she told him as they climbed into the van.

The roadside burned green; they arrived at the dock with minutes to spare. Scott watched the Beaver taxi out, dragging a thick, silky wake behind it, race to take off, dwindle, and vanish into the now radiant sky.

In the emptiness that followed, Scott's phone rang:

'Where have you been, son?' Mac's voice was unnaturally loud and clear, like that of a much younger man. 'Did you get my message?'

'Not yet. How are you?'

'I'm through Stage One. I get to invite a guest to supper. I'm cooking. Six-thirty tonight, okay?' *Cooking?* The water ahead of Scott glistened and trembled, like some kind of hallucination. He was very thirsty.

'Mac. Things are heavy here. I'll have to see what's going on. So I want to, but I can't promise.'

'Please,' Mac said. 'Scotty, I don't ask much of you.'

26

---◆---

THE IDEA, THE VISION THAT ANNA CARRIED was part treasure, part burden. It glowed, but at the same time it was invisible. She carried it out of the floatplane and through the airport, brought it with her into the aircraft. Holding it still, she watched through the small, scratched window the vast corrugation of grey and white mountain peaks below. Then the city was visible, a brown glint of towers, thrusting out of the surrounding plain like some strange crystal in a rock.

She buckled herself in. The elderly woman next to her offered a mint and Anna thanked her and accepted, sucked the sweetness as the city grew suddenly closer, larger, and then vanished, lost in the ordered spaces of the airport itself. The plane's wheels jolted onto the runway and the plane vibrated with frustrated momentum, came finally to a standstill.

It was bright outside and 27 degrees. She reached for her cell phone and switched it off, wanting to keep a clear head. Vik had said he would leave the car for her; she would be at the museum by noon. Could she make the others see what she saw? How much did she really count for there? Depending on the answers to those questions, her plan would be supported, or it would not: it was as wide open as the huge blue skies above, she thought as she set out on the familiar road that seemed suddenly strange, treeless, extraordinarily flat. She must keep her mind on what mattered and forget the rest. Alan Coxtis came unbidden to mind, sitting with his back against the rock. She must be like him, she thought.

It was a shock at first to see that even the overflow parking was full and the constant streams of visitors between their cars and the entranceway, and threading their way over the nearby boardwalks: this was the other half of the museum's purpose: exposing millions of people filled with the wants and needs of their twenty-first-century human lives — their anxieties about status, work, love and the shape of their legs — to the past. They came, Anna knew, mainly to gasp at the reconstructed monsters, but in the course of their day some of them surely would begin to wonder at the intricacy of the ecologies the big dinosaurs were part of, to glimpse something far more terrifying than any T. rex: the sheer enormity of time, the terrible relentlessness of geological and evolutionary change.

She was not sure what people could do with this understanding, the vertigo it brought. But she did like to see people at the museum, spilling out onto the café terrace at lunchtime, or emerging, tired but wonderstruck, at the end of the day. At the same time, she was very glad of her designated space in the staff area at the back.

'Everyone's doing their best to get here.' Brian told her, as he and Jan climbed out of one of the museum vans. 'Had to pick up Jan from the field station, drag him away from his new fish! This is turning into quite the saga.'

'Yes,' she shrugged. 'Sorry!' He offered a brief hug and she took it gladly. Both of the men were grey with sand and dust.

'Complaints have been flying around, apparently.'

'I did omit to contact the St'alkwe̲xtsihn,' she told him, 'But as I've said, there are precedents and I'm sure it can be sorted out.' They pushed through the back entrance, into the even indoor light.

'Who is this young assistant of yours?' Jan asked, removing his sunglasses to reveal brown eyes sunk in sockets pale as twin moons. 'Wish I had one.'

'Scott?' she said. 'He's helping out. A very useful member of the team.' The two men glanced at each other.

'Well, I guess I may as well tell you: Swenson called us yesterday. He seems to think you've, quote, lost your mind over this young man,' Brian said, lowering his voice. 'He's suggesting your loyalties are compromised and that's why the whole protest has got out of hand—'

'I will, quote, lose my mind if he goes around saying things like that!' she said, willing herself past her own sensitivity to the phrase *lost your mind*, to keep on walking. All three of them laughed.

Brian and Jan went to shower while she waited in the boardroom for the others to turn up. Sheila was the first to arrive.

'George is coming,' she said, opening the case and taking out her laptop. 'He'll chair. And Susan from PR. Quite a business!'

'Well, the timing is unfortunate,' Anna said, 'but I think it's a very interesting situation. An opportunity,' she added, getting to her feet to shake the director's hand. Before long the room was full: ten men, two women.

'Anna,' George said, waving his cuffed hand in her direction. 'I'll need dinner and a drink within the next two hours, so please get us started.'

'I have been thinking about the common ground, and I think I have come up with something that might work,' she began. She was nothing like the woman who had sobbed in the blue light of her nylon tent, and she acted as if both Mike Swenson and HD did not exist.

✦ ✦ ✦

Scott knew he would have to make the journey out again later in the day, but even so, he trudged back upriver. The camp and its concerns had become his world — he could not stay away.

They were getting ready to jacket.

Lengths of lumber and strips of burlap had been prepared. Buckets of plaster were dotted around and Jason in a cutoff t-shirt and filthy Carhartt shorts was mixing up another batch. Everyone wore rubber gloves — and there are more people than there used to be, because Mike Swenson and three of his team were there too, some of them chipping away at the rock, Mike himself among the group jacketing the top part of the head.

'What are they doing here?' Scott asked Jason, who paused the drill he was using to drive the mixer.

'Why not?' He used a rag to wipe at the sweat coursing down his face. 'I don't understand Anna's thinking,' he said. 'Don't we all want to get the job done? She's been acting very strangely, and to my mind, Mike has a point. This hasn't been professionally organised, right from the start.'

Greta nodded her agreement. Felix, listening to the animal or bird of the day, worked on. Lin looked tense, but her hands were gloved and ready too.

'There's no harm,' said Maiko, and she and Akira both smiled and beckoned Scott to join them. 'When she comes back, I think she will be pleased.'

'Anna's responsible for this specimen,' he told them. 'There is a reason why this site was divided—'

'Scott,' Mike interrupted, looking up for the first time, 'don't give me shit, okay? Getting the specimen out intact is the point. That's what I'm aiming for. Sometimes a few toes have to be trodden on is all. She'll get over it, or if she doesn't, that's her problem... Where is she?' he asked. 'When is she coming back?'

'You have no right to be here.'

'Right?' he said, and looked around at the rest of them and shot out something between a laugh and a growl. 'That's rich, coming from you. I'm here is what matters. I'm focussed on the work, and I'm going to get it done, despite the idiocy that surrounds us.' He gestured at the cliff.

'Let me tell you something,' he continued. 'I believe in going for what I want, otherwise what is the point of wanting it? You take what chances come your way with both hands, and if you need to fight for your chance, of course you do it. Otherwise, someone else is going to get what you could have had, or mess it up for you. The best thing that could happen around here is if everyone forgets their damn grudges and pulls together.'

'I believe she found it, but offered to share it with you,' Scott said. There was something about Mike Swenson in this triumphant mode that made him reluctant to give the man even the used air in his lungs.

Mike stood.

'Scott,' he said, 'it's not playtime. You don't know diddly-squat about all this. Believe me. We need this out of here so we can get to the other one. That's what we are here for, okay? Come and help.'

'I don't think so,' Scott said, and walked away, knowing that the others would continue working, chipping away the last fragments, pressing the plaster-soaked cloth into the layers beneath.

The project worker, Brianne, let Scott into Phoenix House, pushed aside his apologies about being in his work clothes.

'You are our very first dinner guest. Mac will be thrilled!' she said as she led him to the kitchen at the back of the house, explaining on the way how important it was to teach life skills such as purchasing healthy foods and cooking balanced meals.

Scott had not seen his father in an apron before, and he had never seen him so clear-eyed and well put together: beneath the apron was an ironed shirt, very clean, tucked into new, neatly belted denim jeans; his feet gleamed in the new sneakers, still so white they almost hurt to look at. He had his hair cut. His skin was still blotched red over the cheeks and nose but it was well washed and shaven.

'Scotty!' Mac put the wooden spoon down on a plate and offered a hug. A *hug*: it felt very strange, the feel of him sober, engaging one to one and emanating a waft of soap or aftershave that mingled with the tang of the bolognese sauce bubbling on the stove. Not slumped, but standing. Present.

'Dad,' Scott said, which felt strange, too.

The table was almost ready. Plates, glasses, and in the middle several jugs of iced water, two bowls of salad. A woman in a long brown skirt, with hair dyed a dark red colour, was putting out the cutlery and Mac called out to her:

'Orianna! This is Scott!' She approached, bracelets clinking at the wrist, to shake his hand. Beneath the shoulder-length hair and straight-cut bangs, her face was rounded and somehow childlike, but wrinkled and red with burst capillaries. Her t-shirt had a picture of a tiger on it, with sequins around the eyes.

'Your father's a wonderful man,' she squeezed his hand, and then held it. 'And he wouldn't have got this far without you taking care of him like you have.' She gave him a long, deep look in the eyes and then bustled over to help drain the spaghetti.

'You shake the dinner bell, Scott,' Brianne told him. Other people began to appear and settle around the table: older people mainly, but there were some who might have been in their twenties or thirties. Steam rose from twelve plates.

'Thank you for this good food that we share,' Orianna declared and there were a few muttered amens before those who had waited rushed to catch up with those who had already started their food. Everyone ate as if they were making up for meals missed and the bolognese was good, Scott thought, though something, maybe basil, or even red wine, would help it out.

He tried to fill Mac in on the dig and the protest, gaining in return a few nods, a twitch of the eyebrows and a comment to the effect that it would probably take fifteen years to sort out. Mac's interest, Scott soon realised, was at best intermittent. Most of the time, when his father's eyes were not on his plate they were on Orianna, who sat across the table, smiling now and then at the skeleton of a man who sat next to her.

'Smart woman. Used to have her own floristry business,' Mac told him. 'Jackie would have liked her,' he added next time his mouth was free, 'wouldn't she?'

'I don't know,' Scott told him. He didn't like to think of it, and even if he did, he had no idea who, apart from him, his mother had liked. She was gone before things got that sophisticated.

'She would,' Mac insisted, colouring. 'I'm telling you, she would.'

'Sure,' Scott said, helping himself to the salad passed to him.

And after the dinner, he tried to leave, but no one wanted to let him go and they all trooped into the recreation room to watch *Antz*. Movies and TV, Brianne explained, were only allowed in the evenings. Residents had to discuss and agree earlier in the day what to watch from the limited selection available. At this stage, most of the movies were family entertainment, but if there did turn out to be any on-screen drinking or drug abuse, then they'd pause the movie to discuss it.

Mac, Orianna and Scott sat on the same oatmeal-coloured couch. The lights were low. Scott let his eyes close, half-listening to the voices and soundtrack, and then occasionally willed them open when stirrings or laughter in the room signalled that there might be something worth seeing, though of course, he was always too late.

Beside him, his father and Orianna were holding hands in her lap. Her head rested across his chest, his free arm circled her shoulder; neither of them was looking at the screen.

Scott did not so much glance back to his right until the lights came on again. He passed on the tea, thanked everyone and left. An hour later, in the trailer, he opened all the windows and doors before stretching out on top of his bed. He could think of nothing but the dig, how he did not want to tell

Anna what had happened, how things were about as bad as they could possibly be, though of course in that he was wrong: Barry Sutherland and another officer were in the carpark the next morning, leaning against the side of a single squad car, smoking. A piece of yellow tape had been strung across the head of the trail.

'The area's been cleared,' Barry waved in the direction of the river. 'Some Native kid is threatening to jump off the cliff if your lot don't back down by the end of the day.'

27

---◆---

GEORGE'S JACKET WAS CRUMPLED, his eyes red-rimmed, but he grinned at Anna as she came into the boardroom, and then he dipped his face over his coffee mug.

'I have some good current information on the infrastructure grants,' she said. 'If they did want to apply, and if we were in a position to provide some of the seed money, as well as—'

'Let's wait for everyone else,' George said. 'Excellent Chinese last night, don't you think?' One by one the others came in, saving her from small talk. Brian seemed to have made an effort; he was freshly shaven and dressed in a newish denim shirt buckled into his jeans.

'So,' George said, 'following on from yesterday, I contacted Daniel Wilkinson at the university. He saw the point right away and was keen to be part of such an innovative solution. He spoke to Fleming, the Earth Sciences dean, who also saw the point. I have here...' he reached inside his leather organiser, 'a faxed letter to that effect.'

Everyone around the table made some kind of movement, looked up, shifted position or reached for a pen.

George handed Anna the letter. She saw the embossed crest

at the top, the name at the bottom, could hardly read the words in-between.

'Fleming did express some concern that he had not had a report from Dr Swenson, but under the circumstances he saw the necessity to act quickly. I had a word with Brian here and he's agreed to go along with you, show some institutional support.'

She nodded, wiped the moisture from under her eyes, and looked around at all of them.

'Thank you.' It felt astoundingly good, to have people clearly behind her. 'Brian and I will do our utmost to make this work.'

Sheila bent over her laptop.

'You'll need to leave in an hour's time in order to catch the one o'clock flight,' she said. 'I'm confirming your reservations now.'

'Let's move on, then. What were you saying?' George asked.

'In terms of what we can offer in return for the loan of the specimens, I've been looking at ways in which the museum — and the university too — could support the St'alkwextsihn. Matched funding is available for community infrastructure. It seems to me that there are things they are already working towards which we could perhaps support.'

'Question!' Ken Ruzesky raised his hand.

'With respect, would we be going to these lengths for, say a group of Creationists?'

'So far as I know, those people don't have any kind of land claim.'

'Thank the Lord!' George said, and each of them joined the laughter in his own way, and then waited for Anna to continue.

Everyone was at the hotel, drinking coffee, wondering who was going to pay their bill. Phoning, or trying to. *Message box full*: maybe she already knew? But when was she coming back? Why hadn't she called?

'Just where the hell is she?' Swenson said.

'Don't talk to me that way,' Scott said and turned his back on the man. Jason, too, was losing it:

'Who is this guy on the cliff? No one's telling me anything and I'm supposed to be heading up when she's not here. When's she coming back? What's the point of a cell phone or a direct line if you're not going to answer them?'

Alan Coxtis, on the other hand, answered his cell. He was in the band office, fielding calls on three lines.

'You can come up,' he told Scott, 'if you you've got something to say.'

'Where the hell are you going?' Swenson asked as he left the breakfast room. He passed a CBC van and three squad cars at the entrance to the cliff trail and was flagged down and asked where he was going. Minutes later, he pulled in and parked under a raven carving, leaving a cloud of dust to settle behind him. The office was just the same as it had always been: a low-slung temporary building, with a roof and guttering that needed attention, four creaking steps up to the entrance.

Coxtis came out from behind his desk, grasped Scott's hand, waved at the seating area, though neither of them went there.

'It's Thompson,' Coxtis said, and immediately it made a terrible kind of sense. 'On the edge. He has the bones that were stolen and says he's going to throw them down and then jump himself if nothing has changed by sundown. He'll go through with it.' Coxtis' forehead shone with sweat. He wore the usual jeans and white t-shirt and raven pendant, but looked a very different man to the one who had led the crowd of protesters up to the dig: greyer somehow, his edges blurred, like a reflection in window glass.

'So?' he asked Scott. 'What do you bring to this situation?'

'Anna went to the museum to try and work out an offer. Something to do with taking the specimen as a loan.'

'*Something*? Was that what you came to say?' The phone was ringing again.

'She must be on her way back now!' Scott hoped that this was true, knew he had to make it happen if it was not: there was a floatplane due in at 1 p.m. and another at 5:30. 'She was sure she'd have something worthwhile. Can you tell Thompson that? She really wanted—'

Coxtis walked over to his phone.

'*Meaning well* is not going to help here,' he said as he picked it up. Through the window behind him movement caught Scott's eye: kids were playing on the rope swings that hung from the branches of a stand of large cedars on the edge of the play area. Different rope, bright new plastic equipment in the cleared area, but essentially, the scene was unchanged from when he used to play there as a kid during his mother's visits to her relatives. He had played with Thompson, for heaven's sake. His heart was racing as he raised a hand to Alan and pushed back outside. Kids swarmed over the bars, watched from the bench by one of their grandmothers.

Again, he called the museum's main number. Not in her office.

'Is she in the building? Because I need to talk to her immediately.'

Who was he? they wanted to know. She was in a meeting.

'Can you please go ask her to come to the phone?' There was an appalled silence, finally, a promise to take his number and call him back.

Half an hour later, back in town, the call came. Not her. A man's voice:

'Ruzesky here. Arthropods. Who's this?' it asked, friendly enough.

'One of the volunteers at Big Crow. There's an emergency... a man threatening to jump off the cliff.'

'Anna and Brian just left for the airport, twenty minutes ago. Try her cell,' Ruzesky added.

If she did not yet know what was happening, surely she'd find out on the way? It was 11:45 a.m., 12:45 there. She must be planning to make the five o'clock floatplane, could get to the cliff by six-fifteen. By six-thirty the gorge was normally in shadow, but it was still *light* for hours. Did the sun shining from the west still catch the top of the cliff? Or was the viewing spot in the shade of the hills opposite? Scott couldn't remember. In any case, a veil of white was forming over the sky, like a cataract on an eye.

Ignorant, blissful, damp with the sweat from their dash for the plane, Anna relaxed in her seat. She would call Scott and Jason as soon as they left the plane, on the off-chance that one of them was in town. She'd ask them to keep the news to themselves until she arrived; she and Brian would get a taxi from the dock to the site carpark and walk up. It would be dusk by the time they reached camp and made their announcement.

In all conscience, she thought, Mike Swenson should be taken aside and informed first. He could do nothing. They had a faxed agreement from the Department of Earth Sciences at the university and so it did not matter one bit whether he personally liked their proposal or not.

In the morning, she thought, I'll take the proposal to Alan Coxtis. It's not a foregone conclusion, of course, but I'm looking forward to it, and to having an intelligent man like him at least not *so much* against us. And I'm looking forward to the dig returning to how it should be — a team of people with a common goal that is bigger than all of our ordinary concerns. I'm looking forward to being back in charge, the real me. And I would like to thank Scott for all his help, insight and so on during a time of crisis. I'd like to thank him publicly: an extra word of thanks. *Everyone has been fantastic, but an extra word of thanks...* A long run of complications and bad luck, she thought was about to come to an end. They had an offer. A workable compromise.

Brian, sleeping beside her in the aisle seat, woke with a start as they began to descend. It was only as they drifted through departures that she switched on her phone, realised something was very wrong. A man, she learned, might end his life because of what she had found.

Finally, Scott's phone rang

'Sundown?' she asked him. 'When is sundown?'

'Sundown is whenever he decides it's sundown,' Scott said. 'Can't you get here sooner?'

'*You* must talk to him,' she said, standing with Brian beside her at the edge of a moving throng of people. 'Listen carefully. We acknowledge their claim and would like to support it. We would like to borrow something of theirs. In return...'

28

——◆——

THREE-THIRTY, THE SKY GREY, the sun a blur of white light. It was cool in the car, but the heat hit them as soon as the doors opened. Constable Eileen Donohue and Scott Macleod climbed out of the squad car, nodded at Gus and Garth and the other media types.

No, Eileen Donohue told them, nothing to say. *Good thing,* Scott thought. He could barely speak. Dry mouth, heart trying to get the hell out of his chest. Sweating at the slightest exertion. How had he ended up here? Anna. He met her on the cliff and now he was going back there. The rest of the excavation teams were in the hotel, taking showers and watching TV. He was here, following Eileen Donohue down the trail.

Both of them carried walkie-talkies and his backpack contained a sheaf of papers that Anna had faxed through to Coxtis' office, and, at Thompson's request, some bottled water. Eileen Donohue was pleased about the water. She'd had training in dealing with people who were attempting suicide, but this, she explained, because of the political element, was very different from anything she'd met before. She had spent two hours on the cliff earlier in the day and Thompson had not said a thing to her, nor let her get closer than twenty metres.

'I talked about myself and my dogs and told him how I lost my older brother when I was a teenager, but it didn't work out. He told me to stop. So it's good about the water, that he wants something from us, and trusts us enough to ask.'

Or maybe, Scott didn't say, he's just thirsty. Wants to keep his head clear. Would rather feel good until the last possible moment. They moved into deeper shade, the trail slightly uphill. Eileen was panting a little, and at every step her pant legs rubbed together with a short, brisk sound.

'You've got to remember,' she said as the trees began to thin out, 'we must try, but it won't be our fault if he does it. Warn him before you make movements of any kind. Get his permission before you approach. Before you make any kind of move.'

It was too much. He was going to throw up. *Turn back*, he thought, but they had arrived. The officer Eileen was relieving reported no change and then set off back down the trail. There was Thompson: he had climbed over the rusty bit of fence there to protect the public and was sitting, shirtless, with his back to them, just a metre from the edge, his backpack, t-shirt and a row of jacketed specimens beside him. He appeared to be gazing straight out across the gorge but he turned when he heard them approach.

'Bring the water, Scott,' he said, getting to his feet. 'Just you. Leave her behind.'

It was about eighteen metres to the fence. Standing well clear of it, Scott handed the bottle over. He noticed that Thompson was not wearing a watch.

'Get back,' Thompson said. From five metres away, Scott watched him break the bottle open, tip back his head and drink; once he'd finished, he set the bottle down by his feet.

Almost instantly, it fell on its side and, caught by a breath of wind, rolled over the edge.

Thompson turned back and leaned his elbows on the fence. He had a baseball cap over his half-and-half hairstyle, and the jeans he wore were baggy and belted tight about this waist. He'd clearly been working out for some time. There was absolutely nothing but air behind him and despite the half-grin he wore, his gaze was fierce, and the bones on his face seemed prominent, as if forced towards the surface by the tension within.

'I've got a message and some detailed information from Dr Silowski,' Scott said, noticing Thompson's eyes, not just the power in them but the colour, the same deep brown he'd see if he looked into his own.

'Are they leaving?'

'Look at it. It's worth considering.'

'Who says that?'

'The band council is talking about it right now. They want you there with them to join in the discussion when Anna arrives.'

'Alan Coxtis,' Thompson's face hardened, 'spends far too much time with the wrong people, trying for the wrong things.'

'Maybe he has to.' Without knowing what he was doing, Scott took half a step forward.

'Stop!' Thompson told him. 'A few more acres of upstream land tacked onto the reserve? What's the point? When do we get back downriver where we come from? There are no fish here now. No one wants to hear the truth! It's all horse-trading and back-rubbing, and I don't know why the hell I'm talking to *you*.'

Scott remembered, downriver, a different cliff at the swimming hole, a different kind of hot day long ago. He was new and waiting for or avoiding his turn. Thompson, skinny, dark, slipped down over the edge and lowered himself onto the ledge, and then turned to face out. Sometimes it could be twenty minutes or more before a person finally jumped, but Thompson simply took a breath and stepped right out into the air. There was a modest splash, and then moments later his head shot up from the water. He shook the water out of his hair and then made for the beach in an easy crawl.

He'll step out just the same way here, if he chooses to, Scott thought. He needs to get to the rush as fast as possible, whether that's a fight or a dive, or the top of the speedometer.

From somewhere in the forest behind him, came a sound almost like laughter: the Big Crows. Thompson heard it too.

'My spirit,' he said, his eyes fixed on Scott's. *Hell*, Scott thought. But you can't fly. Not for real.

'She won't be long. Hear what she has to say.'

'What are you doing with those people?'

'Learning, I guess. Can we sit down?' Scott asked.

'Go ahead,' Thompson said, but stayed standing himself even as Scott sat down and reached into his pocket. 'Evolution, science...' Thompson continued, leaning his arms on the railing, 'You're learning that, but what do you know about your own culture?' *Not much*, Scott thought. *Enough*. And what is it, now, anyway? And what do I know about anything? What I know is *I don't want you to jump*. Still looking at Thompson, he pulled out his tin and opened it.

'You can't escape where you're from,' Thompson said.

'No?' Scott said, licking one paper and joining it to another. He managed a smile. 'Wouldn't you rather be somewhere else right now? I sure would.' His hands shook but there was no one close enough to see it.

'I will be, soon,' Thompson replied, as the shadow of a bird passed over the ground between them.

Scott held out the joint. Thompson shook his head, closed his eyes a moment. The wire of the fencing divided his body into diamond shapes.

'People think they can't make a difference,' Thompson said, frowning, 'but we can. People think the only way forwards is to suck it up and get over it, and that's wrong too. And people think they have to follow the script that someone else wrote. But they're wrong, too. I want to do something.'

'Just one thing? Don't you want to do something you can see through?' Scott's heart thudded in his chest. It felt so very close to the surface, as if it might burst through. 'Are you leaving that to the others? Because—'

There was a strange, wet, hollow call from the ravens behind them.

'Don't argue with me,' Thompson said. Scott lit the joint, took a lungful, and held it out, wordlessly. There was a pause, seconds long before Thompson said:

'Okay. Bring it here, then back off.' When Scott had handed it over, he sat back down because his legs were jelly; he watched Thompson pull hard on the joint and exhale looking around him at the trees and the sky. He watched him crouch down, put the joint on the ground, reach for one of the jacketed parts of the specimen, a white lump the size of his own head. Standing again, he threw it up and out. A moment later Scott felt the dull, distant thud of its impact somewhere in his chest.

KATHY PAGE

'Back where it belongs,' Thompson said.

'Anna will be here in less than half an hour.'

'I don't have that long,' Thompson said, just as a pair of ravens passed overhead, close enough for them to hear the creak of wingbeats, feel the wake of disturbed air. Both men looked up, watched the birds rise over the gorge, circle lazily — as if, it seemed to Scott, they were preparing to witness what would come next.

The radio on Scott's belt crackled into life and Thompson's eyes meet Scott's, wide open, bright with fear. He gave the smallest of nods, and Scott brought the radio to his ear: Anna.

'Is he all right? We'll be five minutes now.'

'They're here,' Scott told Thompson. Still, the two birds circled overhead. 'And it's because of what you are doing that they have come up with this offer,' he knew this was not perfectly true, but he figured it could pass — hell, Thompson could come back here later if he wanted to. 'They want to know what you think of what they are offering, and so do the elders, and Coxtis; they need you to be there.'

Above them, the two ravens seemed to hang still, silhouetted against the dull sky. Then, almost as if they had lost the ability to fly, they tumbled in unison down through the air above the gorge. A second later, they beat their wings again, veered and made a twisted double loop in the air, rose, flew steadily back the way they came. From the direction of the roost came more cawing and then a strange, metallic warble.

What would Thompson think it meant? Jump, or don't jump?

'They pulled back,' Scott said. 'They didn't need to go all the way.'

'Go away!' Thompson said. 'Go away and take them all with you! No one comes here, understood?'

Scott turned and walked towards Eileen, one moment confident, the next terrified that Thompson would choose to step out into nothingness. As he and Eileen passed into the darkness between the trees, the ravens croaking above their heads, he willed himself not to look back.

Anna watched Scott emerge from the trail, head up, his face shocked but loose.

'No one to go on the cliff!' he called out. 'No press, nothing. He's thinking it over... I think, maybe, it could be okay.' She breathed in deep, felt as if she too had been temporarily saved. She climbed in next to him in the back of the taxi. Brian, in front, twisted around to introduce himself and add his thanks to Anna's. He hadn't done anything, he said, just tried to pass the time. He'd talked a bit until some ravens flew over and her call came. No one should say anything, he said. The discussion should not begin. They just wait until Thompson made his decision.

She noticed how exhaustion made Scott's face seem older. Traces of the day's exertion and emotion rose from his skin, a salty, bitter smell.

He closed his eyes briefly and then, before supplying the detail, bent to reach into the backpack jammed between his legs; his vertebrae pushed up beneath skin and damp t-shirt, disappeared again as he straightened. He offered the water to her first, tipped his head back and drank. The sound of his swallowing seemed to fill the car, and it was as Anna watched him drink that she realised that Scott was no longer, if he ever had been, a pleasant young man she was giving some work experience in exchange for some of his reassuring manner, a kind of charm against the devil Swenson. He was someone quite extraordinary and could be anything he chose; when he pushed the water bottle between his knees, leaned back in the seat and looked across at her and she had to look quickly away at the road ahead, a narrow ribbon winding through the third-growth conifers.

29

---✦---

SCOTT WAS ONLY DIMLY AWARE OF THE OTHERS. Even in the car on the way to Alan Coxtis' office he had been holding Thompson in his mind's eye. He had imagined him lying on his back on the cliff, watching the light fade and feeling the thrust of the rock beneath him, the pulse of his own blood in his body, while above him the ravens bickered, their noise reaching a crescendo as he stood and made for the trees, ignored the trail and headed directly through the forest towards the village. Scott heard the undergrowth and dry twigs crackle beneath his feet; felt the branches catch at his face and arms as Thompson worked his way through the glowing gloom, a man who almost died.

Now, they waited: an older woman, Susan, who had raised Thompson, Alan Coxtis, Johnny Price and Mark Weatherman; Anna, Brian, Scott. When Susan spoke of Thompson — a loving boy, as a child, she said, very loyal, but grown distant since — Anna touched her arm, poured water into her glass; they tried to talk of other things, fell silent.

Scott saw Thompson emerge from the bushes at the edge of the road, his face scratched and streaked with dust, then start briskly uphill, his trainers gleaming against the blackness of the road.

Inside, they turned on the lamps. The door had been left open and when the darkness outside was absolute, he appeared: a large figure standing in the doorway, damp from the first spattering of summer rain. As vision and reality coalesced, Scott opened his eyes and met Thompson's gaze, returned the small nod he gave. His breath rushed out of him and he leaned back in the chair.

Thompson and Susan embraced, his height folding over her solid, rounded body. He accepted brief hugs from Coxtis and the elders. Coffee, and a plate of crackers and cheese appeared. He ate a little and sat with a blanket over his shoulders, steam rising from the mug in his hands, and everyone was smiling at him, just because he was alive.

He looked across at Anna and Alan Coxtis.

'It's time to talk,' Coxtis said.

'We want you to know,' Anna began in response to his wave of the hand, 'that we will not try to resume our excavation until an agreement is reached.' Her heart thumped in her chest as she said those words: they could not be unsaid, but without them, nothing that followed would make sense.

'We would prefer to make an agreement — one where we offer our acknowledgment of and support for the St'alkwextsiḥn claim to the riverbed, and make a request to borrow the specimens. We would like to prepare them, and make a replica, before returning the originals for you to keep as the band sees fit. In return, we offer financial and other support for the cultural centre that's planned.'

It was something, she thought, though perhaps it could never be enough.

A moth fluttered against the screen. Scott seemed barely

awake; opposite, Alan Coxtis sat straight-backed in his chair. Between the two of them, Thompson, elbows on knees, chin in hands, frowned at the floor. The two elders looked as if they had been carved from wood. Brian, slightly back from the circle, with his legs akimbo, nodded, made the occasional statement to confirm or clarify what Anna said. She didn't need the notes she had brought. It felt, strangely, like one of the most intimate conversations she had ever been part of.

Thompson looked up, his eyes fierce.

'The cliff?'

'We would not touch the cliff,' she said.

'The university has agreed not to expose the part of the second specimen beneath the cliff, if we can come to the agreement Anna proposes,' Brian said. 'Both our director and I spoke to them personally this morning. I have a note of their intentions here. They will fax instructions to Dr Swenson to abandon that part of his excavation.'

Thompson reached for his glass of water and drained it.

'Now we need to talk about this amongst ourselves,' Coxtis said. He stood and waited by the door while they departed. His hand rested briefly on Scott's shoulder as he passed through.

Outside: no stars, no moon. It was still raining very lightly, as if someone's warm breath was condensing their skins. They said nothing as they climbed into the taxi and within moments Scott was asleep, soaring skywards in a dream of flight: he was himself but at the same time some kind of giant winged creature, one of a flock of them rising above the town. He saw the river and the houses and the schools and the mall and the closed-down mill dwindle to nothing as he rose. The air rushed past and all that had been so far — his mother, his father, all their struggles — dwindled to nothing. The great humped island, the vast country beyond spread themselves out below them and as they flew higher and higher they saw more and more of the planet spread out below.

30

——— ✦ ———

A COMMUNAL TABLE WAS SET in the breakfast room. Anna and Brian's cell phones, newly charged and double-checked, lay ready beside their cups and plates, ready for Coxtis' call. Meanwhile they talked about the find and now and then erupted into nervous laughter or reached out to swat wasps away from the food. Maiko and Akira, Felix, the twins and most of Swenson's team were there; there was no sign of Swenson himself, of Greta and Jason or Lin. Scott slept on.

Over a year had passed since the morning when she had sat with Mike Swenson and Colin, pretending that nothing had happened. Now, her mother was dead, and Brian had just told her that poor Colin was in a hospice, no longer seeing visitors, and here they were. This was the end of the road, and there was absolutely nothing left to do but wait.

What if the St'alkwe̱xtsi̱hn said no? She did not want to believe that it was even possible, that after all this, they might simply have to pack their things and leave.

Lin, Gus and Garth arrived and everyone moved out onto the patio and settled under the sun umbrellas. Hummingbirds, *Calypte anna*, as it happened, were dive-bombing the feeders in the yard. Their glittering, weightless bodies shot through the air and then hung momentarily at the sugar water dispenser in a blur of wings, before reversing and vanishing again. 'Twenty-five wingbeats per second,' Anna was telling Felix when the phone rang.

It was the museum, calling to see if anything had happened. She forced her attention back to the hummingbirds, explained about their grooved tongues, their calorific requirements.

Just before eleven, Scott, wearing the crumpled white t-shirt he'd slept in, took a seat at the table. Anna poured him coffee: she felt awkward, uncertain what to say and looked away at the table cluttered with cups, phones and laptops, littered with crumbs and dry leaves blown from the arbutus tree in the yard. She could not bear to be there a minute longer, not knowing whether all they had done and everything they had tried to do added up to anything worth working for, and then, only then, Coxtis called.

'The St'alkwe<u>x</u>tsih̠n,' he said, 'are prepared to accept.' She nodded at the faces around the table, at the same time held up her hand for silence, so that she could hear what Alan had to say: something about mutual respect, about drafting a joint press release.

She closed her phone and the crowd around the table erupted: hammering it until cups and cutlery danced.

'You all deserve a drink,' she told them, 'but just one, because we have to get back to work. Let's re-provision, meet in the bar, and return midafternoon. Aim for three. Dr Swenson's team, of course, are very welcome to—'

'Leave my team out of this.' Swenson stepped through the French doors and into the sunlight. 'What makes you think you can get away with this?' he asked, holding up what could only be his fax from the university, then screwing it into a tight ball. The table juddered as his leg bumped into it and she was glad to have it between them, and to be surrounded by other people.

'We're not getting away with anything, Mike,' she said, keeping her voice low. 'The reverse is true, as you well know.' She was surprised to find herself wanting at the same time to yell a stream of profanities, and to weep like a child. She was even more surprised, a moment later, to find herself recognising the rage and confusion on his face and feeling a sliver of sympathy for the man.

'The way it's all happened is unfortunate. But talk to your dean and you'll see that we hadn't much choice.' Mike gripped the edge of the table as if he might pick it up and hurl it at her; Brian was already squeezing behind the others to get out.

'Let's get out of here,' he said, 'talk it over, eh?' Ignoring him, Swenson leaned towards Anna.

'Anna Silowski,' he said, 'after this, there is nothing I would not wish on you.' Then he turned to Brian and gave a sharp nod of his head; the pair of them walked back through the French doors into the hotel.

Had she heard him correctly? Yes, because Scott, the only person there who understood the true enormity of what Swenson had just said, was on his feet. Anna grabbed his arm, dug her fingers in hard.

'Stay.' She felt stronger than she thought it possible to feel in the aftermath of a curse: *Just words*, she told herself, looking at the shocked faces around the table. No one spoke: there was only the whir of the hummingbirds, the deeper buzzing of wasps and the more distant sounds of voices in the kitchen and traffic on the road.

'I'm sorry the atmosphere on the dig has been so difficult,' she said, as Scott sat down.

Maiko leaned forward, looked around the table.

'A very angry person,' she pronounced. Greta reached for the water jug. '*Big* ego,' she said, 'and attitude problems with women. He's a good guy really. I've read a lot of his papers. Hopefully, Dr Stobart can talk him round.' Felix, still unshaven, his face expressionless, chose the moment to fill his cup with cold tea, tip in three sugars, and stir.

'Mike's just totally stressed out!' said Gunnar. He and his brother Joe wore similar frowns, each pair of blond eyebrows struggling to meet, join into one. The brothers got to their feet: they were going to catch up with Mike and Brian, to see if they could help — why didn't Greta and Jason come along too? Greta shrugged and followed them out. Jason stayed behind.

'I'm no good with scenes,' he said, 'and the way Greta acts with Swenson winds me up. Give me something to do.'

'Help Scott with the supplies, perhaps,' Anna suggested.

She closed her laptop and they left the table behind them, plunged back into the gloom of the hotel, pausing only briefly at the bottom of the stairs. She could not stop smiling. Everyone — almost everyone — was happy. She was looking forward to reading Coxtis' draft press release, to a longer conversation with him, and then to a drink.

'Okay?' she said. 'Scott, are you okay?'

Spaced out, he told her but it was as if his soul had been scoured, his body worn to nothing; it was as if his feet could not touch the ground, however badly he wanted them to. Gratefully, he passed the supplies list to Jason, who had dropped him off home. He gathered a bagful of clean clothes and collapsed on his old bed, listening to Mac on his cell phone:

'I'd *like* to do the optional transition week once the main program is over, Scott. Most people are doing it.'

'Sounds good. Go for it, Dad.'

'But it's not funded. Costs three hundred and eighty dollars — Orianna's daughter is paying for her.'

'I don't have it.' Mac's voice, after a moment's pause, seemed louder, harder. He'd have to ask the church, he said. What was that Price woman's first name? Angela?'

'Andrea.'

'And there's another thing. Orianna can't go back to her old place at the end of the program. Too many bad memories. So I'd like her to come stay with us, if that's okay with you, son.'

Sure, Scott said, his eyes on the grey, cobwebby ceiling. It might be a bit crowded, but why not give it a try? But even as he spoke, Scott began to see the abandoned trailer through the eyes of a middle-aged, female stranger: the boarded-up kitchen window, the ancient range, dead flies and dust everywhere; plus, as he had just discovered, the hydro had been cut off.

'It's filthy. And I don't have time right now to clean it. She'll want a decent bed.'

'We can do all that together,' Mac said, grandly.

After the call, Scott got up, tipped some bleach in the toilet and wiped the windowsills with an old dishcloth, and then lost heart. The thing he hadn't said was how much he did not want to return, whoever else was there, however clean it was. He was glad to hear Jason drive up.

A tapestry of voices surrounded them as they walked in: Joe's bar, cool and gloomy, was fuller than it had been for years.

Both teams and a fair number of the Forest Nation campers were taking up most of the tables. Regulars and other late-comers were standing at the bar or in groups between the tables, and spilling out onto the bright, hot patio. Everyone was talking. By the window, Felix was playing cards with the twins and the Forest Nation leader, Spruce. Brian Stobart, who had clearly finished or abandoned his chat with Swenson, sat with Anna and a woman Scott recognised as the reporter from the local paper. Brian leaned forward awkwardly, cupped his hand to his ear to hear what she was asking him. Swenson was at the bar, with Greta, the pair of them perched on stools.

'Hell,' Jason said, seeing them. 'Look, I'll wait in the van. See you outside.'

Matt flung his arms across Scott's shoulders.

'Hey man! You look different!' Matt, Scott thought, looked just the same, but updated: latest Ray-Bans and jeans, some ex-pensive kind of frayed punky polo shirt with the buttons undone, and a single glass bead on a thong around his neck.

'I already got you a beer. Here. Great body,' he said following Scott's gaze to where Greta sat, very straight, her Lycra top so white it seemed to glow, listening to Swenson talk. Swenson had a shotglass in front of him, and he paused only to tip it back and grin at her.

'Is it true,' Matt said as Scott took the offered beer, 'that you gave Thompson a smoke right in front of the cops? Cool! But what I need to know is where d'you get it from? Who sup-plied it?'

'You. Way back.' Scott grinned at Matt, liked him all over again.

'So I'm part of this too?' As Matt tipped his head back to

laugh, Scott saw Mike lean in, touch Greta lightly on the shoulder, and then run his hand down the top of her bare arm. Perhaps, Scott thought, as Greta slipped off her stool and took a step back, Jason should have stayed? Or maybe not: Mike too was on his feet, still smiling, still talking and he reached out this time for Greta's hand. A glass fell from the bar and crashed at their feet as she pulled away, and suddenly the entire bar was silent, everyone looking over to where they stood.

'I said, don't touch me!' Greta spoke very clearly, as if to someone who struggled to hear. Her jaw tight, she stepped out of the mess at her feet and made for the exit. Mike caught up just as she reached the door.

'Don't!' Greta yelled as he reached for her again. He waited for Greta to push through the door and leave it banging behind her, but she stayed where she was.

'It's bad enough that you think you can *say* this stuff to me, but what the hell makes you think you can just *grab hold of me?*'

There was a spattering of applause and foot-stamping. From the table by the window, Spruce whistled his approval, a piercing, rabble-rousing sound.

'All I meant—' Mike began, and again, Matt laughed. He wasn't the only one. Anna was on her feet, her face blank with shock.

'What you need to do, now, is apologise to me,' Greta said.

'Apologise!' yelled Spruce and his friends, as Swenson pushed past Greta, out into the parking lot.

'Where's Jayce?' Greta asked the crowd staring at her, and a moment later, cell phone in hand, she too pushed through the door.

The bar erupted.

'Please,' Anna said to Brian, 'let me through. Where's Scott? Scott?' But what could he or anyone do? There was a surge towards the door, a crush as they struggled out into the sun.

A horn blared. Spruce was walking backwards, one step at a time, as a white university van inched towards him, revving frantically. Swenson, clearly visible through window, was driving. Jason jogged alongside, beating on the drivers' window with his fists: 'Stop! Open the fucking door!' Greta, her face streaked with tears, stood in her white top and frayed shorts, 'Stop, all of you!'

No one was going to stop.

A-pol-o-gise, Spruce mouthed, slowly, silently, amidst the other yells, his eyebrows shooting upwards on the *o*. The van jerked forward, faster. Spruce, pushing off from the bumper, grabbed a windscreen wiper in each hand, pressed his face against the windscreen glass: *A-pol-o-gise!* His feet lost their grip, dangled, and his body swayed side to side as the van bounced over a pothole towards the exit, picking up speed, not pausing, not signalling, and accelerated out of view. They could hear the sirens by then, and seconds later, the squeal of brakes. Everyone ran towards the noise, the smell of burning rubber.

Spruce, suddenly pale, lay spread-eagled on the ground: 'I'm fine. Let me sit up! It's my fucking *leg*, not my back! These people,' he told the officer who was supporting him while the ambulance came, 'are all my witnesses, right?'

There were thirty of them, wide-eyed, watching Barry Sutherland and his sergeant usher Mike Swenson into the second squad car and drive away, watching Spruce finally pass out as the paramedics loaded him up.

✦ ✦ ✦

Anna was one of the first to be interviewed; Scott the last. It was remarkable, Baz Sutherland said to Scott as he left the station, that so many people were prepared to come forward, and that they had all said more or less the same thing.

'But even that doesn't mean anything will come of it, in terms of the harassment,' Greta told Anna. They were in Anna's room at the hotel, Greta sitting with back to the wall on Anna's bed. 'Though the driving charges will stick. And I'm going to report this to the university. They have a very clear grievance procedure for sexual harassment. I bet I'm not the only one. Why should he get away with it? Will you support me?' Anna filled water glasses from a plastic bottle, and brought them over.

I feel responsible is what Anna had said to Scott earlier, though she had not explained to him why, and she had not planned to tell Greta either: better, she thought, to be simply a witness, not a witness with a peculiar resurrected grievance, a perceived agenda of her own. But here she was, in the same room, or one very like it, and here was Greta.

'You're absolutely right to make an issue of it. It happened to me, actually,' Anna said, and saw the younger woman's face loosen, and then put itself back together. 'I had to hit him. A terrible mess— I didn't make a complaint, though probably I should have. Of course, I'll support you.'

The first time someone knocked, she found Jason outside, and watched him put his arm around Greta, saw how the younger woman turned her head into his chest while he stroked her hair. The second time, it was Scott.

'Just checking in. Everything okay?'

'Thank you.' It was all she could say. And all she wanted to do was sleep. She turned out the rickety bedside light and lay in the almost dark of the room, allowing the events of the day to replay themselves in her mind until they wore themselves out and became the words of the letter she would write: *I have known Greta Hanson since she began volunteering for us four years ago, first as a fieldworker and then as research assistant. Greta is a trustworthy, responsible, mature person...*

✦ ✦ ✦

Swenson's team, not knowing where he was or when he might turn up again, strode ahead, leaning forward under the weight of their packs. Lin, Jason and Greta talked together in low voices. Scott had exchanged packs with Brian who clearly did not enjoy the hike: he was sweating hard, his knee, he said, was playing up; he'd been waiting months for surgery.

The site, when they arrived was dusky and still, their abandoned tents billowing slightly in the breeze.

31

—————— ◆ ——————

THEY ROSE EARLY, WORKED HARD UNTIL DUSK. Kneeling or squatting on the rock, land-bound, they inched towards the moment when they would lever the skull piece, half-covered in plaster, right out of the rock, and, they hoped, turn it over without breaking it.

'A marriage of twenty-first-century science and stone-age technology,' Brian called it, rubbing his creased, dusty hands together as he spoke. Beauty and the Beast, Scott thought when he looked at the pair of them: Brian's sun-broiled bald patch; Anna's hair not just all there, but alive and refusing to stay in the tie. His small eyes hidden in folds of skin; hers huge, alert, shining. His blunt fingers, her agile hands. They had known each other for years. There was nothing between them, or between Anna and anyone, so far as he could tell.

'Dr Swenson has gone back to talk to the university,' Gunnar informed them on his return from a trip to town. Jason drew his finger across his throat. There was laughter; even the air seemed to relax.

'We'll have to pick up some slack,' Anna pointed out, 'wind up for him.'

No one minded that, and she found herself laughing at the slightest of ironies, the feeblest jokes. She touched people on the elbow or shoulder as she talked to them; they worked on, and far above them the ravens reeled out into the impossibly blue sky, teasing with their aeronautic tricks and indecipherable messages, their shrieks, caws, the deep, hollow glugging sounds. It seemed to Scott that they had arrived suddenly, and almost by accident, on Planet Paradise: just the teams and the occasional visitor, working in the silvery morning light, in thick yellow midday sun, the sudden shade that came a little earlier each afternoon.

'Though it's a shame,' Anna told Scott, 'about my brother and the kids. I wanted them to see this. He was going to bring them, but Lesley has complications and he can't make it. Who knows whether I'll get to do something like this again?'

'Don't think that way,' he said, shocked to be reminded of one of the first things he'd known about her, even though it seemed, now, a groundless fear. How to say, don't worry, it will be just fine, without sounding trite? Sometimes, he felt he was starting to hate words: despite the way they proliferated, you could only ever say part of what you meant. Many things that were never said at all.

It is always best, Anna wrote in her personal notes, *to work slowly and carefully, but it's true as well that now Mike Swenson has left, I simply don't want the dig to end. No — I want it to last. The human squabbling is over, and now we can surrender to the task before us.* They could, she felt, allow themselves to open up to the strange, stone-bound creatures they were prising from the earth's grip. These creatures were separated from them by the element they moved in, and by many millions of years, and yet it was possible to feel a kind of kinship with them. Did everyone feel this way? She liked to think so. And while they were not unravelling time, as Felix once rather grandly suggested, perhaps they were at least loosening its grip.

She did not want the dig to end because it felt so good — and also, when it was over and the specimen embarked on the long process of preparation, and she would be left all over again with the question that hovered over her life, with the way things were before the dig began, before she had met Scott Macleod and asked for his help.

She would go home to all that, and Scott would do whatever he chose to do next. Maybe she would be able to help him in some way.

I will miss Scott, she wrote. *I have to admit that I will miss him being a few metres away, miss the knowledge that he's aware of me, just as, increasingly, I'm aware of him. Of the person he has turned out to be, but also of his hands and face the way he moves.*

Perhaps, she told herself, it is good that the dig is almost over.

Chip by chip, they burrowed deep under into the remaining plinth, reaching in where they could not quite see, supporting the specimen with timber joists and cement blocks. They kept fragments of waste rock close by to cushion the impact when it came to flipping the skull piece over. The discard piles were huge now, five times the size of the holes they had made; at the end, they would use the waste rock to fill in, and allow the river to wash the rest away.

'What we do has more impact than you'd think,' Felix told Scott. 'It'll wash up somewhere, make a bank, change the river's flow.'

They nudged through the last bit of plinth, fed ropes through the gap, widened it, inserted joists, levered and propped, this side then that, until the base of the half-wrapped rock lay on a sagging timber cradle just above the main ground level. Next, it must move across, then over.

'If Dr S were here,' Greta said, 'he'd be telling us we're crazy — just saw the damned thing in half!'

'Fingers crossed that he's not actually right!' Anna laughed partly from nerves, also because she could see the absurdity of it all: the rock posed in the middle of a group of sweaty humans who wanted to throw themselves at their task, but could not, who wanted what seemed to be the impossible — until, towards the end of the afternoon, the huge stone-and-plaster parcel slid slowly down the tiny slope they had created and lodged on the edge of the trench.

Good footage, Gus said. Though it would edit down to less than a minute.

'Tomorrow,' Anna explained, no longer angry with the cameras, but including them, 'will be better still. We'll set up more levers, bracing, ropes. We'll make a frame here, hang onto the ropes on one side, and reduce the propping of the other, and slowly, the idea is, we'll roll it.'

She squeezed her eyes as it went over: there was a sound somewhere between a groan and a cry, and when she looked again it was unbroken, ready for the underside to be jacketed and braced.

They eased the huge, irregular, plaster-coated lump of rock onto rollers and pushed it out into the middle of the gorge, taking each roller round to the front as it emerged from the back. They packed the smaller pieces into crates.

It could, Scott thought, almost be something he'd imagined — that old up, up and away thing of his. But it was real: the vibrations of a Sikorsky 61 doubled and redoubled — an impossible, heart-shaking din.

As the grip hook descended, he, Anna and Jason helped the technician from CanCo to thread the nylon straps of the harness beneath the specimen and ratchet them to length. They could hear nothing of what they did. Jason and Scott slipped the fitting onto the grip hook. Anna checked it, and then each of the ropes; returned, looked at them both, her eyes huge. Escaped strands of her hair danced in the updraft: she was thinking of the calculation, the density of shale, her estimate of the specimen's volume...

She signalled that they were done. The cable tightened. Machine and gravity pitted themselves against each other. The noise intensified. Moments passed and it seemed hopeless, and then there was the faintest suspicion of movement, an almost imperceptible wobble as the rock lost contact with the ground. The Sikorsky pulled up and they tipped their heads back to watch, their throats tight and dry.

It cleared the gorge and the treetops and slid east across the sky, dwindling fast. Soon it would be descending by the entrance to the cliff trail, where Felix and Brian and Lin and half of the other team waited with the trucks.

'We did it!' Scott said, his arm across Anna's back. Everyone hugged everyone; the helicopter made four more trips, returning last of all for the portable WCs, dangling over all their heads.

✦ ✦ ✦

They went to Marco's. The tables had been pushed together to make one huge expanse decorated with plastic grapevines and candles stuck into wine bottles. Everyone and his friend was invited to eat lasagne, including Mac and Orianna, who had arrived home by taxi that afternoon and were sitting just beyond Brian and Lin, a tall glass of soda in front of each of them.

Anna rattled a spoon in her glass.

'We are so delighted with how everything has turned out. I hope,' she said smiling at Coxtis, 'that this way everyone has got something of what they wanted.'

There were whoops, whistles and cheers from the unofficial royal couple of the Forest Nation: Spruce and his pregnant girlfriend, Ocean. The St'alkwextsihn elders, Thompson and Coxtis, were more dignified in their response. They were on a long road, Anna thought. This, the end of a journey for her, was for them a tiny, symbolic step.

'I want to thank everyone—' Scott's hand shook as he filled a few nearby glasses, and then his own. It could almost be a dream, he thought, the whole thing from meeting her until now. But now it was over: Anna thanked the protestors, she thanked Thompson for his courageous stand, for sticking to his ground but also being patient and open, she thanked Coxtis and the elders for their willingness to negotiate. She thanked the funding bodies. Her colleagues at the museum. The teams.

'Everyone's contribution was vital in what has turned out to be a huge challenge, but I think it's true to say that without Scott Macleod here, we'd not have been able to succeed in the way we have.' There was clapping and yells: *Scott, Scott!* To begin with, he liked being thanked, but as she continued, speaking of the many ways in which he had contributed, of his hard work, kindness, calm and clear-sightedness, Scott's pleasure faded. It was the end; when he thought how soon Anna would be gone, back to where she came from, his heart ached. He was both angry and sad. He did not want to say goodbye. He did not want the story to end; he wanted another one to begin.

Plates were handed around; they moved through the main course and out the other side of it into chocolate cake. People stood and carried their glasses and coffee cups around the table to talk to each other. Scott went to sit with Mac and Orianna.

'We can't stay much longer,' Mac told him. 'This has been really hard for us.'

'The wonderful thing, with Mac and me,' Orianna said, 'is that we each know exactly how it is for the other one, don't we?' Her eyes were deeply shadowed — makeup, he thought, rather than tiredness, but couldn't be sure. Scott thanked them for coming.

'You've done great,' he told them, yelling against the hubbub. He walked with them to where he had left the truck, handed over the keys

'These people,' Mac said, 'are they going to take you on and pay you now?'

'Don't think so. I don't have the qualifications.'

'You don't mind?' Orianna asked Scott. 'You really don't

mind an old lady taking your dad on?' She needed, she had already explained, to sleep in Scott's room because of Mac's snoring: sleep was very important to people who were recovering. Scott could choose between his tent, the sofa, or Matt's floor. Orianna's hair tickled his face, as she leaned in for a hug. She smelled of some kind of medicinal oil, leafy and good for you. She was okay, he thought, not wonderful but okay.

'Scott,' Alan Coxtis told him when he returned to the party, 'I know you've got mixed feelings about family, about where you belong. But we're emerging from the darkest times. There's support, there's direction. Healing. We're evolving. We're making treaties and we're out there in the cities, everywhere, not just parked on the reserves. Our population is growing fast and in twenty years, who knows? We're re-colonising Canada, and what we need now are young people like you, who can hang on to what's important, but also think creatively. So far as I'm concerned, if you want to, you belong.'

Thompson was going back to school next year, Coxtis said. The band was sponsoring him. He was going to get an education on his own terms, do something with his life.

The room emptied. Anna was on the other side of the table with Akira, Maiko and Brian. Scott had never seen her so relaxed and open. She always drew his attention, but now her face, her skin seemed to cry out for touch. *Forty*, Scott reminded himself. Much educated. About to leave. Though not sick, he was pretty sure of that now.

Greta, Jason and the twins caught him on his way over to her.

'What's next for you, Scott?' Greta asked. She was returning to California, and then next summer she said was, 'TBA, either

China or the Arctic. Jason's trying for the same, fingers crossed.'

'Sounds cool,' he told them. 'As for me— definitely neither of those.'

'You must visit the museum,' Lin said. 'In six months, perhaps, there will be something to see.'

Akira gave him a business card, English one side, Japanese the other and said that he must visit the institute, if he was ever in Japan. Then he and Maiko said goodbye, and a waitress leaned over to clear glasses, and it was really the end.

'Which way are you going?' Anna asked Scott, who waved his arm in the general direction of everything. 'I really can't thank you enough,' she said as they set off towards the hotel. *More gratitude!* he thought. He didn't want it and found he couldn't speak at all. His mouth was welded shut. 'I've really appreciated your support and your—' she hesitated, 'company,' she said.

'We'll be in touch,' she said as they walked past what used to be a store selling outdoor clothing, 'I'll keep you posted about the specimen, and remember, if you need a reference, contacts, anything, you have my email.'

It was, she felt, surprisingly painful, to be doing this. It was unbearable, Scott thought, that they would go on walking until they reached the hotel, and then Anna would thank him one last time. She would cross the road and follow her colleagues inside; he would veer right, and then walk and walk not knowing where he was aiming for, and then start to run, trying to escape from feeling that life was impossible. *No*, he thought. I'm not going back there.

Still talking, repeating herself about the references and contacts that he did not want, she turned a little towards him.

'I'm sure that things will go well for you,' she said, and he reached over and put his hand on her waist, felt its softness, the jut of her hip, the impact of her foot on the ground; she stopped, but did not pull away.

'Anna—'

'I know,' she rested her hand in the small of his back, 'but listen, Scott—' He ran his hand up her side, encountered her ribs, the swell of her breast. The others had turned the corner and they were alone, one moment still looking, the next pressed together so that she could smell the traces of wood smoke on his skin. Their breathing and the small wet sounds their lips made filled each other's ears.

Everything else about them vanished, and they wanted it to. First the Mountain View was impossible, and then it did not matter at all; they slipped through the back way. Scott used an old pass key and let them into a back room.

'Wait—' she said, pushing him away: they were still half-clothed but beginning to move as if they were not, 'Scott, be clear, this is just tonight, okay?' His leg was jammed up between hers and he knew that when he ran his hand over her skin it made it hard for her to speak, and it was the same for him, but he was not wanting at all to speak and *just tonight* was a whole lot better than not at all.

'Okay?' she said, 'I don't want you to—' but it seemed that what she did want was clear enough and he gave enough of a nod that she let him: inside of her, out of himself, everywhere at once.

In the small hours, Scott pulled on his jeans and went to the kitchen to raid the fridge. He put what he could find on a tray. Breakfast rolls, grapes, little packets of cheese, two glasses of orange juice.

She drank her juice and then said that she liked him very much — there was something wrong with the way she said this, and he dimly remembered, then, how things had begun with him having to understand something. But she was still there, naked, the blanket pulled up around her legs.

'Very much... Tonight was wonderful. Now, let's leave it like this. Otherwise, things will just get complicated and painful.' Why those words? Why complicated and painful? Why not *fantastic, wild, intense?*

'It's a minefield. I'm sorry, but don't get involved.'

'I am fucking *involved*!'

'Then stop,' she said and began to get dressed. 'Put your things on and come out with me, don't stay here alone. It's almost morning.' Her hand grazed his back as they left the room, and every nerve, cell and vessel in his body responded.

She went upstairs to her own room, and felt far more sad than she could justify. But it would be all right, she told herself. How else could it be? In a day or so he'd understand; they'd both get over it. Scott sat outside; a few hours later, he watched the floatplane roar away across the water, and then, rise, dwindle and disappear.

✦ ✦ ✦

Pale and puffy, her hair newly cut short, Lesley peered at her family, cheerful as ever. 'It's fixed for Tuesday. They'll only be six weeks early,' she said. 'Three pounds maybe? And then, I'll be able to get out of this bed!' she said. 'Okay, not right after, but soon. It's going to be fine.'

'*When* are you going to come home?' Sam asked. His hair

had grown over his eyebrows and ears; Frankie's was in bunches, not braids. Both children, Anna thought, looked less clear-cut, wilder than usual.

'I'm not exactly sure, darling,' Lesley told him. 'I'm going to have to spread myself pretty thin,' she said to Anna as the kids went off with Vik to buy ice cream, and they both laughed, because she was so uncommonly huge.

✦ ✦ ✦

Even his father had someone, though Scott did not like the way Mac grew restless when Orianna was not there, the way his eyes gravitated to the window or the door, waiting for her return. He had seen that look before, and knew what it could lead to. Though they seemed happy, and she had found part-time work in a garden centre, for which she needed Scott's truck.

'Thank your lucky stars,' Matt told Scott. 'She did you a favour. A woman with problems is not good. It's *them* that are supposed to look after *you.*' They were in the tent Scott had erected on the patch of grass in front of the trailer. Despite the soft light, Scott noticed lines on Matt's face that he hadn't seen before, smelled the dope smoke on his clothes, the coffee on his breath.

'You're insane, man,' Matt said. In his opinion, Scott should move back into his old family house, which Matt had bought for a song, with cash. He could do the necessary repairs and alternations, and set up an operation in the basement on a percentage basis. 'What else are you going to do?'

What did he have? Years at the hotel. Excellent but uncertified computer skills. Basic mechanics but no formal qualification. Catering for a palaeontological dig. Looking after two people with health challenges. He would never be a palaeontologist, a politician, a detective, a guitarist, or a helicopter pilot. He had no computer, no income, was not a real Native, and he did not want to return to the Mountain View Hotel, or to run a grow-op.

He wanted to be with Anna Silowski, and he did not care if he was insane.

✦ ✦ ✦

When Madeleine and Christine were born, it was a week before they could be touched. They were in the NICU, with monitors taped to their scalps, sensors on their feet, drips in their stomachs, and visitors had to scrub and gown to visit them. It was like having *no* babies, Frankie complained. It was like having monkey babies, said Sam.

But soon they could be touched, held and studied up close. At home, a frenzy of feeding, laundry, meals, and since the irrigation had stopped working, watering too. Anna took on the groceries, the cooking and Frankie and Sam, she drove them to their school and play dates, arranged treats afterwards, fed them, made sure they washed their hair, read to them, made sure Vik played with them too when he got in. One story was about a girl who was jealous of her new baby brother, who finally came around when he gripped her finger and wouldn't let go. *He Loves*

Me Too, the book was called. Lesley's mother had sent it.

'But there's only *one* baby, in the story,' Frankie pointed out as she dug herself deeper into her end of the sofa. 'And it's a boy, and anyhow, I'm not jealous. But I want a mountain bike.' A baby on her lap, Frankie's hair slipping between her fingers as she braided it, Sam clinging to her in piggyback, Lesley in her arms half sobbing from exhaustion, Vik's arm flung across her shoulder: there was no time, scarcely a waking moment free of human interaction, never an hour without some kind of touch.

Then Lesley's sister Jo arrived, and it was time to return to her own life: to the documentation of the Big Crow find, to her empty house, to the choice she had set aside before she left. The family, six now, gathered outside to wave her goodbye.

◆ ◆ ◆

Scott's first ride was in a red Jetta — driven by a maniac — but it got him on the ferry and then to a good spot on the road out of the terminal. Then he was in a battered Explorer on Highway 1, heading for Kamloops with Ken, who said he'd take him as far as Hope: easier to find a ride from there, mind you, the Coquihalla was a toll road. Soon the road snaked along a valley between tree-clad mountains, and Ken sped along, making the most of the company. If Scott was looking for work, there was a brother of his in Kamloops, who owned a restaurant and was starting up a ginseng farm.

An hour's wait just outside Hope, then a logging truck going for the pulp mill, driven by Alvin who waved away his ten bucks for the toll. Silence this time: they couldn't hear themselves speak. The mountains now were dry, hot-looking, like in a Western. Signs for the ginseng farm. Alvin dropped him right outside the campsite.

Back by the road, 7:30 a.m., destination Banff: snapped up by two gay men from the US in a shiny white rented SUV. There was *plenty* of work down south for someone like him, said Carl, the driver, had Scott considered modelling?

No. A silence ensued, talk about other things. Food. Cars. The climb towards Rogers Pass — gouged black rock, white peaks, and the bluest sky Scott had ever seen. They vanished into shady tunnels, burst out into the light. At a café near the summit he got lucky with a grey Toyota, driven by Eileen, travelling with her husband, George. They had a son Scott's age, who was backpacking in Europe.

'Lord knows exactly where,' Eileen said. 'Our fingers are crossed.'

Golden. Lake Louise. He called at the grocery store, and then walked to the riverside campsite, which was shady and cool. The year was turning. A few fires burned in the dark, kids yelled and careened round on their bikes or played Frisbee with their dads: the way things weren't, Scott thought. But all that was the past. He had had a bird's-eye view of Anna's place on Google Earth: just out of town, a few miles on from the museum, the only property at the end of a left turn. He would be there tomorrow.

✦ ✦ ✦

She saw him from behind, framed by the windshield, right there, walking the same way she was driving: Scott, with his green backpack. He had somehow stepped from one part of her life into another and for a moment she could only think that she was mistaken, that despite putting him out of her mind, she had somehow managed to dream him up.

Scott?

She passed, pulled over and watched him approach. She saw the loose walk, the set of his shoulders, the smile he didn't even know he wore. Very familiar, yet also strange. He saw a grey Volvo, very dusty; he heard classical music drifting out the open window. He was braced for trouble — for her to yell at him that he should not have come, or drive off.

'Are you okay?' she asked. He shrugged, smiled.

'I need to talk with you,' he said. In the back, Roger gave a couple of sharp barks, and then, when told to be quiet, growled and stayed put. Just for a moment Anna was afraid. But it was *Scott*. She leaned across to open the door.

'I don't live far from here,' she said.

The key stuck in the lock. She had to put her bag down to get in.

He took off his shoes and followed her into the house, noticing only the general feel of the place, a mix of old and new, the weathered wooden floor in the hall, the modern-looking pictures on the walls. He waited while she fed the dog, and then poured two glasses of water from the jug in the fridge and handed him one of them, watched him drink.

'Why have you come all this way?' she asked. Though she knew, stiffened when he leaned towards her.

'But you can't just walk into my life. You know my situation.

And you're — I don't know exactly — young! Can't you see, Scott?' He could or would not see, his point being, you could not just turn something off once it had began. But he liked the way she said his name.

'And I have to come to a decision about testing,' she told him. It was impossible then not to reach out for him.

32

━━━━━━━━ ✦ ━━━━━━━━

HE SAT IN THE WAITING ROOM while she gave the blood sample. Painlessly, the thick, dark liquid filled the syringe and she, the scientist, became data. An object of enquiry. Not quite the same self anymore.

There, the technician said, calmly taping cotton wool into the crook of her arm, as if it was nothing at all.

Four weeks later, he accompanied her to a different part of the hospital to see Dr Hutz. Hutz, short and plump, bald, his face cross-hatched with lines, looked up at him as they shook hands and asked, 'Family?'

'Scott and I have recently become close,' Anna said. Hutz waved them into their seats.

Hutz liked to begin by looking at the family background. Anna talked; Scott took it all in: the Russian grandmother who left her sick husband behind when she emigrated, Mama, Leo falling to bits, Vik and his kids... He listened, but also he watched: he watched the tensing and relaxation of small muscles around her eyes and mouth, the frown that came at every question and then smoothed itself away as she began to talk. He watched the tilt of her head as she listened, the way she closed her eyes when she was overwhelmed by what she was thinking, hearing or saying. It was impossible, he allowed himself to think, that she could be sick: she was just far too much alive. After all this, they would be free.

'Mama kept things secret to protect us,' Anna told Hutz. 'Once I knew, *I* had to protect myself. And her way seemed to be the best way. Now—' she smiled.

'What's changed?' Hutz prompted. 'What's different now?' Anna swallowed.

'I don't think I would be sitting here now, if Mama were still alive.' She sat for a moment as if listening to some kind of private music, her face smooth with surprise. 'And now—' her gaze rested on Scott; he could feel its warmth, 'Now, I need to find out.'

'Not for me. I don't need to know,' he said.

'Because of you, I do,' she replied. Hutz took in a slow breath, let it out. He moistened his lips.

'Whatever the situation between you now,' he said, 'it is liable to change once — if — you have the result, whatever that is.' How did Hutz drag you out of your comfort zone without you knowing until it was done? It was all in that soft, flat tone of voice.

At the same moment, they reached for each other's hands.

Afterwards, they made their way in silence to the elevator, which first refused to depart and then seemed to plummet down. It felt strange to step out into the ordinary afternoon light, the crisp fall air.

✦ ✦ ✦

Dr Persaud, the neurologist, asked Anna to walk in a straight line down the corridor, and follow with her eyes the course of a ballpoint pen, which he moved to and fro in front of her face. He'd looked down to tick boxes on a chart, but otherwise his eyes never left her. He was young and tactful and soft-spoken and was only doing what he'd been asked to do. Scott knew it was crazy to want to rip the damn clipboard out of his hands, but that didn't stop him wanting to.

'A difficult job, though,' Anna agreed afterwards. They sat in the car in the hospital parkade, the engine on for heat.

'Not as difficult as it is the other side of the desk.'

+ + +

She had not told Vik and Lesley about Scott, but the Sunday before the last appointment, she called and told Lesley that she'd be in town on Tuesday, and would like to bring someone to meet them.

Tuesday was a bright, cold day. Juliette met them in the lobby, shook hands, checked that Anna still wished to be given her result, and then called up to the doctor's office. Dr Persaud would open the letter now, she said as they went up in the elevator. He used to do it in front of the patient, but it was unnecessarily stressful. With a soft clatter, the elevator doors opened; Juliette waited for them to step out first.

Even now, she could turn back. Anna's heart thudded in her chest. There was a roaring in her ears.

Why Persaud? Scott remembered the way he had watched Anna walk down the corridor, which now they had to walk again together, following Juliette past door after door, on each a name and its string of letters. But did it matter? Perhaps, even, it was better that the person on the other side of the desk was someone you didn't care for.

The door was ajar.

Dr Persaud invited them to sit. Juliette took a chair by the window. Anna withdrew her hand from Scott's; he reached and took it back. Had their journey over gone smoothly? Dr Persaud wanted to know. Good. Well. He had just a few moments ago opened the letter, he said, glancing down at it and then up again.

He was sorry, but it was bad news.

'Are you sure?' Scott asked, leaning forward to see the paper.

'I'm very sorry, but yes.' Dr Persaud turned the paper round, and pointed with his finger. 'There are forty-three repeats.'

33

———— ✦ ————

THE HOUSE GLOWED CREAM against blue-white snow and a jumble of heavy, purple-grey clouds, its windows already lit.

'Maybe,' Anna said as she pulled the keys from the ignition, 'this is not the best way to do things. Not fair on you. Not fair on them.' But Lesley had already opened the door and was beckoning them to hurry in. They hurried up the icy path that led to the porch.

'Both asleep,' Lesley said as she hugged Anna. 'Come in out of the cold! Great to meet you, Scott.' She shook his hand and they both saw her face freeze, but only momentarily, as she took Scott in: shaved but hollow-eyed, exhausted, not what she expected and nowhere near her sister-in-law's age.

'Hi, Lesley.'

Younger, Anna had told Vik on the phone two days ago. Scott was making fajitas at the time, and he had looked over his shoulder and stuck out his tongue. *I'd like to bring someone I've been seeing. You'll notice,* she had warned, *that he's younger than I am.* So no one could blame Lesley, now, Scott reminded himself, for doing just that.

He tugged off his shoes. Anna watched Lesley watching him: checking that what she had first thought was indeed correct, that the Scientific Sister had finally and outrageously succumbed to lust, or love, or madness, or all three. It was really not the point, Anna thought, but there was no way Lesley could know that, or that she could tell her so right now, standing in the door.

They followed Lesley through the foyer, where the fading light washed down from a row of skylights, and on into the living area: two steps down into the sunken lounge. Gas flames burned brightly behind the glass door of the stove set in its column of river rock. Like something from a magazine, Scott thought. A thick, rough-textured rug spread across the floor in front of the fire and the only signs of Anna's new nieces were two white cloths and a pair of tiny cotton blankets, neatly folded and placed on the arm of the leather armchair nearest the fire.

They sat next to each other on the sofa, held hands. The baby monitor lay on the glass table in front of them and for a moment, before the talking began, they could hear the two babies breathing upstairs.

'Isn't this something?' Lesley smiled brightly. Her pixie cut was beginning to grow out. 'It's falling out, too. Hormones,' she said.

'It suits you,' Anna said. 'You look a little tired, but amazing too. Younger, somehow.'

'Coffee? Wine? And I'll fetch the kids. Vik will bring dinner, so we can relax.'

A moment later the kids burst in, yelling at each other to slow down.

'Frankie, and Sam—' Anna began.

'Who are you?' Sam asked Scott. Next to him, Frankie stood

a head taller, a girl with fierce expression and almost protruding blue-grey eyes. Lesley reappeared with a tray of glasses.

'Scott worked on the dig. He was in some of those pictures I showed you.'

'And now...?' Lesley asked, as she set glasses on the bamboo coasters on the table. *And now?* Pretend, Scott thought, that this is happening to someone else.

'I've been staying with Anna,' he said as Sam climbed onto Anna's lap, wriggled down, elbowed her, thrust one leg out across her knees. She adjusted to the weight of him, eased one hand free and rested it on Scott's thigh. Frankie lay belly down on the rug, stared up at them both with X-ray eyes. Her hair, very shiny, had clearly been braided wet, left to dry and then only recently been undone. Perhaps, Scott thought, it was supposed to be like Anna's? 'Workwise, things are kind of up in the air,' he told Lesley. 'I covered for the bookstore manager at the museum for a couple of weeks, but she's back now. I'll pick something up in town.'

'Can't the museum find something permanent?' Lesley eased herself into the leather chair by the fire. 'I bet Anna could pull some strings.'

A thin wail emerged from the baby monitor. A line of tiny lights pulsed red.

'Can you believe it?' Lesley's glass was halfway to her lips. There was another wail, sharper, louder, and then a shuddering intake of breath. She hurried out of the room.

For a few moments they listened to the crying, then to a stream of whispered endearments, and then Frankie reached forward and turned the monitor off. Lesley strode in carrying one of the twins.

'Would you?' she said to Scott. 'Anna looks like she's already occupied with Sam. Thanks.' The baby felt almost weightless, soft, as if she had no bones. Terrifyingly fragile.

'Maddy,' Frankie informed him, brushing the baby's eager lips with the soother until she took it, and fell suddenly silent, sucking and swallowing, her eyes fixed on Scott's chin.

'It's *not* Maddy,' Sam, hot in Anna's lap, selected a single but large and perfect chip, 'it's Chrissie.' Anna eased her nephew from her lap.

'I won't be long. I'll just go see if they're all right up there.'

So Scott sat with Frankie and Sam, holding the baby; he heard Vik come in. *How the hell did I get to be here?* He'd met Anna on top of a cliff. Agreed to go on the dig. He'd followed her when she ran away: and now he was sitting, totally wired, the bearer of terrible news in a leather sofa in a monster house in Calgary. He was reaching up to shake the hand of a corporate lawyer who was wondering what the hell was going on with his sister, and in the crook of the other arm he was holding the lawyer's baby.

'Pleased to meet you!'

'Likewise. I see you're getting to know the family, Scott!'

A briefcase still dangled from Vik's left hand; his thick black coat flapped open, showing a pale shirt and slate-coloured tie. The room seethed with the spicy scents of the Chinese food he'd brought. 'Where are the rest of them?' Sam attached himself to his father's leg. Frankie feigned indifference. The baby, relaxed now, but still awake, was like a small fire against Scott's arm and ribs. Anna returned to the room, smiled at him, completely forgetting, for a moment, why they were there.

'Do we need to warm this?' Vik gestured at the two bags he'd put on the coffee table as he came in. 'Excuse us a moment, Scott.' The two of them moved up to the kitchen area, packed the food into the oven and scooped cutlery from drawers.

How, Scott thought, *is she doing this?* He wanted to yell and roar, break things. To run out into the cold, shouting. To blow something up. Maddy, Chrissie, or whoever she was, was something to hang on to. *So, who's doing the looking after, here?* he thought at her. Carefully, he carried the baby over to the window. Vik and Anna's voices were behind him, their reflections hovered on the glass; it was dark outside now and wind stirred flakes of snow from the trees and shrubs.

'Maddy's fine now,' Anna said. 'I'll take Chrissie up.' In the bathroom, he wiped the milky spit off his sweater and splashed water over his face. He was nauseous, desperate for the evening to end. But also he wanted to make time stop still in its tracks, and then, with the last of his strength, push harder still and roll it right back.

'Hope you like Chinese, Scott,' Vik said, as they sat down at the kitchen table. 'Should have asked—'

'Great. Looks good.' Frankie served herself and Sam with chow mein. Anna steadied herself by focussing her attention on the wine in her glass, its thick glow, the deepness of the colour.

'Cheers!' Glasses clinked, steam rose.

'Hard to do Chinese yourself,' Lesley said. 'So many ingredients.'

'Lesley's a wonderful cook.' Anna's hand rested on Scott's thigh. We can do this, she thought at him, at herself. Okay, he thought back, if you say so — even though, actually, it was impossible. She was eating, he noticed, not much, but even so, eating. Broccoli. Noodles. Shrimp in ginger.

'Soy, anyone?'

'Yes!'

'Say *please*. And not too much, Frankie. It's basically *salt*. Why,' Lesley asked, 'do they like *everything* that's bad for them? Now there's a bit of scientific research that someone should do!' Vik helped himself to rice and then paused, serving spoon aloft.

'Scott, I missed whatever you said before—'

'They met on the dig,' Lesley filled in: an obvious rescue attempt. Nice woman, thought Scott. Much appreciated: he couldn't put up with much more of this pressing around the sore point of his life, what are you? And especially not now. Yet there it was: the feeling of her beside him, the knowledge that if he was struck blind, he'd know her by touch and scent. So, he told himself, suck it up.

Vik wound noodles on his fork.

'Anna's never much let us into her private life before—'

'Stop it, Vik,' Lesley said. 'You two must feel like you're being interrogated.'

'Well—'

'Really,' Lesley said, 'the main thing is we're so glad you came. Kids, if you've finished eating, I think it's time for bed.'

The two women upstairs, Vik and Scott loading the dishes, and then waiting by the fire.

What could he say now? Why had she left him here? *Come on*, Scott told himself, it doesn't matter. This is nothing at all.

'Anna always says that not everyone has to live the same way,' Vik was saying. 'True, of course, but — may I be frank?'

'Vik,' Scott sat as straight as was possible in the soft leather armchair, 'Let's leave this for now? There's something we have to tell you once the kids are asleep.'

'That sounds exciting!' Lesley called out as she re-entered the room and sat down next to Vik. Two couples in a living room. He was terrified that he would break down.

It was far worse, Anna thought, for the person receiving the news than it was for her, giving it. *News* was the wrong word, she thought, so was *told*. The news itself was like some kind of disease and this transaction, the transmitting of it, the way it was given, announced, inflicted upon the person receiving it was, however you led up to it, an assault.

'This will be a shock. We were at the hospital today and I have just tested positive for HD.'

Telling Vik, she could at last cry. Scott had cried there in the consulting room, and later when they walked together by the river, but she had felt almost detached. But now Vik was holding her and both of them wept, and Scott was dry-eyed as he moved over to comfort Lesley. Perhaps it was the effect of some kind of stress chemical in his bloodstream, but now that the words had been spoken, the news passed on, he had a feeling of almost supernatural power, of an inexhaustible source deep inside him: there was nothing he could not do or make go his way, no bad luck that could not be transformed into its opposite, nothing he could not make happen or protect Anna from.

'Everything is fine now,' he said later when the first wave of shock had passed and the questions began. 'It'll likely be some years before there are noticeable symptoms. The way I see it, it would be crazy to spend all our time thinking about when it might finally get to us.'

'Dr Persaud,' Anna pointed out, 'did detect some saccadic deficiency...eye movements.'

'You don't notice it, though, do you? Do you? Does anyone else?' Scott asked. 'Everything is fine now.'

And when they woke, late the next day, half of the snow had melted. Everything was dripping. A steady, warm wind blew from the west. Rushes of soft wet snow slid down the roof. To the west, above the mountains, stretched an arch of blue sky, while above them a seething, boiling mass of cloud is streamed east. He'd not seen the Chinook before, and called everyone out to see.

They slipped deeper into winter, the whole canyon snow-coated and the hoodoo formations capped with blobs of white. There were pink, cloudless skies to the east.

Almost certainly, Anna thought, she was in denial, but at times it felt as if the most difficult thing was dealing with Vik. Naturally he worried a great deal. He had thought everything through hypothetically for himself, years ago, was only trying to help. He wanted to know her plans and intentions. Between visits and after them, he called.

'The thing is, if you tell the administration at the museum,' he said, 'they'll start thinking about it from the institution's point of view: when and how to replace you.'

'I'm quite interested in that, too. I want to have some input.'

'And as for colleagues — with the best will in the world, most people can't keep anything to themselves—'

'True. And I *know* how I used to be, but now I have the

result, it's suddenly very uncomfortable to have a conversation with, say, Brian, who has always been so kind, knowing he doesn't know. I've worked with him for years... And I really don't think the museum would take advantage. They're not like big business, Vik.'

'Look,' Vik said, 'is Scott around? Can I have a word with him?' Before she knew it, she had slammed the receiver back into the set.

'He always thinks he knows best!' she yelled at Scott on her way upstairs.

Vik called right back.

'Scott? I didn't want to upset Anna, but I'm concerned — after all this time telling no one a thing, it seems as if she might be losing her sense of what's prudent. Maybe you have some influence?'

'I guess she has to do it her way. The people at the museum seem pretty cool.'

'Scott,' Vik's voice was tight, 'how much experience do you have of the politics and backbiting that goes on in an academic institution? And, I've got to wonder, where are you in all this? Where are you coming from?'

'I am your sister's lover,' Scott said, and there were several seconds of complete silence on the end of the line before they both hung up.

'He thinks you're after my money,' Anna explained, 'but he's trained to think that way.'

'Oh, so okay then. No problem!' he said and it was scream or laugh: they laughed, standing in front of the window she'd flung open, with the crescent moon bright in the sky and the cold gushing in like a liquid form of light.

'I wouldn't care if you were,' she said. Though for him it was not comfortable: he had picked up some work but she had twice paid off his credit card. The second time had been a large amount because he'd bought a laptop on sale. And of course she had paid for the courses she had insisted he sign up for. Many were online, but for English, he'd had to join in with the regular high school class in town, twenty-two kids and just one other adult, Norah, seventy-two, wild white hair thinning over a bright pink scalp, who did one course at a time to keep her brain ticking over. Norah and Scott sat together right at the front of the class, and he drove her home at the end of it. The fact was he needed a vehicle of his own, and Anna would get him one — not new, but something he could live with.

She paid for the ski trip, too: three days, taking Frankie and Sam with them to give their parents a break. Scott was shocked by how much he liked it — the drive up through the snow, the weird superclean, overwarm apartment painted almost white to match the outside, the fireplace, and couches, the huge window full of blue sky and mountain, and then, outside, the bite of the air and the sudden freedom of movement, gliding on the skis he had borrowed from Vik towards the lifts, ahead of him the two waist-high kids with their short legs spread absurdly wide. He was grateful that his own legs remembered what to do.

At the end of the first day, they simmered in a vast hot tub, the steam rising all around, and their hair froze on the way back in, even though their feet were still hot.

The kids were booked in at the ski school and so they went higher, into the blues and then the blacks, the slope vertical-seeming, dizzying if you let yourself think that way, but he turned to her and said, 'Right?' and she pushed away. It was still the same, all flow, looking ahead, feeling her way towards the turns and seeing how fast it could be. They each knew where the other was and they wove across each other's paths as they sped on down. All around, other goggled people in other bright jackets wove their way down too, and the entire resort was like some kind of machine in perpetual motion. The snowflakes that started to fall in the afternoon were just another part of it and stopping, stillness, was impossible. At the end of the day they were too tired to speak or sit and fell asleep with the kids in their bed with the TV on.

She could still do it. Scott was right: there was nothing wrong with her at all and in the white glare of the snow, in its vastness and strangeness they forgot everything else that was happening or might be, talked only of the qualities of snow, the runs, of where to go next and tomorrow, what to eat. But on the last day, they dropped the kids for their lesson and returned to the apartment where their skins surprised them, suddenly colourful in the dazzling light reflected from the white walls and the white outside. Hers was flushed with purples and blues; his had become brown, every hair and scar and crease as if freshly inked.

They lay together on the sofa and listened to Mozart turned up very loud because he found he could actually like it that way.

Six months, she had predicted at the beginning, that was how long it would last. But now she thought perhaps nine. He would have finished all his courses by then.

'The heat will go out of it. The situation will sink in. Promise you won't hang in with me out of guilt.' She made him promise formally, say the words aloud, which he did, but somehow managed to make them funny.

'Have you thought,' she said, 'that it might only be because of this disease that I've become involved with you in the first place: *disinhibition*, have you thought of that?'

'No,' he said, taking hold of her foot, letting it wash over him like the music itself.

'Have you thought you might be just a distraction?' The word *just* he really didn't like. But hell, why not. She was weird and wonderful, brave, beautiful, astounding, addictive: it seemed to him that she deserved a distraction, just as she deserved every one of the teams of scientists and graduate students who were injecting viruses into mouse-brains in order to find a way to turn off the HD gene, or working out just exactly what the mutant protein, Huntingtin, actually did, good or bad, and the drugs people, and all those who have gone before them.

She frowned, studied him some more.

'What are you—?'

'What *am I*?'

'What *are* you doing here with me?' What did she think? He widened his eyes, covered his ears.

'Listening to your fucking music!'

It snowed as they left the mountain. Frankie and Sam fought in the back of the car all the way home.

'Shall I drive this monster of yours?' Anna asked as they left Vik and Lesley on the porch and made for the GMC she had surprised him with at Christmas. She laughed at herself as she settled into the too-big driver's seat, got the heat going and set the wipers to scrape off the snow.

Scott pushed his seat back. The aches in his legs reminded him all over again of the whiteout world where nothing mattered except how you took the turn. He plugged into his own sounds, tapped along to the beat.

The road was familiar now: the glittering belt around the city, the sudden emptiness once they turned off. They were going home: that was how he thought of her place now.

The road unreeled ahead of them, dusted white and even quieter than normal. Anna drove on, quite liking the car despite herself. Scott thought how he could sleep, if he wanted to, and thinking it made him want: halfway down a remembered run, his muscles let go, his mind emptied itself. He was almost there, when lights flared to the left.

'Stop!' he yelled reaching for her arm; there was a terrible noise, and then nothing at all.

34

***

ANNA'S LEG WAS IN A CAST, and the first time he saw her afterwards she was in a wheelchair with it stuck out in front of her. His head was bandaged and they both were wore neck supports. He had a black eye; her face was puffy and unfamiliar, cross-hatched with small cuts. Her eyes looked smaller than they used to be. She had a patch shaved along the side of her head and a row of ten stitches in the white-blue skin of her scalp. Between them they had five cracked ribs, a quantity of bruises, dislocations and cuts too many to count, but none of it mat-tered at all, except perhaps, that it hurt to smile. They could be dead. Him, or her, both. Or in a coma, or paralysed, any com-bination of the above, but here they were. It was, Scott thought, the most amazing piece of luck!

'Scott—' her voice was muffled by the bandage that covered his ear. He pulled it off.

'I nearly killed you. I should have accelerated, not—'

'No. The *truck driver* should have stopped. *He* was speeding. Vik says it's absolutely clear.'

Set free, they staggered out of the hospital doors and into the first of many cabs, their pockets stuffed with appointment cards and rattling with pills, and everything, even the concrete, looked bright and new.

'Keep all the receipts, everything,' Vik warned them, 'for the insurance. I will handle all that.'

✦ ✦ ✦

Her hair was a mess as it grew back. Scott shaved his head to keep her company and when they went together to the museum the technicians in the preparation room pushed back their masks, turned off their micro-abraders and drills and, in the sudden silence that fell, made feeble jokes about their casts: what strange specimens these were!

'Are you bringing yourselves in?' Lin asked, offering them both her not-quite smile. 'Where's the paperwork? Humans being so common, you will be way down the line, I'm afraid.'

A length of pterosaur jaw longer than Scott's arm was partly exposed, revealing a strange bony crest at the end and two rows of sharply pointed teeth, widely spaced. On another bench, the slender bones of the left arm and hand were beginning to emerge from the shale: the gifts of stone.

She worked, but not too much: her report on Big Crow, a couple of documents in connection with the Big Crow River cultural centre. She was working on him, too: improving his math, making sure he scored well in tests. To begin with, he fetched things to save her heaving up out of her chair; she typed for him and even once cut up his food, but then their disabilities, even as they diminished, became part of their lives.

Anna received a handwritten envelope, inside it a card featuring tiny flowers in an arctic meadow.

Dear Anna, it said. *I am shocked to learn about your health and the recent accident too. I also am going through a very difficult time. I may have been somewhat abrupt in the past and do hope we can forget our previous difficulties. Best wishes from Lily and myself.*

Yours truly, he had signed it, *Mike.* The tribunal, she knew from Greta was only weeks away. She dropped the card in the recycling bin along with the local news, supermarket flyers and credit card company solicitations.

35

AN ATHLETIC-LOOKING WOMAN with dark hair in a knot at the back of her head met them at the door of what could almost have been a private house, but for the health authority sign and the wheelchair ramp outside.

'Linda Sampson. I remember speaking to you, Anna,' she said, nodding and smiling as they shook hands.

They followed her to a large room with a coffee maker in one corner and some plates covered with Saran wrap laid out on a table by the wall. There was a circle of widely spaced chairs in the middle of the room. Despite it being May now, some tired-looking tinsel from Christmas was still pinned around the windows. It was very warm even with the window wide open.

'Quite a few partners are coming today,' Linda told Scott. 'The partners and carers meet informally in here, while the group takes place in the room across from here — for about an hour. Then we all get together for a social at the end.'

'I believe you were diagnosed quite recently, Anna? Many of the people in the group are further progressed than you. They'll have a lot to pass on.'

There were footsteps in the corridor and voices — a woman's calling out

'Linda, you in there?' and then the woman herself, plump and flushed, her hair in tight curls; her husband, a gaunt man, hollow-eyed, with a fixed stare, his limbs twitching and jerking, in a strange, endless dance.

'Gloria and Ian,' Linda said.

'Everyone's coming,' Gloria told them. 'Full house today.'

Linda briefly clasped her hand onto Ian's shoulder, and introduced the two couples. She spoke slowly, and gestured at each person as she said the names, and then waited, smiling at Ian.

'Pleased to— meet you,' he said after a slight delay, the *s* slurred into a shushing sound, the syllables stretched out of shape. Like a drunk, Scott thought. Like Mac used to be.

'I'm going across to the other room now,' Linda gestured in the direction she was about to take, waited for Ian to accompany her.

Anna squeezed Scott's arm.

'Okay?' she asked, and then, before he could say no, she joined Ian and Linda. He was on his own.

People came noisily along the corridor and into the room, the women putting plates of food on the table and hanging their purses over the backs of chairs.

'This is Scott. His wife, Anna, has just been diagnosed,' Gloria said and the newcomers shook Scott's hand, hugged each other and went to get coffee. Most people were middle-aged women but Jade — her skin powdered white, hair dyed black, three studs in one side of her nose — was probably still in high school, or could have been. She wore black with a purple poncho on top.

'So you're still in shock, then,' she said. 'I bring my dad. He drives mum nuts and we don't get to town much, so she's shopping.'

'Nuts?' Gloria called out, her curls bobbing as she threw her head back. 'Tell me about it.' Others nearby laughed too. 'He *still* won't give up. And he can't do anything much, but it's really upsetting, you know — when you do think, sometimes, at the end of the day that you'd like someone to snuggle up with. And you can remember how you started out.' She teared up briefly, and then shrugged. 'That was another life. What we do a lot of in this group,' she continued, looking at Scott, 'is *complain*. But today, we'll try hard to keep it in check, because you are new, okay?' There was more laughter.

'How are things, Jo?' Gloria asked a tired-looking woman with long mousy hair in a loose French braid. It was impossible to tell her age.

'Well, I've made progress,' she said. 'I made word cards, like Linda mentioned in the email, and we're really getting through. His frustration level's gone way down. He's almost himself.'

'The thing is,' said the trim, silver-haired man next to Scott, 'you have the muscular problems, but also the cognitive deficit, and speech is where they come together, you really have to work to get through. But you can, that's the thing, you can. I'm Carl,' he said, offering a hand. 'How long have you and your wife been together?'

'We're not married. We met last year,' Scott said. But time, he reminded himself, was not the point. What happened in it is what matters. A minute could matter more than a month. 'She's got no symptoms,' he said.

'Good,' Carl smiled. 'That's good.' Some kind of shouting, a ragged sound, reached them from across the corridor.

'Chants,' Carl said, reaching in his jacket for his wallet and flipping it open. 'That's how they begin. There she is.' A woman in a low-cut evening dress with an up-do and earrings looked out of the tiny photograph.

'Twenty-five years,' Carl said. 'Last eight have been a challenge. Gave up work, and so on. Big change. Daughter helps when she can but she's got her own problems. You get to know how you feel...what's important.' Jade tapped Scott on the arm.

'Can't smoke in here,' she said. 'Want one?' Scott went out with her anyhow, stood on the porch while she blew out gusts of fragrant smoke.

'My grandmother used to live with us, and she died of it. One of my uncles has it and my aunt is getting it too. It scared me when I was a kid. Now I think, okay, he's the same Dad underneath it.

'You have to have a sense of humour. Get one if you don't already. Have a laugh. It's okay. I might get tested in a year or two...dunno. Have to see.'

Back inside, Jade made for the washroom. Scott passed the closed door to the other room and stood outside. What was she doing in there? Why had she insisted on this?

Before he knew it, he'd opened the door.

There were more people than he'd expected. He couldn't see Anna, just the backs of heads and a man sitting opposite the door in an armchair, his fingers rising and falling as if he were conducting an underwater orchestra. The man next to him had a bruise on his face and was saying how he hated not to drive anymore.

At last Scott saw her, over to the left, sitting with her hands in her lap and leaning forward to listen, her eyes very bright.

'Is something the matter, Scott?' Linda asked, coming over to the door. 'Distractions create anxiety. Please don't interrupt us.'

Carl was explaining his exercise regime.

'Every morning, I get Sonia up,' he said, 'and I go. Five miles. If the weather's bad, I have a treadmill in the basement. Endorphins. It's the key.'

'I don't blame anyone,' Angela said when Carl went over to talk to Gloria, 'but there just aren't many men who hang in like Carl has. Josef—' she pointed to a man of about thirty, skinny, balding, with several earrings in one ear, who stood by the coffee urn, 'He's a Home Care Assistant.'

Names and faces were beginning to blur by the time Linda appeared at the door. Some went to help their partners, and others pulled the film off the plates and started to fill a cluster of spouted baby cups that had appeared by the drinks. Anna came in just after the man who was talking about not driving — Con, it turned out, who was with Angela. She helped him into a chair, leaned over and put her cheek next to his.

Anna put her arm around Scott, asked for the second time if he was okay.

Anna took Scott around the room, introduced him to Amy, in the wheelchair, to Keith — bright-eyed, beaming — who intended to compete in a triathlon in the spring.

'I'll email Anna a regime. Cardiovascular work and antioxidants.'

Everyone was talking at once. Sausage rolls, quiches, cookies and pieces of chocolate cake did the rounds. Not everyone ate.

Andy was a blob of a man in t-shirt that said he was *Not mad, but getting there.* His wife left him and despite his symptoms he was still looking after two teenaged kids: 'We work it out. Keeps me going.'

Greg, Sharon, Ben. Company director. Teacher. Unemployed.

Carl was sitting next to a bone-thin woman in a wheelchair who looked twenty years older than him and nothing at all like the Sonia in the photograph.

How long? was what Scott suddenly wanted to know. How long did it take to get like this?

'People are getting tired and time's running out for those of you who came on the bus. Let's have our song.'

Gloria stepped forward, looked around and began. Her voice poured out of her: it was like a creature that lived locked inside her and had been let out for a rare minute or two. *I'm singin' in the rain, just singin' in the rain...* Her eyes moved around the room, settling briefly on someone and then moving on. Before the end of the second line, other people were joining her: high wavering voices, grumbles in the boots, monotones. Scott raised an eyebrow at Anna, and then thought *Why not?*

I'm laughin' at clouds... So dark up above...

He heard Anna's voice, high but steady, part of the inner core of coherence surrounded by the notes that were off, the notes two beats too late: *Come on with the rain, I've a smile on my face.* Some people meant it, some hammed it up and somehow, it sounded all right: *Just singin', singin' in the rain!*

After the applause at the end people gathered up their be-longings and prepared for a mass exodus for the disability buses outside.

'Do you celebrate Easter?' Carl asked, his hand on Sonia's shoulder. 'My daughter will be visiting. And I'm taking a short break with a lady friend of mine, someone I met online.' He winked, made for the door.

'So very difficult,' Anna said in bed that night, 'to know I must change so much.'

'But when it happens, you'll be good at it.' He said *when* but was thinking *not yet,* and he was also thinking *if,* because it was true that at any point there could be a breakthrough: if not cure, treatment. Thinking *if* did not mean that he was running away from things. In a way, it was more realistic, not less. You had to hold it all in your mind at once and it was hard to do.

Later he sat up in bed while Anna slept. His head was full of the people from the meeting: Carl and Sonia, Jade, Gloria, and also of the people he and Anna might each become.

He thought, too, of his father, now living a sober life with Orianna, attending church every week, meetings every day, and, because of Orianna's seasonal affective disorder, already plan-ning next winter's trip south to an apartment in Puerto Vallarta she could borrow from a friend of her daughter's. *Perhaps you and your lady-friend will visit us, son.* Maybe it wouldn't last, but who would have thought it could happen at all?

It was strange to think of himself as say, ten years older. Heavier, the first lines. The way he felt and saw things would change slowly, over a period of time, likewise for Anna, and then a day would come when they had to acknowledge that it had become something different. He had to accept that what was between them now would in the end turn, as one of the booklets Anna had sent for from the society had explained, into *a relationship of dependency and care, which is often very difficult for one or both partners to adjust to.*

He understood why she had insisted on going to the meeting, even though they had no need of it yet, why she had put herself through it, for him. She's telling me I can leave, he thought. I can leave tomorrow, if I want to and I know she won't blame me.

Yet he didn't want to. He wanted to go all the way. Further out, deeper in, and on to the bitter end, which he would somehow make sweet.

36

———◆———

THEY HAD CELEBRATED HIS EXAMS and Greta's victory in the tribunal. He had been living with Anna for ten months when she came and sat next to him in the kitchen and quite simply told him it was over.

'I don't want to continue... So what I'm thinking,' she said, very slowly and carefully, 'is that you could use Mama's room while you decide what your plans are.'

What she was saying did not match her voice.

'I do believe what you say, absolutely,' she told him, 'but I want you to have another life.'

When he reached for her she shoved him away and his hip glanced on the corner of the counter: it was a shock to feel her fight him and then he wanted to fight her back. He had her by the arm, would not let go. A chair clattered to the floor. His heart punched at the walls of his chest, he was ready to overcome her, wanted to hurt.

'No— I can't stand this! I just can't!' she shouted. The shock of what he was doing loosened his grip and she twisted free.

After that, he would not stay there, not one night. He took a bag of stuff and the letter she'd written him and drove back to Big Crow even though he knew Mac and Orianna were staying with her daughter, even though he knew being there was likely the worst thing he could do. He drove when he should have slept, put miles behind him — between him and her — as fast as he could.

The window had been fixed. The lights worked. The refrigerator and the stove had been unplugged; Scott hooked them up again, unloaded his beer and vodka into the fridge. There was no plan, except to knock himself out, to obliterate his memory of Anna any way possible. And perhaps as well as that, to show her: Did she think of *this* possibility? Was this what she had meant by *another life*?

He had a good example to follow, and he did a thorough job of it, stretched on the sofa with the drink within reach, watching TV and forgetting it as he watched, falling asleep, drinking some more, emerging only for liquid supplies, a bottle and a case, from the liquor store. Some time passed.

It seemed very early, but was actually around noon, when knocking on the door dragged him back into the room: he was on the couch. Light shimmered painfully through the lace curtain. Scott yelled to go away. He lay there, still, his skull throbbing, and whoever it was outside began knocking again. He pushed himself up and negotiated a path through furniture that seemed to lurch at him; he reached the door, struggled with the matter of opening it. Who the hell?

'Thompson.'

'Long time. Alan said to look you up. You look rough. Can I come in?' Thompson looked the opposite of rough: he moved easily and talked freely. His hair was longer, washed and shiny, caught in a ponytail at the back. He glanced around the trailer, and then kept his eyes on Scott.

Scott reached the sofa again. He closed his eyes.

'Got coffee?' The sounds of Thompson washing cups and scraping coffee out of the tin seemed to Scott like some kind of personal assault, though the smell was surprisingly good; he opened his eyes, warmed his hands on the cup; he thought that he heard for a moment or two the sound of the ravens' wing-beats, felt the air on his face as they soared up above the edge of the cliff. Things had been very different then. Now, all that felt like an imaginary world, a fantasy.

Thompson watched him drink.

'You could get stuck in this shit,' he said. 'They say alcoholism is partly genetic. It's a physical thing. You especially don't want to be doing this.'

No? Exactly what did Thompson think he should be doing, then? It was a mistake, Scott realised, to have asked because just like everyone else on the planet, Thompson had a plan for him, one he had heard before: Scott should study.

'Open up, man. The point is, get wise and get a degree at the same time,' Thompson said. 'Anthropology, Law, Education, whatever. Look at your cultural background, the history and politics of it, past, present and future. Develop skills and re-connect to your mother's side of the family, and at the end of it you're qualified to do something worthwhile.'

'So where are you sending me?' Scott asked, his head back in the cushions, every inch of him committed to gravity: 'You got that picked? I can't,' he said. The c word had lost its terrors; it was a friend after all. 'I can't do it. Leave me be, okay?'

Feeling Thompson's eyes on him he was aware, suddenly, of how he must look: stubble, red eyes, slept-in clothes. A tsunami of self-pity engulfed him as he watched the other man put down his cup and make to leave. But at the door Thompson turned back:

'Look Scott,' he said, 'forget the detail. Why not just come back to the city with me and take a look at things. There's a spare bed in our house right now.'

37

——— ✦ ———

HE WORKED AT A RESTAURANT CALLED FLUX, hung out with Thompson and his student friends. It was months before he could bear to slip the CD Anna had left for him into the drive, to allow her words to appear in clinical Verdana on the screen of his laptop and hear the voice they conjured up, telling him about what was now the past.

I have woken each day and felt my spirits lift because you were there beside me or somewhere in the house. But increasingly, as the reality of this diagnosis sinks in, I need to set you free of me. That day at Vik's when the Chinook blew and you stood there with your shirt flapping and your head craned back to look at the clouds, I thought my heart would burst, but also I knew that if need be — if things did not come to a natural end — then I must do this.

I believe you when you say you could cope with what is ahead of me, but because I believe you, I want your life to be otherwise. I want to know that you are out in the world, and that countless other possibilities are ahead of you. But it is only with great effort that I do what does sometimes seem perverse.

You've altered me. Everything is the same yet different. There is a shine to things that there was not before. Even now.

I'm no longer afraid, or never for very long.

I will miss you, and I hate to make you sad. I want you to know how glad I am that we have been together for these past months. If I am honest, I do not want you to forget me, but rather to understand, and to see this parting as a kind of love. And I want you to know, too, that I will be all right.

Scott hated the letter, but did not destroy it. Sometimes he thought he hated Anna too, but when he read that genetic manipulation looked likely to halt the progress of HD in mice he still wanted to be able to dance around the room together, crying out *You see? You see?* Teams of people were working on it all over the world, but this piece of research was happening right here in the university Thompson attended. Could he do something like that? Wear a white coat and chop life up under a microscope or whatever it was that they actually did? Save her, so that she would have him back? Though it was people he liked, not the bits they were made of, not the pieces of code: he liked the girl with the white cane whose mother came every day to meet her at the bus stop right outside their house; he liked Simon B, a Haida performance poet who was going to move into their house, and Helena Michaels, mother of three, studying law part-time for the next god knows how long, and his co-worker Aidan who was building a straw bale house over by the Centre for Horticultural Studies. Thompson himself.

'Why so heroic? Hundreds of communities don't have a physician,' Thompson pointed out. Why so expensive? Scott countered. To be one of those took about ten years and countless thousands of dollars, not to speak of dedication and ambition; highly educated, amply supported middle-class kids murdered each other for places, for the right to dissect corpses and fill their well-disciplined minds with Greek and Latin words. Though it was true, also, that he had stood on the hot shale and laughed with Anna about the bones of the arm and hand; he did know that words were just squiggles on the page, wave patterns in air which vibrated the eardrum, stimulated the nerve and somehow, in the depths of the brain, became sounds, the names of things you didn't ordinarily see — that they were no more and no less than that. He could learn them when he wanted to, could like it, even, so long as it took him to a place that made sense.

Don't push me, he told Thompson.

A BSc, perhaps, at most, he privately thought, and if he got that far, think again. Months before he even considered signing up for his first class, he ordered a life-sized skeleton with moveable joints and display stand, which arrived in pieces in a box the size of a dryer; he spent the next two days in the living room of the shared house on East Fifth, assembling it with the aid of the diagram. It was a 3D jigsaw; it was simple mechanics, a list of words; but also, it implied a person, someone whose problem you could fix, improve at very least. Once he had the bones and the joints filed in his brain, he could begin to visualise the large muscles and their attachments, could find the things themselves on Thompson or any other willing body; could feel them, glowing, illuminated inside himself as he pushed up the hill on his bike or wove between the tables at Flux.

38

———— ✦ ————

ANNA WAS BACK FROM A WALK, hot and exhausted, and if she had known who was calling, she would not have taken the call. But the ringing continued, and she pressed *Talk*.

'Is that you, Anna?'

He had to ask, she knew, because her voice was different. It was slower, and it seemed to belong to someone slightly drunk who was trying very hard to appear sober. And also Roger stood watching her, panting and needing water. She was sweating hard, her heart battering in her chest. But Scott's voice was absolutely the same, and she did not hang up.

Yes, she agreed. It was a very long time since they had spoken. Were things going well for him? Yes, he said, they were.

'I'm wondering if it's possible to visit,' he said. Even then, she was going to say that no, she still thought it best, from a purely selfish point of view, to just leave things in the past. 'I have a friend, Lenni,' he told her, 'who would like to meet you. I think you'll like her.'

He travelled with Lenni by bus from Calgary, back into the landscape of his former life. They shared his MP3, listened to the same music — but they were not together: she had the window seat and stared calmly out at the shimmering blue sky and the golden or glaring yellow fields to either side; he was sweating silently beside her, his eyes mostly closed as they proceeded down the road that he and Anna had driven many times, as they passed the exact junction where the truck had blindsided them.

She sounds quite something. A hard act to follow, Lenni had told Scott when they arrived at the History Stage — that sticky moment when a woman he'd been seeing would look into his eyes and then away again, then back, maybe stroke his hand, or fiddle with the fringe on her jacket or bite at a nail, then stop herself, start again. Perhaps she'd cry a bit as she explained how her ex two-timed her, or she him; how it stopped being fun, or how he was so jealous and it was stifling, or she wanted to live together but he didn't or they did live together but fought all the time, or alternatively never fought at all but the spark went right out of it... Then she'd dry her eyes, smile, say: 'What about you?'

Like, forty? That's kinda weird.

But it doesn't sound, you know, like it could have gone anywhere.

How sad.

'I'd like to meet Anna,' Lenni had said. 'Seriously, I would.'

But why? And what the hell was he doing, going along with it? Why, four years — *four whole years* — down the line, when he had finally gotten over her, had he dialled Anna's number? Why was she allowing them to visit? Suppose he had brought Lenni all this way just to discover that he still belonged to Anna, always would? Suppose he lost her, too?

She sat quietly next to him, studying the landscape, reading the names of signs. An important part of Lenni, Scott was beginning to understand, was that if she was afraid of something, she would neither run away nor ignore it. She would quite deliberately turn and face it, get to know it as intimately as she could.

Lenni made me do this, he told himself.

Because physically it was not a good day, Janice had driven Anna downtown to meet them at the Greyhound stop by the convenience store. It was very warm still, the light was just fading. Most of the town was closed and still, but they could hear the highway traffic and some music from a café down the street. Anna was torn between excitement and dread. What would it be like after all this time, to see him? What would it be like for him to emerge into the gritty light and heat of summer dusk and see Janice standing close to a suntanned woman in loose khaki shorts, much thinner than he remembered? Who had grey in her hair and looked older, now, than her age? Would he notice the difference in her eyes, the stare? That between movements, her face looked somehow stiff?

Of course he would — and now the bus was upon them and its doors hissed open. She concentrated, frowning up at the passengers as they emerged: two large women in bright track pants, an assortment of old men and boys, a young woman carrying a backpack, tall, and alert in the way that creatures are and people often are not. Then Scott.

Should she have been surprised that he too looked different? That at first she couldn't speak, and then all she could do was shout out his name in her new voice?

'Scott!'

The hug was not a simple thing; she knew it was awful for

him to feel the unwelcome dance inside her, whereas, through the damp fabric of his shirt, her hands registered only a strong back, the familiar protrusions of his spine.

'There,' she told him, sensing tears before she saw them. 'Don't worry. I'm doing well.' They stepped back from each other and Lenni offered her hand.

'I'm very pleased to meet you,' Lenni said, and her large grey eyes sought Anna's as she spoke, and did not shy away. She wanted, Anna felt, to know exactly how things were.

In the car, when Anna turned to answer a question about the museum she saw them together: dark and light, Scott's hand on Lenni's thigh, the way they leaned into each other without meaning to, how they didn't need to look at each other in order to communicate, and yet could not stop themselves from doing so, and she cursed herself for allowing the visit. She saw Scott, his strong back and his complex history, fully awake now and connected to his own life, who would commit and mean it, fight for what he wanted, suffer and recover, transformed, if he should lose: a man who'd called her name out in the night, who had wanted to walk alongside her on her own difficult road. Who could have done so, who would have found a way, somehow, eventually, to something good, to whom she had eventually said, *No.*

His face was a little older now: the planes of it more defined, the gaze steadier. He wore his hair longer, but there he was. And she saw the other woman in all her glory, passionate, intelligent, and curious. Lucky, young and whole.

This was what she had wanted. But it was so far easier to know about in the abstract than it was to accept in the flesh. It took strength to get through dinner: the serving of the food

Janice had prepared, the pouring of wine.

That night she lay in her bed and heard the low murmur of their talk in the room below, a burst of laughter, the running of water in the shower, the opening of a window, and wept. It was as if stones were in her chest and she had to push them out. It felt like a kind of work. Eventually she could breathe normally again, felt her face relax, her body dissolve into a strange, empty lightness.

Scott was sleeping with his girlfriend Lenni in her mother's room below. They would eat breakfast together in the morning, and then she would show them around, and not forget to invite them to the opening party next June.

After the preparation room and the moulding facility, where technicians were already working to make resin replicas of the skull and other finished parts, the three of them wandered through the newly completed Cretaceous garden. The path wove through a crush of ginkgos, huge ferns and horsetail, then past a waterfall, and a pool with spiny, greyish fish. The air, warm, saturated, had a tang of must and rot about it. Water dripped from the ferns and dogwoods on the bank above the benches they sat on and with no warning, warm mist hissed from concealed valves, drenching them, coating all the leaves.

39

——— ✦ ———

AT SIX, THE LIGHT IS STILL STRONG, the rock and asphalt throw back the day's accumulated heat. Scott parks the old Volvo in the staff lot next to Janice's Honda and he, Anna and Lenni climb out and then walk together along the sandstone path, past the pond habitat and the fountain. Anna's movements are pretty much constant now, and they slow her down. She wears flat shoes, and, in honour of the occasion, black pants and a new raw silk shirt, exactly the kind of thing Mama would have liked. Together, the three of them approach the visitors' entrance to the museum (this — the sun warmed stone of the wall, the sudden shade as they pass through the first doors, Scott's hand on her elbow, Lenni's gasp as they see the display, Brian shouting out their names — all this might not have been, she thinks, but is).

In the entrance hall, just where she always imagined it, the pterosaur swoops down above them, big as an airplane, its spike-toothed jaw partway open, its vast cartilaginous wing membranes suggested by the long bones of the arm which seem to run straight into the tapering wing finger on each side. The vertebral column cuts a diagonal line through space, diminishing towards the tail. The legs are tucked back and up — all of it has been coated unevenly with a gold finish that here and there catches the light from both above and below. As Scott looks up he could almost hear and feel the rush of air.

'Nylon wires...much heavier...than the original,' Anna explains to Lenni, 'Resin. Much stronger too... One of four made. Had to...fight like blazes to have it coloured that way... Alan, Thompson! Good to see you... You know... Lenni, of course.' Beneath the swooping pterosaur the much smaller people in the room hug and shake hands, move towards the tables at the back of the room.

'Maybe she's after our canapés,' Lin says, looking up, before she slips a cube of cheese into her mouth.

'Looks like a guy to me!' A reporter from the *Globe* grins across at Greta, who is wearing a skirt with a matching jacket; she nods back without returning the smile. *Curator, Marine and Flying Reptiles*, her name tag announces. *Director, Preparation* reads Lin's. *Palaeontologist* is Anna's description. She does have an official institutional title: *Research Associate*, which means whatever Greta and she make of it, but perhaps Andrew, when making up the tags, felt it was more tactful to generalise.

'The actual specimen,' Greta tells the reporter, 'along with one of the replicas, will go back to Big Crow as soon as the new Cultural Centre is finished. You must talk to Dr Silowski about that story. She's the one who—'

Though Anna is wary of too much talk now, of too much of anything. The room is filling fast and she has to say a few words later. Her voice does well enough, but as she tires, she becomes slower. She has to wait for the words to come to her, and sometimes they won't and she grinds to an impossible, in-furiating halt. So, champagne later, but water for now: *I'll need what's left of my faculties*, she thinks. And should she spill, there won't be a mark. You have to think this way.

Linda Sampson from the HD Society has driven all the way from the city to bring Keith from the group.

'You're looking good!' he says, as he hugs her a little too hard and too long. The entire museum staff, along with Janice and Don; Vik, Lesley, Frankie, Sam, Maddy and Chrissie — the twins waist-high now — are already here. Felix has brought a friend; the celebrity guest, Ben Morris, is flying in from the US and must be somewhere on the road right now; Maiko and Akira have been here most of the week. Friends, colleagues, the great and the good — the PhDs, the VIPs — it seems that everyone she is connected to, past, present, future will be in this room, although Michael Swenson, working again now in Alaska, did not reply to his invitation.

'If he accepts,' Scott said when he heard that Anna, in con-sultation with Greta, had actually *suggested* inviting him, 'I can't promise he won't suffer for it.' Even now, part of him is ex-pecting the bastard to materialise like the bad fairy at the birthday party. He keeps checking the door.

On the right-hand wall, just where the entrance hall leads on into the galleries proper, a small red velvet curtain hangs at head height, the string ready for Anna to draw at eight, when every-one will be here. Meanwhile the hosts and their guests cluster around the tables set out in the centre of the entrance hall, their voices lost in the huge space.

Lenni, far taller than either Alan or Thompson, leans forward slightly to talk.

'I saw the drawings for the Cultural Centre,' she says to Alan. 'Looks wonderful.'

'Did...Ai Lin take you to see the...real fossil yet?' Anna asks him. 'It's through that door... They left the lids off the...crates. You must see it, Lin is right there, she'll take you.'

Ben Morris strides up. His eyes are bright and inquisitive, his voice warm as he congratulates Anna on her splendid achievement. He has forgotten, she thinks, that he once mistook her for Swenson's assistant — and so will she: it's wonderful that he, the foremost expert in this field, could come.

'Thank you so much for making the trip. This is Alan... Coxtis and Thompson from the Big Crow River First Nation... And Lenni, who's...currently conducting a feasibility...study into a biodiesel bus link between here and downtown Calgary in the summer months... And Scott Macleod, also originally from Big Crow... He was one of our...volunteers.'

She watches as Morris pumps Scott's hand, and asks him the question he used to dislike so much:

'What's your field, then?'

'We have bones in common. I aim to qualify as a physio next year, and specialise in neurological rehabilitation.'

'Anna,' Andrew from Events whispers in her ear, 'just to say don't worry, there *is* a microphone on its way.'

She leans forward to take a sip of water, puts the glass carefully down and then makes her way to the back of the room, where a thick maroon rope, hung from two gold-coloured posts, is looped across the entranceway to the galleries. She slips behind one of the posts and sits on the bench in the half-darkness of the display on geological time. Her movements are not too bad; they may even decrease little, or feel as if they have done so, if she can just relax.

It's the dark, perhaps, that reminds her of the cave her father took her to all those years ago, before he was properly sick, before she knew or suspected anything. There was a long hike, just the two of them, on baking limestone, and then the sudden damp darkness of entrance.

She remembers the earthy smell, the roots pushing through the rock above their heads, the goose bumps that suddenly covered her arms. How she asked him what would happen if the lamp on his helmet went out, and he said that it would not, but even if it did, they would simply feel their way back out: everything would be all right.

They moved forward through a tunnel on their hands and knees and at the end of it entered another underground room, filled with a chalky, wet smell and dripping sounds. Slowly, her eyes became accustomed to the light from the lamp her father had brought, and she saw the forest of stalactites hanging from the roof of the cave like so much melting wax, a creamy colour, here and there streaked with orange. Below them, the stalagmites, softer and growing more slowly, rose to meet them. Occasionally, a mite and a tite had touched, grown together. Everything glistened. For the longest time, she and her father crouched side by side and watched.

'Anna,' Scott says now, sitting next to her in the dark and taking her arm. 'Ready now?' She nods, lets him help her up, lead her back into the bright room that smells of wine and food and warm freshly washed skin.

Scott takes his place in the front row of the crowd and Anna stands near the microphone while Greta introduces her: her career, the find, and her qualities as a scientist, as leader, a colleague, her new work for the HD Society since she retired.

The woman standing not quite still by the microphone is still Anna, Scott thinks, but she has changed, is changing all the time. There are losses ahead, and the endless question of how best to deal with them. He still wishes he could have saved her, knows, too, that she would say that he did. He is glad that he has another life, and also that she is in it.

Anna taps the microphone, coughs.

There are so many people to thank, and a winged creature to offer up — a fragment of the history of life carrying in its narrow pelvis yet another discovery: a single egg, mango-sized, the find within the find, Lin's.

'I'll keep this *very* brief,' she smiles at the faces turned towards her, at Frankie straight, tall and so much grown up, but as eager as ever; at the twins, quiet but not still, at Sam who stares solemnly at her, then suddenly smiles. At Vik. Brian. Thompson. Lenni. Scott.

'First another introduction—'

She pulls the cord and the red curtain draws back, revealing the sandstone plaque, the name incised into it:

'*Agas-to-pte-rus magni-corvi-ensis*: the amazing winged beast... from Big Crow.' She says the name she has chosen part by part, then, gestures at the glittering fretwork of bones above. No mistakes, she thinks, as applause ripples around the room and she too is airborne: blood surges through arteries and capillaries, her lungs fill; air infiltrates every part of her, pushes right into her bones. This world, she thinks. This moment. The people in it.

'I am sure she will continue...to change all your lives and thoughts, as she has mine...' Anna smiles, finds Scott's eyes, studies the card she has propped on the lectern, and then looks up again; cameras flash, magnesium white.

Thanks & Acknowledgments

In retrospect, I can see that this novel was inspired by two things: the beautiful skeleton of an elasmosaur which hangs, invisibly suspended, in the Courtenay & District Museum, and a couple of sentences about genetic testing in an article about biogenetic intervention entitled 'Bring Me My Phillips Mental Jacket,' by Slavoj Žižek, published in the *Times Literary Supplement* and sent to me by my friend Sue Thomas. Between the spark and the finished book are countless hours of daydreaming, reading, research, writing, and rewriting — a huge enterprise, requiring support of many different kinds. I wish to thank all of the people and organisations who helped me, as well as those I do not have space to name here or have forgotten, and even those who did not realise that they were helping. None of them, of course, are responsible in any way for how the book has turned out, or for any errors that I have made.

One of the bonuses of writing fiction that requires research is meeting, face to face, on the page and online fascinating people with knowledge, experience and approaches to the world very different to my own, and being offered a glimpse into their lives. Lorna Cameron and Shari MacDonald were very generous in sharing their experience of coping with HD as sufferer and carer respectively; likewise, generous were Linda MacLaren,

Loretta Young and Dr Michael Trew, who shared with me details of their work in genetic testing and the ongoing support of families with HD. The websites of the Huntington's Disease Societies of the US, UK and Canada were excellent resources. *Mapping Fate* by Alice Wexler was invaluable not just for the scientific and historical background, and as an inspiring story of ongoing collaborative work, but also for the personal material it contains, which deepened my understanding of the emotional and moral complexities of making a choice about genetic testing for a condition that is, currently, incurable.

In every novel, there are many seams between the real and the invented. The work of local historian Chris Arnett opened my eyes to the richness of local First Nation' history and culture, and to their ongoing struggles (the place where I live and work is part of the land claim of the Hul'qumi'num), but Big Crow is an invented town and the First Nation band, the St'alkwextsihn, or Stallquakseen, and their particular language, situation and stories are imaginary. Likewise, parts of *The Find* take place in the National Museum at Greentree, Alberta, a place in many ways like The Royal Tyrell Museum at Drumheller, but fictional rather than real. Staff at the real museum were extremely patient and helpful, and especially so were Don Brinkman, Jim McCabe and Marty Eberth. Monique Keiran's book *Reading the Rocks* was an inspiration; likewise Wayne Grady's *The Bone Museum*, Jack Horner's *Digging Dinosaurs* and *Fossil Legends of the First Americans*, by Adrienne Mayor. I would also like to thank Walter W. Stein for his take on the way palaeontology works, author David Spalding for the many useful references he gave me, and Rolf Ludvigsen for his book *West Coast Fossils*, as well as for his advice. Author Brian

Brett directed me to the works of naturalist Loren Eiseley, where I discovered not just a mind at once rigorous and passionate, scientific and poetic, but also a man who may well have refrained, for fear of inheriting or passing on his mother's mental instability, from having children of his own. Richard Hebda helped me with technical questions about permissions. Kathlyn Stewart was extremely patient with my queries about the vocational aspect of palaeontology, and steered me away from a major error. Chris Harvey, at www.languagegeek.com was a pleasure to correspond with, as were the experts at www.translatum.gr.

The writing of *The Find* took several years and it could not have been done without the generous financial support of the Council for the Arts. Lesley Thorne, Anne McDermid, Kim McArthur and Svetlana Pironko each offered crucial advice about this book, which would never have been completed without the friendship, support and draft-reading capacity of Vicky Grut, Margaret Thompson, Helen Heffernan, Gillian Campbell, Maureen Moore and Jen Howe. Pamela Erlichman dealt valiantly with the typos.

Of course, the biggest thanks of all go to my husband, Richard Steel, whose love, support and faith in me enable me to continue to write. Marriage to a writer entails not just compulsory manuscript reading and many hours spent discussing people who do not exist, but also, in our case, frequently looking after the house and children while I work: it is impossible to thank him enough.